WINDWALKER

BY

DINAH MCCALL

Book cover: Kim Killion of HotDAMN Designs
www.hotdamndesigns.com

With regard to digital publication, be advised that any alteration of font size or spacing by the reader will automatically change the author's original format.

Dedication

As with all of my stories, this was a dream. It is meant to entertain, not to depict any historical information used in this story as fact. Some of the references are true to different Native American tribes, but none of this story is based on any legend.

I am dedicating this book to my Bobby. He gave me the dream, and now I'm sharing it with you as the story was meant to be told. Rest in peace my brown-eyed warrior and know my heart is with you until we meet again.

Dinah McCall

Chapter One

New Orleans, Louisiana: The witching hour

The gang zeroed in on the lone woman like the curs they were and the moment Layla Birdsong saw their faces, she knew was in trouble. There were nine of them, three blacks, four whites, and a couple of Asians - an odd amalgamation of affirmative action losers armed to the teeth.

She was never going to see home again.

The skinny white man with the pock-marked face rubbed his fly.

"Come to Papa," he jeered.

"Back off, Rabbit, I get her first."

Layla's gaze jerked to a skin-head wannabe with a swastika tattooed on his neck. Where in hell were the cops when you needed them?

Thunder rumbled overhead as the storm that had been approaching drew closer.

"Hell to the no, Fuck-face, you went first on the last one," another man shouted.

Layla tried to dodge the black man but it was to no avail as he grabbed her breast, squeezing it so hard she screamed. Then he shoved her backward, laughing as Fuck-face swung a knife. He crowed as it cut through the fabric of her blouse into the smooth brown skin on her belly. As she turned away, he danced around her and swung again, this time slashing the back of her arm from shoulder to elbow.

Layla screamed. "Nooo... oh God... stop! Someone! Anyone! Help! Help!"

"That's how I like 'em, screaming and bleeding," he said in a sing-song voice, and moved a step closer.

Layla's belly and arm were burning where the flesh had been cut. When she swept her hand across the point of pain and it came away covered in blood, panic shifted into rage. She didn't have a weapon and didn't stand a chance, but she came from a long line of warriors. If this was the day she died, they would have to take her in a fight.

She shifted her stance, looked down at the blood on her hand and in a moment of defiance, swept two fingers across each cheek, leaving behind two swaths of blood as war paint.

Now she was ready. All she needed was a weapon and launched herself at the one with the knife.

The impact took him by surprise as they went down in a tangle of arms and legs. The others whooped with delight as Fuck-face's head bounced off the pavement. All of a sudden he was seeing double and on the defensive.

Pulled by bloodlust, the gang drew closer, shouting out encouragement to their man while telling the woman in every vulgar term they'd ever heard what they would do with her before she took her last breath.

Layla heard nothing but the grunts and curses of the man beneath her as she battled for control of the knife. She had hold of his wrist with both hands, using every ounce of her strength to turn it downward, until the knife was only inches away from his face.

In a panic, he began cursing and yelling at his friends, 'Help me, damn it, help me. The bitch is going to put out my eye."

She had his wrist in a bind, pushing it continually downward in an abnormal position, and no matter how hard he hit her with his other fist, she didn't give.

Her eye was swelling and the cut he'd opened on her cheekbone was bleeding. A rumble of thunder rolled across the rooftops as she lunged, and when she did, her blood dripped into his eyes, momentarily blinding him.

It was his loss of focus that gave her the edge. She threw all her weight onto his wrist and heard the bone snap as the blade plunged downward into his neck.

Fuck-face's eyes bulged, then rolled back in his head. His body was still jerking in death throes when she crawled to her feet; the bloody knife in her hand. She was bleeding profusely, but there was a rage in her eyes.

"Who's next?" she shouted.

Thunder struck before she got an answer. A blinding flash of lightning hit the street behind them. A gust of wind exploded within their midst then rapidly turned into a whirlwind, spinning violently as it grew larger before their eyes. The force of the wind pinned Layla up against the wall. The knife dropped at her feet.

One gang member flew backward, slamming into the light post and snapping his neck like a toothpick. Another went airborne a good thirty feet up before he came down. The sound of his body hitting pavement was lost within the roar of the wind. Another man's clothes were ripped away. He was screaming in blood-curdling shrieks as the skin began to peel from his body.

And that was when she began hearing drums – Native American drums. That's when she knew this was more than a storm.

The whirlwind ripped through the gang, leaving one after the other lifeless. When they were dead, it moved toward Layla and then stopped, hovering feet above the ground.

Her heart was pounding – her gaze fixed on the swirling mass. Breath caught in the back of her throat as the whirlwind shifted, then parted like curtains, revealing something inside!

She could see brown skin and black hair and a flash of fire where his eyes should have been. The pull between them was strong and almost familiar, and then her focus shifted to the hand he extended. She never thought. She just acted. One moment she was an observer, and then the next she was within the wind, face to face with something for which she had no name.

He wrapped his arms around her and then they were gone.

****

The alarm was going off when Layla woke. She rolled as she reached out to stop it, then winced at the pain in the back of her arm, and shut it off with her other hand. Then she saw the blood - all over the sheets – all over her.

She flew out of bed, her muscles protesting as she tried to stand. There was a pain in her belly as sharp as the one on her arm. Her head was throbbing, and she had an overwhelming urge to cry. She staggered to the mirror; staring in disbelief.

One eye was swollen shut, there was a cut on her cheekbone, and her face was a mass of dark bruises and abrasions. Even more puzzling, she was still wearing the clothes she'd worn yesterday to the conference on early childhood education. She remembered going to dinner afterward with some of the other teachers attending the conference, and leaving the restaurant just before midnight to go back to her hotel. But then she took the wrong turn out of the parking lot and got lost. Before she could find her way back, the rental car died. So how had she-

And then it hit her!

The gang!

The attack!

She turned her hands palms up, looking at them for answers. They were covered in scrapes, bruises, and cuts.

Did she really kill a man or was it all a bad dream?

Did they rape her?

How the hell did she get to the hotel?

She began tearing at her clothes as if she could remove the horror along with them, and when she was naked she looked back in the mirror.

Shock rolled through her as she stared at her body in disbelief. She looked like she'd been in a battle and vaguely remembered thinking she had prepared herself to die. There was a cut across her stomach that was still seeping blood, as was the slash along the back of her arm.

The man with a knife!

She remembered fighting with him, then plunging the knife into his throat right before the storm hit. It brought wind – a wind so strong it had peeled the flesh off a man's body. After that, everything was a blur.

She began to shake. So how did she get here?

Suddenly her ears popped as the air inside the room began to shift. Then she saw movement in the air behind her; and watched in disbelief as an image began to appear.

She blinked, and when she looked again, there was a man with skin as brown as hers, dressed like a ghost from the past. He was naked from the waist up with hair as black as a raven's wing, hanging well below the middle of his back. He wore buckskin leggings and a breech-clout down to his knees. A large chunk of turquoise hung from a rawhide strip around his neck, centering the span of a massive chest, and once they locked gazes, her panic ended.

At the least, she should have been embarrassed. She was naked and yet felt protected as she turned to face him. When she started to cross her arms over her breasts, she stopped. He'd already seen all there was to see. The moment that thought went through her mind, his eyes narrowed.

"Am I dead?" she asked.

"No. Spirits do not bleed."

"Are you a spirit? Was it you who saved me?" she asked.

"You will call me Niyol, and you, Layla Birdsong, saved yourself."

The rhythmic cadence of his voice was as hypnotic as his physical appearance. It did not go unnoticed that his name was also the Navajo word for wind. A coincidence? She thought not then realized he was still talking.

"You need to prepare yourself for what's going to happen. You will be questioned. Answer as truthfully as you know how. They already have proof of what happened to you. It will be seen on what you call security tapes. You were out-numbered, and yet you fought bravely and killed your enemy. You are a red-feather warrior."

Layla had heard the term before, from her Muscogee father. It meant that she'd killed an enemy in battle, but thought it pertained only to men. And then the realization of what he'd said about tapes sank in.

"The police will come? Am I going to be arrested?"

"No, but I must warn you. These tapes will appear on all of your communication devices. You will be called a hero, and a witch, and a woman not of this world. People will come looking for you... bad people. Do not be afraid. When it is time, I will come back for you."

"What do you mean, *you'll* come for me?"

His eyes narrowed even more as his nostrils flared. "You belong to me. When it is time, I will be back."

Panic shifted through her. She didn't want to be claimed by anyone, especially some spirit from another world.

"I belong to no man," she muttered.

"I am not any man and you are a red feather warrior. We will be together," and then he took a step toward her.

Despite the pain she was in, Layla felt heat between her legs, like he was already there. He was before her then moved through her, as if she was smoke.

The joining was shocking and instantaneous. Her legs went out from under her as a bone-jarring climax dropped her to the floor. She was on her hands and knees, still shuddering from the impact when his hand, or what felt like his hand brushed down the length of her back. Another climax rolled through her, shattering every concept she had of human existence. When it had passed, so had she. She was belly down, unconscious on the hotel floor.

****

Two blocks of city streets had been marked off with yellow crime scene tape. What was left of the nine gang members were right where they'd fallen – some of them in pieces, a couple of them too damaged to identify. The one with the skin peeled off his body was the most puzzling, but the Coroner, Dr. Chin, was already doing initial observations with the detectives right behind him, hoping there would be identification in the clothing.

Detective Billy Wallis of the New Orleans P.D. was a twenty-year veteran on the force; fifty-one years old with a thick head of graying hair and a body as square as his jaw. He caught lead on the case, and met up with his partner, Thomas Pomeroy on scene. They'd been trying to make sense of it ever since. Pomeroy was leaning toward it being some kind of gang fight caught by the storm, when a beat cop appeared with a handful of security tapes that blew through the theory.

"Technology at its finest," the cop said. "All of the businesses on this street were closed when this happened, but four of the nine coughed up security tapes. I think you need to see these. There was another person here. I saw her on the tape and I think you need to see it ASAP. Also, there's a purse and a knife over there behind that trash can pertaining to the case."

"A woman was in the middle of this? Son-of-a-bitch. We've got another body to look for."

Wallis walked over to the trash cans and looked behind them. Sure enough, there was a woman's tooled leather purse right where he said it would be, and a pig-sticker knife with a wicked looking blade.

"There's a purse here all right, but some pickpocket could have dumped it there after stripping it clean. If there was a woman in all this, then where is the body?"

The cop shrugged. "Watch the tape and figure it out for yourself."

Wallis frowned. "This is no time to go all mystic on me. What do I need to see?"

The cop shrugged. "On the tape, it looks like she got sucked up into some kind of whirlwind and disappeared."

"Fuck," Wallis muttered, then yelled at his partner. "Hey Pomeroy! Call the weather bureau and ask if there was a tornado down here with last night's storm."

Pomeroy pulled out his phone as Wallis waved at a crime scene tech.

"Yo! Rivera. Come get a shot of this purse and knife, then see if you can find any ID inside the bag."

The crime scene tech stepped back from the bodies he'd been photographing and moved over to where the detectives were standing.

"Where?" he asked.

Wallis pointed.

Rivera took a trio of shots, then moved the trash can, bagged the knife, and squatted beside the purse. He lifted the loose flap with his pen and poked inside.

"There's a wallet," he said, then gloved up and pulled it out by the edges. It fell open, revealing the face of an attractive young woman with an Arizona driver's license.

"Layla Birdsong, twenty-eight years old, out of Arizona. Name and face looks Native American. What in hell was she doing down here?"

Rivera saw the edge of a plastic room key sticking out of the wallet and pushed it out with the tip of the pen.

"Here's a room key. She was staying at the

Marriott."

"Hold that wallet still," Wallis said, and took a photo of the driver's license and room key with his cell phone, then stood up as Rivera bagged the purse as well. "You got a couple of extra evidence bags?"

Rivera dug them out of his shoulder pack.

"Security tapes," Wallis said. "I'll log them into evidence after we stop by the hotel. We'll be viewing them in investigations later today."

Rivera made a note in his notebook. "Anything else you want me to shoot here?"

"No. Carry on," Wallis said. "Pomeroy and I are going to the Marriot from here." Then he waved Pomeroy down and headed for the car.

"Find out anything from the weather bureau?" Wallis asked, as Pomeroy slid into the seat beside him.

"Definitely no tornado warnings, only what they called a brief downburst as the storm cell collapsed."

"What about top wind speed?"

"Gusts up to 40 to 45 mph. Nothing out of the ordinary."

Wallis frowned. "That does not help the theory of a storm causing this bodily destruction."

"Maybe it'll be on those mysterious tapes," Pomeroy said.

"Maybe, but I'm stopping at the Marriot first. If we're lucky we'll find answers in Birdsong's hotel room."

It wasn't far from their crime scene to the hotel. They pulled up at Valet Parking, flashed their badges as they got out, strode into the hotel and up to the check-in desk where they flashed their badges again.

"We need to speak with your manager," Wallis said.

A clerk hastened to fill their request. Moments

later, a tall, elegant black man appeared, smiling cordially.

"Detectives. I'm John Samuels. Would you mind coming to my office so that we don't block check-in lines?"

"Lead the way," Wallis said, as he and Pomeroy followed the man into his office.

"Please, have a seat," Samuels said. He sat, then leaned forward. "How may I be of assistance?"

Wallis pulled up the photo of Layla Birdsong's driver's license and room key.

"Do you recognize this woman?" he asked.

Samuels shook his head. "No, but I just came on duty today after two days off. Is she dead?"

"We don't know where she is, but she's a person of interest in a case we're working," Wallis said. "Would you please see if she's still registered in this hotel?"

"Of course," Samuels said, and swung his chair around to the computer and typed in the name. A few moments later he paused and looked up. "She's still registered here. Room 404."

Wallis nodded in satisfaction. "We need to see it."

Samuels opened his desk and pulled out a master key.

"If you'll follow me."

They were on their way out when a clerk burst into the room.

"Mr. Samuels! One of the maids found a body in Room 404. She doesn't know if the woman is dead or alive."

"Call 911 and have hotel security meet us there," Samuels snapped, and increased his stride.

"Shit," Pomeroy muttered, following Samuels out of the office.

"This way. It's faster," Samuels said, and headed for a service elevator.

The ride was short. As they got off the elevator they heard a woman screaming and ran. It was the maid, squatting down in the hall with her hands over her head, praying between shrieks. Hotel security came out of a stairwell at the other end of the hall and joined them.

Samuels picked out a man from their security and pointed at the maid. "Take her to the break room. The police will want to talk to her."

As it turned out, they had no need for the pass key. The maid had gone in to change the sheets and the door was still ajar. As they entered, they saw the woman's nude, bloody body lying on the floor. She wasn't moving.

"Oh dear lord," Samuels said, and took a step forward.

"Stay back!" Wallis snapped, then countered the order with an apology. "Sorry. Didn't mean to bark. If you would direct the rest of the officers and crime scene techs to this room when they arrive, we would greatly appreciate it."

"Of course," the manager said. He shuddered as he gave the body one last glance and quickly left the scene.

Wallis squatted down beside her to check for a pulse, expecting a flat-line. When it thumped beneath his touch, he rocked back on his heels.

"She's alive! Call a bus!" he yelled.

Pomeroy grabbed his phone as Wallis leaned closer. He wouldn't move her for fear of exacerbating the injuries, but made sure there was no obstruction to her breathing. When he was satisfied her airway was open, he assessed the visible injuries.

The bruising on her body was massive, and there was blood, both dried and seeping in different locations. One eye was swollen shut, and there was a long slash down the back of one arm, as well as cuts and scrapes on the palms of her hands. What he couldn't figure out was how she got from the crime scene to here, or why she was still alive when everyone else on the scene had been decimated?

"Bus on the way," Pomeroy said, as the sound of an approaching siren could already be heard.

Wallis touched her arm. "Hang in there, lady. Help is coming."

Pomeroy had been moving around the room, and from what he could see, nothing made much sense.

"The bed is bloody as hell, and so are the clothes on the floor. At one time, she was obviously in bed in this condition, because there's too much blood in too many places, for it to be scatter."

"I agree," Wallis said. "We'll leave this for the crime scene techs to figure out. Right now we've got a live witness. I just need her to wake up and tell us what the hell happened out there."

Moments later they heard footsteps running down the hall. Pomeroy stepped out to flag them down, and then moved aside as they rushed inside.

Wallis gave the woman up to the EMTs, and the room up to another team from crime scene, and as soon as they transported her, he and his partner followed the ambulance to the hospital.

****

Pain was the first thing Layla felt as she began to regain consciousness. Her eyelids were heavy, like she'd been drugged. She heard someone calling her name and struggled to wake up.

"Layla! Layla Birdsong! I'm Dr. Toussaint. You've been injured and are in the emergency room. Can you tell me where you hurt?"

Layla licked her lips, her voice just above a whisper. "Everywhere."

She heard a woman's soft, Cajun voice near her ear.

"We're taking good care of you, cher."

Layla tried to take a breath, but her belly hurt. She reached for her midriff, but someone grabbed her hand. It was the same woman with the soft voice.

"No, baby... don't move. Let Doctor Toussaint work his magic on you."

The doctor was talking, but Layla lost focus when she began hearing the drums again. He was near! She could feel it. And there was something else that she knew. He didn't belong in this world.

Chapter Two

Detectives Wallis and Pomeroy were waiting for Toussaint when the doctor emerged from the exam bay.

"Is she conscious?" Wallis said.

"She's in and out," Toussaint said. "We're moving her upstairs as soon as a room is available."

"Can we talk to her? I have nine bodies in pieces out in a street and she's my only witness."

Toussaint frowned. "You can try, but if it rattles her, you're out."

The detectives nodded and quickly strode into the room. There was a nurse checking vitals that gave them a sharp glance, then saw their badges and looked away.

Pomeroy paused, shocked by the brutality she had endured. "It's a freakin' miracle she's still breathing," he muttered.

Wallis moved toward the bed.

"Miss Birdsong? Miss Birdsong? Can you hear me?"

Layla heard the voice and registered the question, but it was a struggle to answer.

"Um... hear."

"I'm Detective Wallis, and this is my partner, Detective Pomeroy. We're with the New Orleans Police Department. We need to talk about what happened to you."

"Gang," she mumbled, and then reached toward the pain in her belly.

The nurse stopped her. "Don't touch it, honey. There are bandages."

"Hurts," she whispered.

"Doctor Toussaint ordered pain meds. They'll be here shortly," she said.

Tears rolled from the corners of Layla's eyes.

"Can you tell us what happened?" Wallis asked. "Do you remember?"

She shook her head. "Not much."

Wallis persisted. "Tell us what you do remember. It's very important. You said there was a gang."

She thought back, remembering the dark street and the oncoming storm. The men! They'd come out of the shadows without warning.

"One grabbed me here." She touched her breast. "Another had a knife. Cut my stomach... my arm. Thought I would die."

Pomeroy glanced at Walllis, sickened by the violence she was describing.

"What happened then?" Wallis asked.

"Not sure... I fought. I think... no, I know that I killed the one with the knife."

Wallis's eyes widened. "You took one down? What did the others do?"

She frowned again, trying to remember. "Watched. Shouting. Laughing...until he died. Then the storm came."

"Did you see what was happening during the storm? Think hard. What tore those men up?"

She finally opened her eyes. Both men were leaning over her bed, waiting. She heard the drums again.

Answer truthfully.

"The whirlwind... it was a whirlwind."

Layla exhaled slowly then closed her eyes.

The nurse frowned. "She's had enough. You need to leave now."

Wallis nodded. "If we have any other questions, we'll come back tomorrow."

Layla didn't answer. Like she had a choice? The man – the spirit - whatever he was, said there would be tapes. He said they would be leaked and bad people would come. It was beginning, just like he said it would.

She was scared – as scared as she'd ever been in her life. The only thing that kept her from coming undone was the promise he'd made to come back.

****

They'd watched the tapes – all of them. Some were better than others depending on the angle of the cameras, but they all told the same story. A gang of nine had come out of an alley and attacked Layla Birdsong. What she had neglected to mention was that after they'd cut her twice and were about to close circle and finish her off, she backed off like she was gearing up for a race, smeared her own blood on her face and gone after the one with the knife without hesitation.

Wallis had gotten chills watching, and was resisting the urge to rewind it again. She was one tough cookie. Once she and her attacker went down, the gang had moved in. The cameras didn't catch how she'd managed to win the battle, but it was all too clear she was the only one who got up when it was over.

And that was when everything got weird.

There was a huge flash of light on the tape, which

they took to be lightning, and then all of the shots from the cameras became blurry as the air became filled with debris. By the time it cleared enough to see what was happening, the wind had begun gathering, spinning and turning into a swirl of contained power unlike anything they'd ever seen.

It wasn't a tornado because they could see the top and the bottom of the whirlwind moving violently and independently of the storm. It appeared to be targeting the men one at a time, which should not have been possible.

Even as Wallis doubted his own perception, he watched one man thrown backward into a light post with such force that his feet and head touched behind his back. Then another was lifted a good thirty feet up and unceremoniously dropped, splattering brain matter all over the street. The clothes on another man came off like a snake shedding skin, and then the wind went deeper.

Pomeroy groaned and then grabbed his partner's arm. "Oh hell, Wallis. Look! Look! Son-of-a-bitch! It was the wind that peeled the bastard's skin. It was the wind! How fast does it have to blow to make that happen?"

Wallis's gaze was still fixed on the screen as the wind moved toward the woman pinned against the building by its force. The whirlwind was still turning, but when it stopped forward motion, and appeared to be hovering, Wallis gasped.

"That's not fucking possible."

Then just like that, she was gone. As she had said, the whirlwind took her. But how? Where? All of a sudden it was nowhere in sight. Not on any of the tapes. They should have been able to see it moving away – not completely disappear. What in hell were they to make of this? And, it still didn't explain how she got to the hotel.

He had a feeling she knew more than she was telling, but whatever happened to the gang members, it was the storm and circumstance that had done them in.

He reached for the remote and turned off all the screens.

"So does this close the case?" Pomeroy asked.

Wallis shrugged. "As far as I'm concerned, it does. We know exactly how the nine men died, including the one she fought with. She took one down and then the storm hit. She lucked out there, or it would have been a different story."

"But how did she get to the hotel?" Pomeroy asked.

"Hell, maybe she flew like Dorothy in the Wizard of Oz. I don't know. If she doesn't remember, it still doesn't matter. Our job is finished here. Mother Nature took care of the criminal element in this case. "

"Want me to get the Captain?"

Wallis nodded. "He needs to see this. He'll be the one to make the call, but there's no doubt about it. Layla Birdsong is guilty of nothing but being in the wrong place at the wrong time."

****

Doctor Toussaint was making morning rounds as Layla was shoving breakfast around on the plate. He walked into her room just as she was trying to take a drink of juice through swollen lips.

"You need a straw for that," he said, and yanked the straw out of her water and poked it into the cup of juice.

Layla took a sip and then set it aside.

"Thank you."

Toussaint nodded. "Let's check out your eye," he said, nodding with what she hoped was satisfaction. "The swelling is beginning to subside. Can you see anything out of it?"

"A little, but it's still blurry."

"That should clear up as your eye continues to heal. Let's see how your stitches look, shall we?"

His nurse removed the bandages on her belly, as well as the ones on the back of her arm.

"Looking good," he said. "The seepage has stopped. No signs of infection." He scanned her chart as the nurse began applying fresh bandages. "Slight elevation in temperature but that's to be expected. How's the pain tolerance? We can up the meds a bit if you're uncomfortable."

"I'm managing. So how long do I stay here?"

He smiled. "I can understand your lack of empathy for our fine city, but you're going to have to bear with us for a few more days."

"I have a job to go back to on Monday."

He frowned. "Not this Monday. Call whoever you have to call and tell them you have been delayed."

She thought of the school on the Navajo reservation and her first grade students. Although teachers were supposed to start work on Monday getting classrooms ready, classes for the fall semester didn't begin for a couple of weeks. Surely she would be well enough by then to work.

"Yes, I'll make some calls," she said, including one to her grandfather.

She had been calling him every day since her arrival in New Orleans. He was probably worried that he hadn't heard from her today; such turmoil from an innocent conference on early childhood education.

She waited until the doctor was gone and the food tray removed and then pulled the phone into her lap. The last thing she wanted to do was cry when she heard her grandfather's voice, but they were all the family each other had left, and why she was in Arizona teaching on the reservation instead of back in Okmulgee, Oklahoma where she'd been raised.

Thinking of Oklahoma made her think of Donny Boland, the man she'd once dated. When the need to move to Arizona to take care of her grandfather arose, Donny got mad. He told her to put the old man in a home somewhere and stay there with him. He kept saying life was for the living and her grandfather's life was nearly over. Why give up her future to babysit an old man?

She'd been stunned by his callousness, and then so angry she'd tossed him out of her life and told him never to come back. Even now, she regretted ever thinking she loved such a jerk, let alone having sex with the man. It still made her feel dirty.

However, today was about the present, and Donny Boland was in the past. She took a deep breath, gathering her thoughts and her emotions, and made the call.

****

George Begay had been sitting by the telephone since before daylight, waiting for his granddaughter's call. He knew she was in trouble, just like he'd known the day his wife of fifty-seven years would die. When the phone finally rang, he was relieved. One way or another, he would know what had happened. He didn't say hello. He didn't even wait to see if it was actually

Layla who was calling.

"What happened to you?" he asked.

Layla sighed. She should have known it would be so. Grandfather always knew when something was wrong.

"It's a long story," she said. "Just know that I am okay... or at least I will be."

Once he heard her voice, the fear slid from his heart.

"Are you hurt?"

"Yes, but I'll heal."

He focused in on her voice and closed his eyes. Within seconds he saw men and blood and wind.

"You were attacked?"

It was the fear in his voice that was her undoing. Even though she tried to hide it, her voice was trembling as she began to explain.

"My car broke down on the way back to the hotel. It wasn't far and I started to walk it. But it was late and there was a gang. I thought I would die, but I did not."

"You fought."

The lump in her throat was getting bigger. "Yes, I fought, and I killed the one who cut me."

The silence was telling. George Begay did not trust the white men or their courts. "Are you in trouble?"

"No. There were nine of them and only one of me."

"How did you get away?"

She thought of the whirlwind and the spirit that was within it and knew it was something that could not be explained, especially over the phone.

"There was a storm. I will tell you more when I come home."

He closed his eyes and concentrated on her voice, then struggled against the shock of what he saw. It was not a storm, and they both knew it.

"When will that be?"

"I'm not sure. The doctor is going to make me stay a while."

George grunted softly. "You are hurt worse than you are saying. I will call the school and tell them to look for a substitute."

"Thank you, Grandfather. I was about to ask if you would do that for me."

"You will give me the name of your hotel and the phone number to the hospital."

"Why?"

"Because I am coming there to be with you."

Layla frowned. "There's no need, Grandfather. They're taking care of me. When I'm well enough, I will come home."

"No. You are going to need me. It wasn't a storm, Layla, and you know it, but the storm is coming. You are going to need all of your people before this is over."

Layla's heart skipped a beat. Everyone on the rez accepted that George Begay knew things others did not and she could do no less.

"What are you saying, Grandfather? What did you see?"

"That was no storm."

The skin crawled on the back of her neck. "It was a whirlwind."

"No, granddaughter. It was a Windwalker. You have been chosen. I don't yet know why, but you will be in danger. I will come. Tell me where you are."

She gave him the information, because there was no refusing this man once he'd set his mind to a task. And she didn't want to think about what she'd heard in his voice, and she didn't want to know what a Windwalker was. Not yet. She needed to heal before she let herself go there again.

****

The local newspapers were covering the story of the gang members' deaths, trying to tie their ethnic mix into a battle of rival gangs. Even in a city rife with crime, the fact that all nine of them had died in such brutal fashion was one for the books. A local television station had a brief interview of the cab driver who'd stumbled onto the bodies after dropping off a fare. Someone had leaked the fact that there was a survivor, and now the media was all over the Police Chief during his news conference.

"Chief Warwick! Chief Warwick! What about the woman? What's her name? How did she survive the storm when the others did not? Is it true she killed one of them in self-defense?"

The questions were coming at him right and left, but he'd been through far more controversial issues without losing his cool, and this was no exception.

"Yes, there was a survivor and she has been completely exonerated of any wrong-doing. There were nine of them and one of her. She fought back, but it was ultimately the onset of the storm that turned the tide for her."

"About the storm. Why was it so centralized? The damage is very obviously contained within this two block area."

Warwick laughed. "Seriously, Stanley? You're asking me to explain weather patterns? You need to be asking those questions of a weather expert, not a cop."

He disarmed them with laughter and brought a quick end to the questioning. After viewing the footage, the less he had to comment about this incident, the better. They'd run the tapes by the local district attorney who'd come to the same conclusion the law had. The gang assaulted a woman who'd fought back. The storm was the turning point. How the woman got back to the hotel and into her room, when she'd left her purse and room key behind, was beside the point. As far as the law was concerned, guilty parties had already been punished, and as soon as the Coroner confirmed the identities, the bodies would be released to family members.

Case closed.

Until a copy of one of the confiscated tapes was aired on the evening news, and another wound up on YouTube that they didn't know existed, and Layla Birdsong became marketable goods.

After that, they came out of the woodwork.

Paranormal buffs claiming it was a demon that had interfered with the attack, while others claiming it the work of voodoo.

Crazies gathering outside the hospital who were getting 'messages' from outer space that Layla Birdsong was from another world, and her 'people' had come to save her.

She'd gone to bed in a state of shock at what was happening, and was still big news when she woke up. By noon, the crowd outside the hotel had grown to such proportions that it became a public nuisance, and the police had been dispatched.

Layla stood at the window overlooking the parking lot, watching as the police dispersed the crowd from hospital grounds. Instead of leaving, they simply congregated on the other side of the street in growing numbers. She couldn't help wondering where this would end - how it would end.

I will come for you.

"When?" she whispered. "What is going to happen to me before you do?"

****

It was just after noon when a woman walked into the hospital. After a couple of lies and ten dollars to an orderly, she located Layla Birdsong's room. The first thing out of her mouth was begging Layla to pray for her son who was dying from cancer.

Shocked, Layla rang for help and the floor nurse called hospital security.

Layla was almost asleep when it happened again.

She didn't actually hear the door open, but she was aware that the noise from the hall had just become louder. She opened her eyes just as a skinny white man with dreadlocks slipped into the room, holding a pair of scissors.

Layla flashed on the gang and the man with the knife, and panicked. She rolled toward the far side of the bed to get away, tangled her feet in the sheets, and fell out of bed screaming. A metal tray hit the floor with a crash. The pitcher of water on her tray table went flying, and still she was screaming.

The man's expression was a mixture of shock and dismay. "No, lady, no! Don't be afraid!" he yelled. "I'm not gonna hurt you. I'm not gonna hurt you. I just need a piece of your hair."

The orderlies took him down, the police put him in handcuffs and hauled him away, leaving Layla with three torn stitches in her belly, and two on the back of her arm. By the time the stitches were fixed and fresh bandages in place, she was in tears again.

Even though a policeman now stood guard outside her room, she was afraid to close her eyes. It wasn't until a nurse came in and administered a sedative that she finally passed out.

"Walk with me," he whispered, and when he took her hand, her heart stopped, then started up again in rhythm with his. She felt his energy surge through her as surely as she felt the Arizona wind upon her face. Within the space of a heartbeat, they were standing on a mesa overlooking a part of the Navajo reservation.

"What's happening to me?"

He laid his hand over her breasts where her heart beat was the strongest.

"I am happening."

"Why me?"

"Because you are strong enough to do what must be done."

Wind swirled around them, brushing the length of her legs like a lover's touch then lifted his hair until it appeared to be floating behind his back.

The sexual pull between them was frightening. Layla wanted to feel him inside her - to take her, here – now – right where they stood. She didn't understand it, but she couldn't deny it. He was a fever in her blood, but a fever without a cure, and she could tell by the way he watched her that he knew every thought going through her mind.

"You are not yet strong enough for what will be. Your grandfather knows. He will help prepare you. Listen to him. Learn it well. It will be what saves you."

Tears burned the back of Layla's throat. "I thought you said you were going to save me."

The wind was stronger now, and was no longer a whistle but a whine as it came barreling toward them through the canyon.

"I said I would come for you when it was time. I did

not say that I would save you. This you must do for yourself."

"Layla."

Her eyes flew open. Her heart was pounding and there was a dryness in her mouth, like she'd been in the heat too long without water.

"Grandfather! You're here!"

Even though he was shocked by her appearance, he still saw his granddaughter beneath the swelling and the bruises. He kissed her forehead; afraid to touch her anywhere else.

"I said I would come," he said, and then kissed her again, just to make certain she was still in one piece.

Layla held tight to his hand, grateful that he was here. She had always thought him a handsome man, and still did despite his age. His features were even, his forehead broad. Long gray braids and a black hat only added to his presence, as did the turquoise and silver Conchos on the belt at his waist.

She didn't realize he'd come with company until she spotted another familiar figure standing just inside the door and another outside the room. It was the Nantay brothers; officers from the tribal police.

She frowned. "Why are they here?"

"To help me keep you safe."

"But the police are-"

"White man's police cannot help you," he said softly, then sat down on the edge of the bed. "Give me your hands."

Layla did as he asked, watching as he turned them palms down, then palms up.

"You are like your father," he said. "I was not happy when my Lena fell in love with Jackson

Birdsong, but I think now it was a good thing. You are taller than your mother ever was, and far stronger."

Layla waited for him to continue, but he did not. Finally, she leaned forward, her voice lower so as not to be overheard.

"He said you would prepare me when I was stronger. Prepare me for what, Grandfather?"

The words were shocking to George. For a moment he felt as if he'd been shown her death sentence, and yet he knew it was also her fate.

"When we go back, you will no longer teach children."

"But I-"

"No, Layla, this is so. You will revisit the old ways; hunting with bow and arrows, making fire without matches, eating less and enduring hardships; learning how to find water where there is none.

Layla's heart was hammering so hard against her chest she felt she would faint. She was thinking back to when her father was still alive, and how obsessed he'd been about teaching her things usually left to men.

Like many hunters in Oklahoma, both white and Indian, she was proficient with a bow and arrow, could build a fire without matches, catch fish with her hands, and knew how to field dress a deer. But this was surreal; as if Jackson had known what she would need to learn and prepared her in advance.

"Why is this happening? I don't understand. He said his name was Niyol, but he's not from this world, is he, Grandfather? Is he a spirit? Is he one of the Old ones?"

George hesitated, answering somewhat cautiously. "I think he is a Windwalker. They move between both worlds as they see fit."

"Why did he save me?" Layla asked.

"He saw the warrior in you. You have been chosen for your strength and courage. It is an honor, Layla."

She thought about what her grandfather said. Nothing was ever going to be innocent or simple again. Her eyes welled.

"He said bad men would come."

George frowned. "We will protect you. For now, all you need to do is get well.

Chapter Three

The next time Detectives Wallis and Pomeroy came by the hospital, it was to return Layla Birdsong's personal property. With the case closed, there was no further need to retain her purse and its contents for evidence. As they approached her room, the cop stationed outside her hospital room stood up. When they started inside, he stopped them.

"Knock, then you wait and let them admit you."

Wallis frowned. "Them who?"

"You'll see," he said, and sat back down.

Pomeroy knocked.

The door swung inward, revealing two uniformed men at the door and an older man sitting in a chair beside Layla's bed. When he saw the police, he, too, stood up.

Layla recognized them and motioned for them to come in.

"Grandfather, these detectives are the ones who were working my case. I'm sorry, but I don't remember your names. Detectives, this is my grandfather, George Begay, and Montford and Johnston Nantay... officers from our tribal police."

"Nice to meet you," Wallis said.

Pomeroy acknowledged the uniformed officers with a nod, but they didn't respond.

Wallis accepted that the New Orleans police department had been judged and found lacking here, but it was what it was. He handed Layla the evidence bag.

"Your purse and contents," he said. "Sign here and it's all yours."

She signed her name on the release sheet, wincing when the healing stitches on the back of her arm began to pull.

"Thank you for this," she said. "I thought for sure it was gone."

She dug through the purse, even more surprised that both her wallet and money were still there.

How have you been?" Wallis asked.

She shrugged. "Despite the woman who snuck in my room wanting me to heal her child of cancer, and the nut who wanted some of my hair for a voodoo ritual, not bad."

Wallis blinked. Working homicide, he hadn't heard of the incidents.

"I'm sorry to hear that. We can-"

"There is no need to trouble your officers further," George said. "The Dineh take care of their own."

Pomeroy frowned. "Who are the Dineh?"

"It is what the Navajo call themselves," George said bluntly.

Again, Wallis felt the slight, telling him they were performing a job he could not. Still, he understood how they felt. If she'd been his family, he would have been pissed at what happened to her, too, and chose to ignore it.

"So, Miss Birdsong, the swelling in your eye looks much better. Is your sight okay?"

"Yes. As soon as all my stitches come out, I will be gone. Thank you for returning my things."

"We're very sorry you had such an unfortunate incident in our city. Hope you don't hold it against us,"

Pomeroy said.

"It was more than an unfortunate incident, and unless I am forced, doubt I'll ever return," Layla said.

Wallis was done here. "Have a safe trip home."

He left without looking back.

****

Federal Bureau of Investigation
Quantico, Virginia

A phone rang somewhere inside a brightly lit research lab. A balding doctor was entering new data into the computer to rerun a test. When the phone continued to ring, he yelled without looking up.

"Somebody please answer the phone!"

There were footsteps, and then background murmurs that faded from his consciousness. When his assistant walked up near his elbow, he frowned again.

"Not now," he muttered.

"I'm sorry, Dr. Winters, but Emile Harper is on the phone. He needs to speak to you now."

Winters couldn't imagine what the Director of Foreign Intelligence would want with him, but he wasn't the kind of man to put off.

"I'll be right there," he said, and continued to type until he was satisfied he'd gotten to a stopping point, then moved into his office and picked up the phone.

"This is Winters."

"Dr. Winters, I sent you a link. Open it, look at it, and tell me what you see."

"Now?"

"Yes, now."

"Okay, I'll call you back as soon as-"

Harper frowned. "No. Open it now while we're both

on the line."

"This better be important. I'm in the middle of something," Winters said.

"You're always in the middle of something. Do you have it open yet?"

"No, okay... here it is. Just a second while it loads."

Winters watched a few seconds. "You want me to watch a tape about a woman being attacked?"

"Winters, for once, just shut the fuck up and do what I ask without giving me grief."

Winters grinned. He made it his business to give people like the director grief.

"I'm watching a woman being confronted by a gang of men. Oh shit. They just cut her... twice. Wow, gutsy move there. Okay, she went after the guy with the knife. And they're on the ground and I can't see what's going on because- Are you kidding me? She's on her feet! Son-of-a-bitch. That means she must have-"

There was a flash of light and then Winters forgot what he'd been going to say as he watched a whirlwind forming. When it began to move through the gang, the hair stood up on the back of his arms, and when it began picking them off one after another, he stared in disbelief. What he was seeing was impossible.

"This isn't real. It can't be real. Someone has tricked this out," he muttered, and then gasped when the woman and the whirlwind disappeared before his eyes.

"So, have you seen it all the way through?" the director asked.

"Yes," Winters said, as he dropped into the chair behind him and then hit Play again. "It's interesting, but it's obviously not real."

"But it is," the director said.

Winters felt everything he knew about physics shifting gears without him on board.

"Impossible."

"I have the original tape. Every expert at Quantico has seen and examined the tape and to a man, swears it's pure. So given that's a fact, what am I looking at?"

"You're asking me? Find yourself a mystic. He'd have as good a guess at it as I would."

There was a moment of silence and then the director cleared his throat before speaking again – a subtle hint as to how uncomfortable he was with the subject.

"What do you know about Native American lore?"

"You're kidding."

"No, I'm not kidding, damn it."

"I'm a scientist. I work with facts, not fairy tales. If you want to talk about witch doctors and shamans, call Lydia Foster. She has an office at the Smithsonian."

"We never had this conversation," Harper said.

Winters went back to the lab, but he couldn't get the image of that whirlwind out of his head. Later, he realized he hadn't asked what happened to the woman, and assumed she was no longer alive.

****

Lydia Foster was out of the office when Harper called. He left a message, asking her to view the link that he'd sent and then to call him ASAP.

When Lydia returned and sat down to check her messages, she frowned. She didn't like Emile Harper, but he was the Director of Foreign Intelligence, which meant protocol ruled.

She opened her email, clicked on the link that he'd sent, and was watching absently while digging through her desk drawer for the Hershey bar she'd tossed in there yesterday. All of a sudden she stopped and leaned forward, her blonde hair sliding over one eye as she stared at the screen in disbelief. She watched it four more times straight through and then called Harper's number. He answered on the second ring.

"This is Harper."

"Lydia Foster, here. I got your message. I've seen the tape. Is it verifiable?"

"Yes. Untainted in any way."

"Oh sweet Lord," Lydia whispered, hit loudspeaker on her phone and headed for the bookshelf behind her desk.

"Hello? Lydia? Are you still there?" Harper yelled.

"Yes, yes, sorry. I put you on loudspeaker so I could get to my bookshelf."

"What is it on that tape? We already know it's not a tornado. In fact it's not anything the National Weather Service has ever seen."

"That's because it has nothing to do with weather," Lydia said, then found the book she was looking for and hurried back to her desk.

Harper gave a nervous laugh, as if embarrassed to be saying this aloud.

"I have someone here in the office saying it has something to do with a Native American prophecy."

"Yes, yes, sort of... here, here it is," she said, running her finger down the page of the book she'd just opened. "Windwalker: Man/spirit that can exist both in the world of the living and the world of the dead. It's something like a Guardian and appears only when The People, and in this case it's referring to the indigenous people, not people in general… when The People are about to experience great deprivation, or are in danger, say from something that could threaten their extinction."

Harper frowned. "So how does that connect to the woman who disappeared?"

"What happened to her afterward?" Lydia asked.

"They found her in her hotel room, naked and bloody as hell from the fight with the gang, but alive."

Lydia jumped up and began pacing. "Oh my God, that means she's been chosen."

Harper rolled his eyes. "What the fuck does that mean?"

"Something is coming that will be of great danger, maybe to this country, maybe to the world, but the Windwalker's appearance would pertain only to the Native American people and what would happen to them. She's been chosen to lead them to safety."

Harper snorted. "So what are you saying… that she's going be some kind of female Moses and lead her people through a wilderness?"

Lydia heard the derision in his voice and was immediately insulted.

"You called me for information. I gave it to you and now you decide to be a smart-ass? Go to hell, Harper."

Lydia hung up, then began re-watching the video as her phone began to ring.

"Asshole," she muttered, and let it ring.

****

Prince Institute
Binini Island – West Indies

Landan Prince believed in all things magic and things unseen. It had driven every aspect of his adult life to the point that he'd abdicated his British title and dissolved the accumulation of centuries of family holdings to fund the institute bearing his name.

Twenty-four years of experiments in breeding and research had yielded some interesting, if less than profitable results. The paperweight on his desk was a perfect square of yellow crystal supposedly meant to move people between dimensions, although none of his experts had ever been able to decode it.

He invested his billions according to psychic predictions and it paid off more often than not, which was proof to him of their validity. His office was a museum of maps, diaries, and ancient parchments yet to be examined. There was an octagon-shaped box on his desk that he couldn't open, made of a metal purported not of this earth, and an old, tattered cloth with rusty stains that were supposedly blood stains from a victim of Jack the Ripper. He was convinced that if he could find the right medium to channel the victim's spirit, he would discover the Ripper's true identity.

A misshapen fetus with an abnormally large head and tiny undefined limbs floated in a large jar of embalming fluid on a back shelf of his library that was supposed to be the offspring of a woman and an interplanetary alien. He'd bought stolen treasures on the black market and raided tombs, all in the name of science, but it was actually the secrets they held waiting to be unlocked that turned him on.

Twelve years ago he'd paid an inordinate amount of money to a gypsy psychic and a man who felt no pain to study a healthy child born of their union. He'd gotten two for the money when she gave birth to twins she'd named Adam and Evan.

Something the woman 'saw' after their birth had given her pause for thought and at the last minute tried to back out on the deal. Prince had been kind but firm, and when she persisted he made her disappear and took the twins.

Twelve years later all he had to show for her murder were two boys who conversed only with each other, and in a twin language no one else could understand. The only reason he had yet to dispose of them was his belief that they might still manifest some kind of powers at puberty.

He held séances and ghost hunting forays with a woman on his island named Madam ReeRee who practiced the occult, and when he wanted something he could not get legally, he had her call up the devil, and promised another small piece of his soul in trade for the prize.

He had a team of investigators who combed the internet daily for anything related to the paranormal, and when they sent him the YouTube video of the Layla Birdsong incident, he was immediately intrigued.

The first thing he'd done was try to track down and buy the original video, but it had already been seized by the U.S. Government, which meant he was going to have to hustle to beat them to the woman. Prince set experts to the task of breaking the video down frame by frame, and discovered some confusing aspects that could not be confirmed.

To identify a wind speed that would peel the flesh of a man's skin was impossible because it had never been measured.

To have a whirlwind move independently of present wind was an impossibility of physics.

But it was the brief glimpse of something reaching

out of the wind to pull the woman in that made his heart pound. If he had the power to control something like that, there were no boundaries to what he might be able to achieve. At that point, he sent a team to the United States to find her, but when they finally reached New Orleans, she was gone.

****

They arrived on the reservation just before dark. Layla watched the sun set in a wash of colors from the backseat of her grandfather's pickup. Her heart was heavy with fear and regret. Even though she was coming home, it felt as if she was already separating from the safe and the familiar.

Her grandfather was asleep beside her.

The Nantay brothers occupied the front. There was no conversation to speak of between them and Layla Birdsong. They knew she had a quest before her that neither would have wanted to face, but at the same time, were in awe.

They'd seen the video. They'd seen her swipe bloody war paint on her cheeks in a defiant gesture and go for the man with the knife. She'd killed her enemy as valiantly as any man could have done.

But there was something Layla knew that the others did not. Ever since they'd crossed the border into Arizona, she'd been hearing drums, and the closer they'd driven to the reservation, the louder they had become. Right now they were so loud that she felt like she was at a powwow, and could almost smell the dust from the hundreds of feet circling the ceremonial fire.

The neighbor's dog barked as they drove past the house. The children still playing outside near the porch were students in the school where she taught, and then she amended that thought. Where she used to teach.

There was a moment of sadness for what she was losing. Not only the simplicity of her life, but the freedom and anonymity. She didn't yet understand what would be expected of her, but accepted it, just as she'd accepted death that night before the storm.

George Begay woke up when the dog barked.

"We're home," he said, as he scrubbed the sleep from his face.

When they stopped, the brothers jumped out ahead of them. Johnston helped Layla out, while his brother Montford helped George.

George paused to shake their hands. "Thank you," he said softly.

"No thanks necessary," Johnston said, and set their suitcase on the front steps while his brother carried their own bags to the truck they'd left at George's house a week earlier.

"Call if you need us," Montford said, gave Layla a brief glance and then quickly looked away.

Layla watched them leave with relief. She and her grandfather were finally alone. After all the chaos and crowds and the crazy media attention, the quiet here was both startling and welcome.

"Are you okay?" George asked.

"I'm fine, Grandfather, and you?"

"Tired, but home looks good."

"Yes, home looks good," Layla said, as they went inside.

The house was simple in furnishings, but comfortable enough for one woman and an old man, although not the same house it had been when her grandmother, Frances, had been alive. She'd always had something good cooking on the stove, and a pitcher of George's iced tea chilling in the refrigerator. Now it was as if the house had forgotten how to breathe.

It smelled a little musty from being shut up so long. George wasted no time turning on the window air conditioner as Layla went to her room. All she wanted was a shower and her bed. She dug her nightgown out of the suitcase and headed for the bathroom, when George met her in the hall.

"You need to eat something. You didn't eat when we bought sandwiches at the last gas station."

"I'm too tired to eat, Grandfather. I think I'd rather just take a shower and go to bed."

He patted her arm. "Are you in pain?"

"Not too bad," she said, fingering her cheek where the scar was beginning to form. "I'll take a pain pill before I lay down."

"Then you will need some food in your belly. Take your shower and then come to the kitchen. I'm going to scramble eggs."

She hugged him. "As usual, your suggestion is a good one, and thank you. I won't be long."

When George smiled, it always made him look like his eyes had disappeared. As a child, she'd thought his face looked like he was hiding secrets. Now, she knew she'd been right.

She stripped quickly then stepped in front of the mirror, ignoring the heavy curve of her breasts and narrow waist to check out her war wounds. The scar on her cheek would eventually fade some, but it wasn't going to go away and she didn't care. It would be a lifetime reminder to never quit when the going got tough.

She turned from one side to the other, eyeing the length of the healing cut down the back of her arm and the changing colors of her bruises, then faced the mirror and traced the other new scar forming on her belly.

"Not quite stripper material," she muttered, and carefully stepped into the shower.

A few minutes later she was at the kitchen table eating eggs and toast with her grandfather, who ate with one eye on small television set on the kitchen counter, and the other on her plate. Every time she made a decent dent in her eggs, he spooned another bite or two from the bowl onto what was left.

"Good for you," he would mutter, then keep watching the news.

Layla laughed. "That was anything but subtle."

He shrugged. "There is no need for subtlety. I am a straightforward man. Eat your eggs."

"I'm eating, I'm eating," she said, then got up to get jelly out of the refrigerator.

All of a sudden she heard the drums. They were faint, but nothing to ignore. She turned quickly but saw nothing of which to be concerned. And then she noticed the picture on the television screen and froze. That image of her face with the blood streaked on her cheeks was now being sported by hundreds of 'Birdsong fans'. Were they serious? She had a fan club of people who wore war paint? Why couldn't she be old news?

"What are they talking about?" George asked.

Layla carried the jelly back to the table and sat it down with a thump.

"Crazy people," Layla muttered.

"What do you mean?" he asked.

She frowned. "It seems that I now have a fan club. It's wrong to celebrate a death, even if the man deserved what happened."

"Is that in New Orleans?" George asked.

Layla sighed. "And in Dallas, and in St. Louis, and Chicago and obviously all over the country. It's what they call going viral, thanks to YouTube and Twitter."

She spread the jelly on what was left of her toast and then ate without tasting it. She was gathering up her dirty dishes when she caught George looking at her curiously.

"What?"

"It's already beginning, isn't it?" he asked.

She ignored the fear that shot through her.

"I don't know what's happening," she muttered, and carried the dishes to the sink. "I need to lie down, Grandfather. I'll see you in the morning, okay?"

"Sleep well. We will talk tomorrow."

He was running water to wash dishes when she left.

She crawled between the covers, rolled over onto her side, pulled a pillow over her face to hide the sound and cried herself to sleep.

****

He stood before her, silhouetted by a light so bright that all she could see was the outline of his body.

"They are coming for you."

She wanted to be angry for what he'd caused, but the sexual pull between them was too strong. She fell to her knees and rocked back on her heels, pounding her legs with her fists.

"You started this by saving me. Why didn't you let me die? I can't stay here and bring danger to my grandfather and the people on the reservation."

"In a short period of time all that you know will begin to die. Your cities will lose power. Your water will

be fouled. There will be riots, and there will be death, and then the earth will burn."

"Why? What have we done?"

"You did nothing when it mattered most."

"I don't understand."

"You will."

"What is expected of me?"

"Tomorrow you will look to the East. Be prepared and say your goodbyes."

"Am I going to die then?"

"No. I am going to teach you how to live."

Layla woke up with a gasp and looked at the clock. Only a couple of hours before dawn. The reality was crushing. She'd come to the reservation to take care of her grandfather, not to abandon him. She didn't understand the warning, but felt powerless to stop it.

Her heart was heavy as she got out of bed to dress, and when she was through, braided her hair into one thick rope and fastened it off. She packed her sturdiest clothes and hiking boots into a backpack, tossed in pain meds and toilet articles, added soap and shampoo, then dug a smaller bag from the back of her closet and laid the items out on the bed.

It was all she had left of her father's things – a knife for skinning and filleting fish – a big Bowie knife he always took hunting – and a silver chain with a bird charm that he'd worn until the day he died. When she pulled the chain over her head, the small charm settled in the valley between her breasts. It was good to have all she had left of her father that close to her heart. She packed the knives into her bag then carried it into the living room.

He had said look to the East. The sun was only

minutes away from making an appearance when she heard the floor creak behind her.

"What are you doing, Layla?"

Her grandfather was standing in the hallway with a frightened expression on his face.

"I have to leave."

She watched his eyes widen in surprise then his voice began to shake.

"No. We will protect you here."

"He said something bad is going to happen to the world."

George flinched. Then what he'd been seeing must be true.

"Then you should stay with us. We'll find a way to be safe."

"That's not my path, Grandfather, and I won't be alone. He's coming for me."

George's shoulders slumped.

Layla glanced toward the window. The sun was up. She opened the door and carried the backpack out onto the step.

At first, all she could see was the glare of new sun upon the bare earth, and then the shadows it made as it continued to rise. She sat down on the step. Sound carried in the desert, and the sound of a motorcycle in the early morning hour was unmistakable.

George sat down beside her and put a hand on her shoulder. His voice was trembling.

"Be strong, Layla. Stay alive."

Tears welled as she threw her arms around his neck, wishing she could turn back the clock, wishing she'd never gone to New Orleans.

"I love you, Grandfather."

"I love you, too," he said.

The sound was louder. She looked into the

morning sun and saw a dark blur on the horizon. As it grew closer, the sound of the engine grew louder.

The motorcycle was visible now, but she was looking at the rider – coming closer – coming faster – coming for her.

Chapter Four

Layla stood up.

George stood with her, his gaze focused on the rider in the distance.

"He comes as a man, not a spirit."

"What does that mean?" she asked.

"That you will be able to interact with him as you do with me."

Layla thought about all that implied then stepped out into the sun, shading her eyes as they watched his approach. The rumble of the bike was louder. They could smell the rooster-tail of dust billowing up into the air behind him.

"He is in a hurry," George said.

Layla's heartbeat was accelerating as her anxiety increased.

Fear has no place between us.

She staggered slightly, as if the world had suddenly shifted on its axis, and then the feeling was gone along with the anxiety. She slipped her arms through the straps of her backpack and shifted it to a comfortable position.

The neighbor's dog trotted out to the road as it did every time a vehicle approached, then inexplicably turned tail as quickly as it had come and disappeared.

George's legs were shaking. Looking upon a Windwalker, even in human form, was frightening, but George was more afraid of losing Layla.

The rider slowed the bike as he rode through the street between the houses, rolling it to a stop only a few feet from where Layla was standing. The quiet that came when the engine rumbled then died exacerbated George's panic, and yet as the man of the house he stepped forward.

The rider toed down the kickstand and dismounted. He was wearing old boots, denim jeans and a blue, long-sleeve shirt open halfway to his waist. Long hair fell out onto his shoulders and down his back as he removed the helmet and hung it on the end of the handlebars. When he turned, his gaze went beyond the old man in front of him to the woman behind.

Breath caught in the back of Layla's throat. She was caught in the stare, like a mouse between an eagle's talons. He'd been unforgettable in spirit, but in the flesh, he was formidable. Not until his gaze shifted, was she able to move. She watched as he approached her grandfather.

"I am Niyol."

"Welcome," George said.

He moved forward and put a hand on George's shoulder. "Even though I will take your granddaughter?"

"Will she come back?" George asked.

"Do you know what's coming?"

"I see things in my dreams," George said. "Will they come to pass?"

"Prepare your people. Once again they will leave their lands. Tell them to bring hand tools and knives. They will be needed."

"What is to become of us?" George asked, as Layla walked up beside him. When she slipped her hand into his, he gave it a squeeze, but wouldn't look at her face.

He couldn't without begging her to stay.

Niyol's gaze slid to Layla, like a snake watching its prey.

"She will save you. When she returns, you must all be ready to follow."

George blinked.

One moment Layla was beside him, and then she was on the back of the bike, her arms wrapped around the rider's waist. Tears were running down her face as she gave her grandfather one last look, and then she buried her face in the middle of Niyol's back and they were gone.

****

Lydia Foster walked into her office carrying her briefcase and what was left of the skinny latte from lunch. A lock of her hair had escaped the knot she'd put it in earlier in the morning. She could feel it tickling the back of her neck as she crossed the threshold, then immediately frowned.

Someone was waiting for her in the outer office, which meant her assistant had gone off and left her office unlocked, something she did not appreciate. They would be discussing this at a later date.

"Hello? Can I help you?" she asked.

The man looked up from the magazine he'd been reading, and when he did, her frowned deepened. As she lived and breathed, Emile Harper, the Director of Foreign Intelligence, himself, was sitting in her office. She should have known he wouldn't give up.

"Lydia Foster?"

"Emile Harper."

Emile blinked. So she recognized him. Whatever.

"Yes, I'm Harper. I wonder if I might have a few

moments of your time. It's rather important."

She sailed past him into her office, leaving the door open behind her. He followed without hesitation.

She laid her briefcase on the end of her desk, set her coffee near the phone, and dropped into the chair.

"Take a seat. I have exactly fifteen minutes to give you and then I'm gone."

Harper sat. It was obvious she was still pissed, but he didn't have time to be cordial.

"We didn't get to finish our conversation the other day."

"I was through."

Harper frowned. "I was not. This isn't about a pissing contest here. This is about national security."

Lydia rolled her eyes. "You're not serious. Since when is a Native American legend classified as national security? Surely you haven't run out of terrorists to hunt down."

Harper had the grace to flush. "Look, I'm getting flack from superiors. I need answers. I came to you for help and as a citizen of the United States of America it is your duty to-"

Lydia pointed a finger. "Do not preach at me! I don't work for you, so don't start pushing your weight around. I already told you what I knew about Windwalkers, which is what I personally believe was on that tape."

Harper pinched the bridge of his nose; a gentle reminder to himself not to shout.

"I need more than a legend to-"

"Why? What do you think you're going to do with this Windwalker if you find it? Surely you don't think you can control it? I would have assumed even you spy-phobes would know human control of anything paranormal is impossible."

Harper leaned forward. "And you seriously believe what was on that tape was paranormal?"

Lydia rolled her eyes. "In a word, yes. The spirit world and the entities in it exist in a different dimension, and when it suits them, they travel between this world and theirs. I live in a haunted house. Spirits tug the blankets off me when it's cold just to hear me curse. They turn lights on and off to remind me they are there and ever so often, I hear them talking. I'm not psychic, but I darn sure believe there are people who are."

"Crap," Harper muttered.

Lydia wasn't finished. "With regards to the legend of the Windwalkers appearing during times of crisis, there are actually legends in other cultures that are similar, and back up the possibility of a world crisis. You know how everyone has been freaking out about the Mayan prophecy since someone interpreted it as predicting the world end in December 2012."

"Are you saying that's not the case?" Harper asked.

Lydia frowned. "I'm drawing parallels in different ethnic mythologies, Mr. Harper, not making predictions about the end of the world."

She got up from her desk and, once again, scanned the books shelves before pulling out another tome.

"This is a book of Gypsy legends. There is a similar prophecy written in here that predicts an event, similar to what might bring a Windwalker into this world."

"What kind of prophecy?" Harper asked.

Lydia sat down and leafed through the pages until she found what she was looking for.

"Okay, this is from something called The Gypsy

Chronicles written in the late 13th century, and predicting a catastrophic world collapse, although it does not date when it could happen.

It's actually interesting to note that it was written around the same time that the Anasazi Indians disappeared."

"The who?"

Lydia frowned. "Anasazi. A name given to Pueblo Indians who were supposedly as strong and vital an empire as the Mayans and Incans, and yet tens of thousands of them disappeared without a trace. No one has ever been able to do more than theorize as to what happened to them."

"Well they're already gone and I'm concerned about what's happening now," Harper said. "About that Gypsy prophecy, please read it," Harper said.

Lydia nodded, and as she began to read, the words had a rhythm-like chant that made the prophecy quite eerie.

Sky turned dark.
Sun did die.
Earth was seared.
People cried.

Rivers bled out.
Mountains roared.
Trees shed leaves.
Heavens poured.

Run while you can
And don't look back.
What was is gone,
You must make tracks.

Look for the cleft
Twixt earth and sky.
Go far – Go deep
Or all will die.

Harper swallowed.

"That reads like some damn nuclear holocaust."

Lydia looked up. "Yes, it does, doesn't it? So are we hovering on the brink of a disaster of which only big governments are aware?"

Harper frowned. "Not that I know of."

Lydia shrugged. "I shouldn't have asked. You wouldn't have told me even if it's true, and your fifteen minutes are up."

Harper swiftly shifted focus. "Look. This doesn't help. It only adds to the confusion."

"And that's why it's called a prophecy. It has yet to become a fact, Mr. Harper. Go tell the suits to leave Layla Birdsong alone. She can't help you."

"We'll find that out for ourselves when we bring her in for questioning," he snapped.

Lydia gasped. "You are seriously going to run down that woman and haul her into the nation's capital as if she was guilty of some kind of treason? If they don't laugh you out of a job, you'll have the Bureau of Indian Affairs so far up your ass it'll take a bulldozer to get them out."

His eyes narrowed angrily. "Not if they don't know it is happening."

Lydia tapped her desk with the end of her finger. "Here's something I do know. There is not one Native American living that is unaware of what just happened to Layla Birdsong. And the young ones, who might not know all there is to know about legend, have already been filled in by the tribal elders. If they know where she is, they'll protect her. And, if the United States government sets foot on Indian land to look for her, you will have an uprising the likes of which you've never seen. A Windwalker is holy. Reservation land is sacrosanct, and the United States government has no authority or rights there."

"But I thought you said the Windwalker's coming was like a warning to the world?"

"Windwalkers are Native spirits. They help *their* people. We're all on our own here."

Harper's eyes widened.

Lydia shrugged. "If you look at it from their viewpoint, it could be the ultimate payback for every treaty we broke, every acre of land that we stole, every innocent Indian who was killed in the name of progress over the past several hundred years. If you buy into the Windwalker theory, and if we're about to blow ourselves up, then they'll be the only ones who could ultimately survive it."

Harper stood up. "This conversation will stay between you and me," he said.

"Again, I am not your minion. Go play with your spies, Mr. Harper, and leave me to my students and my studies. If we're all going to perish in the next few months, then we will perish. I just don't want to know about it ahead of time."

He strode out of her office, slamming the door behind him.

Lydia dropped into her chair, then leaned back and covered her face with her hands. She'd run a good bluff and he'd gone for it. But she was sick at heart and already making plans. She'd always wanted to go to Greece and had never taken the time. She'd given her entire adult life to the study of ancient prophecy, and after what she'd seen on that tape, she fully believed it was now or never.

****

Binini Island – West Indies

It was five minutes to midnight and Madam ReeRee had just walked naked out of the jungle into the light of the bonfire burning deep on the island. The flames were waist-high and roaring, sending a shower of sparks up into the air as she approached and Landan Prince was standing only a few feet away from the heat, waiting for the ritual to begin.

ReeRee knew Prince was as intrigued by her naked body as he was the power she claimed to possess, and she didn't intend to disappoint him. She began to move, calling out to the dark ones as the weight of her breasts rolled from one side of her body to the other. It was a turn-on for Prince and she knew it. She was role-playing now, rolling her eyes and moaning and stomping, leading him to believe that's what she did to bring up the spirits. What he didn't know – would never know – was how the true rituals worked. That was for her. This was for show.

Prince kept her in fine food and a house superior to any other locals on the island, so when he wanted to play with the spirits, she happily obliged. It was, however, her personal opinion that the man was a fool. Even though she had never called up the devil for him, Prince thought she did, and in a way he gave life to the promises he made to dark entities by simply speaking them aloud, without caution or care for the day when his reckoning would come.

Earlier today he'd shown her a video that was frightening and puzzling, even for her. She knew nothing of Native American spirits, but none of the spirits she conjured were remotely capable of this. This was big magic – magic she wanted no part of. And yet Prince was here, demanding answers for questions he had yet to ask. So tonight, a chicken would die. Beyond that, she made no promises.

****

Prince had a remarkable hard-on. It was a side-effect of the adrenaline surge he felt during these ceremonies and always wondered why he never thought of bringing a female with him until it was too late. Maybe his lapse was subconscious; knowing the personal power he gained would be sapped by giving it away through sex.

ReeRee was in fine form tonight, already communing with the spirit side. He wanted them to tell him where Layla Birdsong was hiding. If he had her, he would have access to the entity that had spirited her away, and that would give him untold power.

He already knew she taught school on a Navajo reservation in Arizona, and that she'd checked out of the hospital in New Orleans and left with family. He also knew the United States government was looking for her, which meant he had to be careful. He got away with what he did because he made it a point to never be a physical presence at the scenes of his acquisitions or piss off foreign governments.

All of a sudden ReeRee shrieked.

Every muscle in his body tensed as she picked up a chicken and wrung its neck. When she swung the carcass toward him, lacing his clothes with fresh, warm blood, he froze.

She tossed the carcass aside. It was flopping in

death throes as she flung its head into the smoke and began to move around the fire in a wild, frantic rhythm - stomping her feet in the blood and the dirt – chanting incantations in her native patois.

He closed his eyes and opened his mind; ready for whatever she conjured to come in.

****

Niyol liked the feel of heat and wind upon his face. With the woman's breasts against his back and the tight grip she had around his waist - only inches from his manhood - it was a struggle to stay focused. It had been a long time since he'd walked in the human world, and he was hungering for all that it offered, including this woman. He'd already given her a taste of what their union would be like, but he was anxious to experience it as well. Much was riding on how well he prepared her for what was coming, and wasting time with bodily pleasures would have to be carefully paced.

She didn't know, but he could hear her thoughts. He also felt the power of her energy. She had a warrior's heart. It would be important that she stay strong when it mattered most.

A rabbit darted out of some scrub brush as they flew past, a narrow miss in becoming road-kill.

Niyol threw back his head and laughed. He'd felt the rabbit's heart skitter to a stop and then thump forcefully as it leaped. Odd little creature, but he remembered they had a good taste.

The roar of the engine was loud in Layla's ears, and yet she still heard the sound of his laughter and smiled without knowing why it happened.

You will love me.

Layla's smile froze. Dear God. Was that a promise

or a warning?

It will not matter. It will be what it will be.

Again, the simplicity of his answer was what calmed her. He was right. Like water, love found its own level.

****

They rode without stopping until almost noon. Layla was faint from pain and hunger when he suddenly aimed for a line of small trees down in the canyon and rolled the bike to a stop. After the roar of the wind and engine, the silence was startling.

She slid off the back of the seat and then staggered to the shade and dropped. He was beside her within seconds, water in one hand and food in another.

Layla was unable to read the expression on his face and gratefully took what he offered. The water wasn't cold, but it didn't matter. It was enough to wash down a pain pill. The bread was fresh, the jerky smoked and salty. It reminded her of the deer jerky she and her mother used to make for family snacks when she was growing up.

He sat down beside her and ate like he was starving. All of a sudden he looked up at her and smiled. She forgot to breathe.

"Starving. Isn't that what you say when it's been a long time since you last ate?"

She nodded.

He laughed, his teeth white against his sun-toned skin.

"Then yes, I am starving. It has been at least five hundred of your years since food has passed my lips."

Layla thought he was kidding until she realized

not only had he commented on what she'd been thinking, but that meant he must have, once again, read her freaking mind. That was something she needed to remember.

"So how does this work?" she asked, as she tore off another bite of bread with her fingers and put it in her mouth.

"This? You mean us? Why I am here with you like this?"

She was about to nod an assent when all of a sudden her food went flying and she was flat on her back in the sand. His hands were around her neck and she could feel the heat from his breath.

"When you are good enough, fast enough, deadly enough, to not only see an attack like this coming, but defend yourself against it and kill your enemy, it will mean that you are ready for what comes next. It is then that I will leave you."

Layla's heart was hammering so hard against her ribcage that it was hard to breathe. She slammed her hands against his shoulders and pushed him back and then off, picked up her food and began angrily brushing off the dirt.

He laughed, which only made her madder.

"You don't fight fair," she muttered.

His laughter ended. "And neither will your enemy. If you don't learn this well enough and soon enough, you and your people will die."

It wasn't the first time he'd referred to a cataclysmic event, but it was the last time she wanted to hear about it without an explanation.

"You've said that before," she snapped. "Explain yourself or stop talking about it."

His eyes narrowed. There was strength in her words, as well as her actions.

"In a very short time what you call a meteor will fall from the sky and it will hit earth and destroy it forever."

The bread in Layla's hand fell from her fingers into her lap as she stared at his mouth, watching the way his lips formed the words that were ending her world. Later, she would remember thinking how could such a dire and horrifying warning come from a beautiful mouth?

"Before it happens, water will foul. The electrical power that runs your country will end. Food will become a most valuable commodity, and man will turn against his brother for water. For a while, the predators will rise to the top of the food chain while man, who once held that place, will become helpless to protect themselves."

Layla didn't know she was crying until he reached out and wiped a tear from her face.

"Death is always a sadness," he said softly. "Even the death of a dream."

Then he leaned forward, cupped the back of her head with his hand and pulled her to him.

She knew he was going to kiss her and she welcomed it, but was not prepared for the impact of his mouth upon hers. The moment they touched, she not only felt the pressure of his lips, but smelled the sweat on his skin and the sexual urge thundering through him.

She moaned.

Moments later he was out of his clothes and she was beneath him. As he pulled down her pants and yanked off her shirt, she was trembling, desperate for the moment of impact.

Chapter Five

He took her in hunger, more than ready for the powerful rush of blood he knew would surge through his body. Her legs were parted, her body trembling in anticipation. He fell between them and slid into her hot wet depths without restraint, then buried himself as deep as he could go. But when he began to withdraw for a second pass, she locked her legs around his waist and pulled him back.

Layla was already half out of her mind then she heard him laugh. The joy he found in human existence was an aphrodisiac she had not expected. He'd eaten his food with blatant pleasure, and at the moment, he was so high on making love she couldn't have stopped him if she'd tried.

Once he'd brought her to a climax with nothing more than a sweep of the energy that had brought him into her world, and now he was taking her to another level of lovemaking from which she might not recover.

He was big and he was hard.

She was hot and she was wet, and together they were about to ignite.

Niyol rode her without restraint, too hungry for the climax to prolong it. She was reaction to his action, building passion, building energy mass until he became so full he overflowed. She felt him shatter, but was not prepared for the impact to her when it happened.

Not only did he send her into orgasm, but while

he was coming, she felt his as well. She screamed until she had no voice as he spilled his seed. The climax blew apart their capacity for thought. There was nothing they could do but hold on and wait for the pieces of their minds to settle and make them whole again.

****

The sun had moved just enough to burn through a gap in the leaves above them and down onto Niyol's back. He groaned, reluctant to move from the comfort of her body.

Layla felt him shift and held him tighter, unwilling to turn him loose. He'd said that she would love him, and he'd been right. He was a virtual stranger, and yet there was a bond between them stronger than a lifetime of living could have forged. He'd already warned her he would leave, which made her desperate to cram that lifetime together into whatever days they had left.

When he raised himself up, his hair fell down around his shoulders, forming a barrier between her and the heat of the sun. His gaze raked her face and neck as he eyed the silver chain with the tiny bird, and then lower, looking with pleasure at the slim build of her copper-colored body, burnished by the sheen of mingled sweat. When his penis began to stir and then engorge, he inhaled sharply.

"It is good to be human," he said softly, and once more began to move, only this time in a slower, more dedicated rhythm.

Layla closed her eyes and arched her back to meet the thrusts, concentrating wholly on the feel of his body within her depths. When the climax came again, she was in his head. He was right. It was good to be human.

****

Sunset was a few hours away and they were now all the way down into the gorge of Canyon de Chelly. The floor of the canyon was surprisingly fertile and green compared to the land above it. The occasional rock spire rising up from the canyon floor was as a lone King on a chess board. But the canyon floor was not deserted.

It was also home to many of the Dineh who lived and worked the land – herding sheep, growing crops, living a rural life far away from the group housing that constituted reservation living.

Niyol and his woman did not ride through unnoticed, but their presence was not questioned, not even when they scattered grazing sheep.

The motorcycle engine was a steady roar in her ears. Although she was now wearing the bike helmet and Niyol's hair was bound into a ponytail at the nape of his neck, her skin was sere; her eyes dry and wind-burned.

The first time they passed a site of pueblo ruins, the drums were suddenly loud in her ears and she wondered what that meant. Niyol heard the thought.

The Old Ones acknowledge your presence.

Layla gasped. *You mean they know who I am?*

Both sides of the veil know your name.

The burden of what she'd been given was finally sinking in. It was both a frightening and sobering thought to know so many lives rested on her ability to survive what was coming.

Remember, I am with you.

And just like that, the burden lifted. He was right. She wasn't in this alone. A Windwalker makes anything possible.

It was nearing dusk when Niyol brought the motorcycle to a stop in a canyon deep between two massive walls of rock towering above them on both sides.

The canyon valley was both narrow and flat, peppered with sparse scrub brush and a thin line of small trees running through the middle where a thinner ribbon of water flowed.

The canyon looked like Mother Nature had taken a cake knife to the land and carved out a huge slice for herself. Except for a couple of shallow caves along the canyon floor, the walls on either side appeared impenetrable.

"We stop here," Niyol said, pointing to a small pool beside the nearest cave. He pushed the motorcycle all the way inside and began unloading it.

Layla dropped to her knees beside water and drank until she had quenched her thirst. After she splashed her face and neck to wash off the dust, she stood, relishing the quick breeze. As soon as she carried her backpack inside the cave, she went back to help.

They worked together until the bike was unloaded, and then she went to gather dry wood for a campfire while Niyol began setting up camp.

He stopped once to watch her, satisfied she took the initiative without complaining or being told what to do. He knew how Jackson Birdsong had raised her. Long before she'd proven herself worthy, he'd known everything there was to know about her, but he'd forgotten how much he would love her again. When she started back to the campsite, he turned away, a little confused as to whether it was appropriate to let so much of his feelings show. Being human was, at times, also confusing.

"This should be enough to get the fire started," Layla said, as she dumped the armload at his feet. "There's more dry wood down by the trees along the wash."

He glanced up at the sky. "It will be dark in a few minutes."

She shrugged. "We'll need the fuel. It will be cold when the sun goes down. Light the fire and I will have a beacon to follow back."

As she strode off in the direction of the trees, he gathered up some dry grasses then began building the fire near the front of the shallow cave.

He started with a four-foot circle of loose rocks gathered from inside the cave, then twisted the dry grasses into knots before laying them on the bottom. He covered the grass with small sticks, then larger ones, until he had a decent-sized stack ready to light.

He paused, looking out in the twilight. She was on her way back. He put a match to the woodpile, watching intently as the flames began to eat through the grass, then the smaller sticks, to the larger ones on top until they had fire. Night had officially arrived as he walked out of the cave. He couldn't see her, but he knew she was near because he could feel her heartbeat.

Layla's vision adjusted to the dark as the light slowly faded. The canyon wall went on forever. It was so high it would have been easy to believe it was where the world ended.

The cave to which she was headed was an even darker shape against the night until she saw a glimmer of light.

The fire was alive.

The armload of wood she was carrying was awkward and heavy, but she lengthened her stride, guided by the light in the darkness and the man silhouetted before it.

Then she blinked, and when she looked again he was gone. She heard the sound of footsteps then he was before her; taking the burden she'd been carrying. She relinquished the limbs gladly, but winced as a stray limb caught against the back of her healing arm.

He heard her gasp.

"You are hurt?"

"It's nothing, and it's getting cold."

"You go. I am behind you."

She jogged toward the cave and the brightly burning fire. Once inside, she pulled her backpack closer to the fire then took off her shirt to inspect the healing wound on her arm. It stung from the new scratch, but nothing had burst open. She dug out the medicine she'd brought with her, spreading ointment down the length of the new scar. Keeping it supple would aid the healing, and there was too much at stake for her to get sick from infection.

Niyol was almost to the cave when he saw her kneel and take off her shirt. He stumbled, caught by the beauty of her body in the firelight and stopped to watch from the shadows, remembering she was his. By the time he came into the cave, she had put her shirt back on. He dumped the wood near the fire then walked up behind her. He ran a hand beneath her hair as he turned her to face him.

"You are hurt?"

"Just a slight scratch. It's okay."

He felt guilt, a human trait he did not enjoy.

"I am sorry you were given no time for proper

healing."

She slid her arms around his waist, willing herself not to weep.

"Time is my enemy," she said softly. "The time will come when it will take you away from me."

Pain rolled through him so fast her image blurred before his eyes. In sudden panic, he pulled her into his arms.

"Being human also hurts."

Layla stifled a sob.

Somewhere beyond the cave a coyote yipped, and another answered nearby. They'd seen the fire. They'd sensed the human element in their midst. But like the dog in her grandfather's village that had seen Niyol coming and run, the coyotes also sensed a being not of this world, giving him and the fire a wide berth.

Later, after they'd shared more jerky and water, Layla slipped out to go to the bathroom, feeling her way along the canyon wall until she was satisfied she'd gone far enough.

Squatting to relieve herself in such a place, and in this way, reminded her of her life back in Oklahoma when she had hunted the woods with her father. As a child she had been afraid of the dark, and yet she loved Jackson Birdsong so much that when he took his dogs out to hunt at night, she begged to go with him.

With no brothers or sisters, her parents had been her world, and her world grew smaller after her mother's unexpected death at an early age. She and her father had cried together when it happened, and given no other options, faced life without her.

Halfway back to the cave she saw a streak of light up in the night sky and paused, watching as a shooting star sped across a dark palette awash with heavenly bodies.

Skywalker.

Layla turned. Suddenly Niyol was standing beside her and she hadn't even heard him approach.

"You mean that's not a shooting star?"

He shrugged. "It is what you call it, but with a passenger on board."

Layla looked back up at the sky. "Always?"

He took her hand. "It is cold. Come back to the fire."

"Which means you're not going to answer my question, right?"

"Some things are best left unsaid."

She let him lead her toward their camp, but her thoughts were tumbling one over the other. It was suddenly obvious how ignorant humans were, living in this world without thought for things unseen.

****

George Begay felt the same anguish he'd felt the night his Frances had died. He didn't believe Layla was dead, but she would never be his granddaughter again. She'd been set up as a sacrifice, and at the same time, a savior. He'd seen the men in his dreams – the men who would come after her. He'd seen fighting and blood and death, but they had not shown him the faces, so he didn't know her true fate. And so he grieved for what was already lost, as well as what was yet to come.

The Dineh knew she was gone. A few talked about hearing a motorcycle that morning, but no one had seen the rider. They already knew a crisis of world proportion was imminent before Layla even returned to the reservation. The council fires were burning; the elders warning what was imminent, and the younger people confused and afraid.

The Dineh knew the history of their people and what had happened at the Bosque Redondo in 1864. The Navajo called it the Long Walk. The U.S. government called it relocating some Indians, and took the Dineh off their lands, forcing them to other land in New Mexico. It was often compared to the Trail of Tears the Cherokee endured when they the government took their lands in the East and sent them halfway across country to Oklahoma territory on foot.

Many of the Navajo escaped the soldiers' roundup by hiding in the canyons and the high mesas and continued living as they always had. But thousands were taken, and thousands had died. Only that was then, and this was now, and they couldn't believe something that dire would happen again. The appearance of the Windwalker left families in turmoil, and a tribe divided by fear and the unknown.

But the Navajo wasn't the only tribe in crisis. It was happening all over North America, from the east coast to the west coast, from the southern border of the continent to the northern most boundaries. They'd all seen the video and the believers were waiting for another sign – the one that would tell them it was time to run.

****

It was a sound, a breeze on her face, an instinct that something wasn't right.

Layla's eyes flew open, saw a moving shadow on the floor in front of her, which meant someone was behind her. She rolled out of her bedroll onto her feet; her father's hunting knife clutched tight in one hand.

Niyol was holding two skinned rabbits already spitted and ready for the fire.

"Most impressive," he said. "I bring food."

Layla groaned, holstered the knife, and ran her fingers through her hair in frustration.

"I could have killed you," she muttered.

"You are not yet that good, but it is of no importance because I cannot die," he said bluntly, then leaned the spitted rabbits against the stones, angling them toward the fire. "It will take a while for them to cook."

"I know that, and believe it or not, after a long night's sleep and nearly scaring me half out of my mind, I need to pee."

He grinned as she strode past him. He had forgotten that humans were also funny.

****

Two black SUVs drove onto the Navajo reservation just before sunrise with the location of George Begay's house already set in the GPS.

Emile Harper knew they were there because he'd sent them, but they were flying under radar, and technically had no backing or approval of the United States government. As for the men, it wasn't their first rodeo. They considered any confrontation the locals might cause to be of no concern, and picking up one woman and taking her back to D.C. a simple task.

They were driving eastward and topping a hill just as the sun breeched the horizon. For a fraction of a second the driver was blinded by the day's first light, but his vision cleared just in time to slam on the brakes. The second car, which was driving in the dust trail of the first, barely missed rear-ending it.

All of a sudden the walkie-talkie in the first car squawked. The driver in the second car was pissed.

"What the fuck, Conroy? Over."

Conroy was still staring out his windshield as he picked up the radio. There were thousands and thousands of acres on the Navajo reservation, and a good three hundred armed men right in front of them. All he could think was how the hell did they know we'd cross here?

"We've got trouble. Over."

He was trying to figure out how to put a spin on their presence as he headed toward the tribal policemen, who he hoped were in charge. Law was always better than mob rule, and there was a seriously large mob in wait. He couldn't decide whether to play dumb or pull a pissed-off attitude, but he kept flashing on an old cowboy movie he'd once seen, about a small caravan of covered wagons trapped down in a valley by the hundreds of Indians mounted on horseback, lining both sides of the rims above.

Granted he and his men weren't in covered wagons, and there were no mountains directly around them, but they were fucking trapped by a wall of Indians in vehicles as far as he could see. Emile Harper had seriously underestimated the Navajo nation.

As the officers started toward him, he heard the doors opening and closing in the SUVS behind him and knew the men were getting out. So they'd been made. Big fucking deal. He would get them out of it. He opted for a happy face and raised his hand in hello.

"Hey guys, what's going on? Looks like quite a reunion here. Hope we didn't mess up the group picture."

No one laughed, which meant he wasn't going to

be talking his way out of this.

At that point, the tallest officer stepped up.

"Johnston Nantay, Navajo tribal police. I want to see some identification."

"Look, no hard feelings here. We obviously are somewhere we don't belong. Our bad. We'll just turn around and leave the same way we came, okay?"

"No, not okay. Hand over your wallets, all of you."

Conroy heard a distinct click behind him, like someone had just released the safety on a gun. He pivoted quickly, his hand up in the air.

"No weapons! No weapons!" he yelled.

When he turned around, not only had the officers pulled their weapons, but there were three hundred plus Indians spilling out of their cars, armed to the teeth. If he didn't defuse this situation and fast, they might go down in a history repeat of Custer's last stand.

Conroy waved at the men he'd brought with him.

"Drop the guns and hand over your wallets."

His men shifted nervously.

The sound of several hundred rifles jacking shells into the chambers breeched the sudden silence.

Conroy threw down his wallet and handgun, and turned to face Nantay.

"I'm unarmed, I'm unarmed! Don't shoot!"

Nantay's men began gathering up the wallets and weapons while he turned his attention to Conroy.

"I would be interested in hearing what you thought you were going to do here," Nantay said.

"We have obviously taken a wrong turn," Conroy said.

Nantay didn't respond as he began flipping wallets open, and the more he looked, the angrier he got.

"You're either a very stupid white man, or you

think we are," he said, as he tossed the wallets into an evidence bag and handed them to another officer.

Conroy took a deep breath, but said nothing.

"Handcuff them," Nantay said.

"Look here, you can't-"

Nantay finally smiled. "Well, yes we can, because this is our land and you, Mr. Washington, as well as Jackson, Truman, Jefferson, Adams, and all the other presidents you've brought with you, are going to jail."

"We've done nothing but take a wrong turn on a hunting trip," Conroy argued.

But the officers were through talking. They handcuffed the eight-man crew, tossed them in the back of two vans, and headed for the jail as the hundreds of other Navajo climbed back in their vehicles and began dispersing in different directions.

Many rough miles and an hour later, the vans pulled up at the jail. The officers began removing their prisoners, who were complaining loudly of the ride and their rights.

As they started into the building, an older man with long braids walked out, then stopped in their path. The officers yanked their prisoners to a halt as the old man approached, and then began moving from man to man, eyeing each one of them carefully.

"What do you say, George?" Nantay asked.

George Begay nodded. "Yes, these are the ones," then he walked toward his truck, got in and drove away.

"Who the hell was that?" Conroy asked.

Nantay poked his rifle in Conroy's back. "That was the man who told us you were coming, now walk forward, Mr. Washington."

Conroy frowned. "What do you mean, told you we were coming?"

Nantay paused. “The Pony Express has long since disappeared. How did you think we found you?” he said, and hauled them into jail.

****

When Conroy and his men never called in, Emile Harper knew something had gone wrong. These were men who knew if they got caught, they were on their own. However, if they’d been made, then it was all the warning the Birdsong woman would need to hide out, which meant next time she would definitely not be in her grandfather’s house. So much for brute force. Moving on to technology.

****

Binini Island – West Indies

Thanks to Madame ReeRee, he knew something the U.S. government did not. He knew where Layla Birdsong was hiding, and he thought it a place most fitting. According to ReeRee she *was* still on the Navajo reservation, but not near any settlements. She’d already gone to ground and was holed up by water in a place called the canyon of death. It was ironic that he’d been able to confirm the existence with a voodoo queen and Google, although he found out later that the correct translation was the Canyon del Muerto. The internet was a wonderful invention.

But, just as he was about to celebrate an easy retrieval, further research brought his premature celebration to a halt. Canyon del Muerto wasn’t just a little spot on the map. It was miles and miles and miles of land in a remote part of the reservation.

However, anything worth having, was worth fighting for, and he knew just who to call.

He ordered some bread and cheese and a bottle of his favorite wine to be brought up from the wine cellar, then settled into the most comfortable chair in the library to make the call. It was a silly little ritual, but Prince believed in bad luck, so repeating a ritual that had brought him good luck was needed to offset the bad.

He took a sip of the wine, rolling it around in his mouth and then sucking it under his tongue to get the full bouquet before letting it slide down his throat. He allowed himself a small moment of ecstasy at the perfection of the taste, and then broke off a piece of bread, slathered on some of his favorite soft cheese, and took a big bite. He was chewing as he punched in the numbers, and swallowed as the call went through. One more sip of wine as the phone began to ring, and if everything in the universe was aligned as it should be, his call would be answered before the third ring.

One ring, then two. He was holding his breath as the third ring began, then a click, and the voice he'd been waiting for came online. He smiled.

****

Maurice Tenet was an oddity in the world of humans. Being an albino meant always being the one who stood out in a crowd – never being the guy on the beach with the buff bod and oiled-down pecs. Women were nice to him, but mostly through curiosity. He had sex when he wanted it because he could buy it, and liked the setup far better than all the crap that came with a 'relationship'.

But the older he got, the more serious his eye

condition became. He lived with the risk of blindness, not to mention suffering with the skin conditions that were a result of his affliction. He could have become a bitter man, but instead of feeling like he was missing out, he had, instead, created a world around him in which he was the norm, and anyone else he let in became the odd man out.

He drove a white car with white interior and wore only white clothing. He lived in an oversized white beach house in LaJolla, California in which all the walls, furniture and floor coverings were white, and both his maid and his personal chef were people who'd also been born with albinism.

The art on his walls was black and white, and the light fixtures were either all white milk glass or glass with no color at all. Today was Tuesday, which meant it was feeding day for Winston, his pet albino boa. And, keeping with the décor, he was, at the moment, feeding Winston his bi-monthly diet of white mice. He dropped the last mouse into the snake's mouth, watching absently as the boa began swallowing it whole. He never got bored watching the little mice wiggle, even after they were well inside Winston's body.

Satisfied that task was over, he slid the lid back onto the boa's glass case and then walked out of the game room into the library just as the phone rang. He waved at the maid, indicating he wanted a drink. She knew the routine and scurried away as he answered the call.

"Tenet here."

"Maurice, it's Landan. How are you?"

Maurice leaned back in his chair and rubbed his belly, as if contemplating a meal he was about to eat.

"Landan, I haven't heard from you in ages. I'm fine, and you?"

"The same, always searching for a new and better world."

Maurice laughed. "Ever the dreamer," my friend. "So to what do I owe the pleasure of this call?"

"What? You think I don't call just to say hello?"

"You haven't yet and I'm thinking you're past the age of changing your spots. What do you need of me, Landan? What curiosity do you have need of this time?"

"It's not a thing, it's a person... a woman actually."

Maurice's eyes narrowed thoughtfully. Acquiring people required more skill than finding relics.

"It will cost you, you know," Maurice said.

"Money is not an issue," Prince said.

"Well, it is with me. So talk. Who is the woman? What trick is she capable of pulling that might warn her in advance of my arrival?"

"Her name is Layla Birdsong. As for abilities, I'm not exactly certain. I have a tentative location and a photo. I'll email you the particulars."

Maurice frowned. "I know that name. Why do I know that name," he muttered, and then it hit him. "Oh shit! You want me to go after a woman with an evil genie in her back pocket that peeled the skin off the last man who got near her? I don't think so."

Prince frowned. He didn't like to be told no.

"What would it take for you to go after her?"

"Everything you have on what you think she is, and 24 hours to think about what my life is worth to me."

"Done. I'll call you this time tomorrow and just so you know, I expect a positive answer."

Maurice frowned. "Don't threaten me, Landan. Not even subtly. Do we understand each other?"

Prince sighed. "Yes, and I apologize for that. It's just very important to me."

"Yes and so is my next breath. I'll be in touch. Nice talking to you."

He hung up before Prince had anything more to say and smiled at the maid who brought in his drink.

"Thank you, Pet. You're the best."

Petula Sims smiled and giggled, then scurried off before her boss got that look in his eye. They didn't love each other, but shared the occasional meeting of the minds and bed for a twenty minute stretch, after which Pet had the job of removing dirty sheets and remaking the bed, while Maurice took himself off to the shower. He always compensated in her paycheck, she banked the extra for hard times, and that was how it worked in this house.

Chapter Six

One week later:

Layla and Niyol ate once a day, usually rabbit; occasionally a prairie chicken or snake. When they'd first reached the cave, he'd started her out drinking water three times a day, and now she was down to two without feeling thirst. She needed to be physically able to withstand hardship for the days ahead, and there was not much time to prepare her.

Layla had always been fit, but after the week in the hospital, and now the rigors of the training he was putting her through, she was losing body fat at a rapid rate. Her jeans were old and soft, but they were hanging low on her hips. Sometimes she wore a loose shirt, but more often than not nothing more than a gray sports bra and her daddy's necklace dangling between her breasts. She kept her hair braided, or in a ponytail at the nape of her neck, and her smooth brown skin was getting browner. The cuts on her belly and cheek were mostly healed and the scars were noticeable, but she didn't care. The cut on the back of her arm was healed, but tender.

This morning Niyol had sent her out to run the canyon, beginning from the cave all the way to where the wall began to curve - and back again. She'd been running for only a short while when Niyol waved her in. She jogged in gratefully.

"That wasn't much of a workout."

"It wasn't meant to be," he said. "I had things to

do that you aren't meant to see."

Layla stared, first at him and then at the floor of the cave behind him.

"Where did all that come from?"

"From me."

Her eyes widened. "You can conjure up physical things?"

"It is not conjuring. It is a simple matter of acquisition from one place to another."

"I am impressed," she said, eyeing a spear and the bow and quiver of arrows – nice ones with a fine metal tip, a lot like the ones her father had used. There were other knives, although she preferred the hunting knife she wore around her waist, but no guns or ammo.

"Why all the old stuff? Why not some guns and ammo?"

"Because you will fight the old way, or the Old Ones will not deem you worthy."

She walked past him for a closer look, heard a slight shuffling of feet and reacted, but not fast enough. Once again she was on her back with Niyol on top of her.

Layla sighed in frustration. "Crap."

"You are-"

"Don't say it. I know, I know. I'm dead," she muttered, as she pushed him off.

He was frowning as he helped her up. "You are not paying attention. You can learn anything if you just pay attention, and there's not much time."

Layla nodded. "I will do better," she said, and slid her arms around his neck, as if to hug him, but tried to trip him, instead.

She saw his eyes widen just a fraction of a second before she moved, but he was grinning.

"I wasn't expecting that, but you gave yourself

away."

"How?"

"Your eyes always close when we're about to kiss. This time they widened slightly as you mentally assessed what you were about to do."

"Crap again."

He laughed, and this time swung her up into his arms. "I want to make love to you."

Layla's pulse kicked. "The feeling is mutual."

"But this is not the time."

Her disappointment was physical. "Then put me down and pay attention to what I'm going to tell you."

He frowned slightly, but did as she asked.

"Here's the deal, Windwalker. When you walk in human shoes, you don't tease a woman with heaven, and then pull back and tell her the dishes aren't done."

His frown deepened. "I don't understand. I did not ask you to do these dishes of which you speak."

This time she was the one grinning. "It's an analogy. What I'm saying is, don't turn a woman on and then walk away. It's called teasing."

His expression lightened. "Ah. Teasing. I get it. I will never tell you to do dishes."

All of a sudden Layla felt like crying because she knew that to be true, and it was probably the saddest thing she would hear all day.

Her eyes welled as she turned away, but Niyol saw. A sharp pain pierced his chest and his hand moved to the pain without thinking. It had been a long time since he'd felt regret, and was remembering he hadn't liked it then, and didn't like it now.

"I am sorry for hurting you," he said. "But I am here to keep you alive, and you must learn many things before it's too late."

She shrugged and wiped the tears from her cheeks before she would face him again.

"I just over-reacted. You do your job and I'll do mine, and we'll say goodbye without making it a big deal. So what's the next lesson?"

The pain in Niyol's chest grew more intense. He couldn't bear the look on her face another moment longer without trying to explain.

"You are wrong. It will be, what you call, a big deal. Standing in this body, feeling what I feel, it will be a most cruel and unjust goodbye. I will mourn your loss as great as you mourn mine. What you must never forget is that you belong to me. You have always belonged to me. As you take your last breath, look up. I will be standing beside you, waiting to take you home."

A sob rolled up Layla's throat as she threw herself into Niyol's arms.

"You break my heart," she whispered.

Niyol buried his face in the curve of her neck, then began taking off her clothes.

"I thought you said this wasn't the time," Layla said.

"I was wrong."

He shed his clothes as if they were water and laid her down on the bedroll. Deep in a cave in the Canyon del Muerto, surrounded by an arsenal of weapons, he showed her how very wrong he had been.

****

Against every ounce of good sense he possessed, Maurice Tenet gave into his greed and accepted the job Landan Prince offered him – to the tune of five million dollars, plus expenses.

After the dossier Prince sent on Layla Birdsong, Tenet caught the first flight out to Arizona, rented a car in Phoenix, and headed toward the Navajo reservation armed with a camera, his usual protective garb from the dangers of sun and wind, and wearing an assortment of Native American jewelry to make it appear he was both a fan and an admirer.

He wheeled into a gift shop on the reservation, booked a tour to see the pueblo ruins in Canyon del Muerto, and insinuated himself into a faux friendship with the driver along the way.

The oddity of his condition always made it easy to strike up a conversation. People were curious about the pasty-white man garbed from head to toe, wearing wrap-around sunglasses.

All he had to do to get a reaction was take the sunglasses off. The moment they saw his eyes, no matter how hard they tried to hide it, they freaked. With no pigmentation to color the irises, all that was visible was the blood behind the lenses, giving him the appearance of a living, breathing vampire.

As they rode, he listened to the tour guide's spiel, while eyeing the landscape and scoping out the places someone with Birdsong's issues might hide. The good news was that he was here, but the bad news was how vast the canyon actually was. Unless he got very lucky, a search by air would be required.

The guide stopped in several places for the tourists to take pictures. Tenet bailed out with all the others, and snapped pictures at random while watching for his next opportunity to get information. He didn't have long to wait.

The tour guide, a Navajo man who introduced himself as Leland Benally, was standing at an overlook answering the tourists' questions when a woman drove up in a truck. Tenet watched her get out on the run, heading for their guide.

After a hurried conversation between the two, Leland announced to the group that there was a family emergency at home and that his wife, Beverly, would finish the tour for him. He took off in the truck she'd driven in, and she began moving among the tourists, introducing herself and making them feel at ease. When she got to Maurice, she couldn't help but stare at how covered up he was in such heat. He quickly put her at ease with a brief explanation of his condition.

"Wow, that's something," Beverly said. "You know, in an ironic way, I understand a little bit about how out of place you feel. I'm a white woman, married to a full-blood Navajo and living on the rez for almost fifteen years. We have three kids together, but there are times when I still feel out of place."

Maurice nodded sympathetically, but the wheels were already turning. An outsider might be the way into any secrets they were keeping regarding Birdsong, especially if there was money involved. He took a step toward her and put a hand on her shoulder in a gesture of sympathy.

"It's hard being different, isn't it?"

Beverly rolled her eyes. "You said it."

"So is it also hard to live with spiritual beliefs that are usually quite different from the white community. You know... like the white buffalo and shape-shifter stories, that kind of thing. I studied some about this in college and it's very fascinating to me."

Beverly glanced over her shoulder to make sure they weren't overhead, and then took a step closer.

"Everything is hard. It took years for me not to make a fool of myself in certain situations, but there are still people who don't like me, and it's all because of the color of my skin. If it wasn't for Leland and the kids, I would have already been gone. The conveniences other people take for granted are miles from here, like eating out at nice restaurants and running down the street for groceries, shopping for fashionable clothes, malls, movies," she rolled her eyes. "Don't get me started."

"That's so sad," Maurice said. "So I take it money isn't easy to come by here."

She waved her arms out at the stark but beautiful vista. "I don't see any factories or shops, do you?"

He frowned in commiseration. "I see what you mean. And there's the big deal everyone is talking about now that you must be facing. I don't know how you keep it together."

She frowned. "I don't know what you mean."

He lowered his voice. "You know. That Birdsong woman. The one on that video. I think everyone in the entire world has seen that by now. Was she one of your friends? I'd think everyone must have really been freaked out for her, being attacked and then rescued like that."

An odd expression came and went on her face, and for a moment, Maurice was afraid he'd said too much too soon. But the woman was obviously in need of a sympathetic ear.

"She was a teacher for one of my kids, but she's not a friend. She had the audacity to suggest that my youngest girl had issues, and asked me if Leland and I had trouble at home. We don't get along, but that was none of her damn business."

"Wow. Teachers weren't that forward when I was in school. But it's about time for a new school year to start. At least your daughter won't be in her class again."

Beverly shrugged. “It doesn’t matter. She’s gone. Quit with no notice and took off up here somewhere to commune with nature or talk to spirits, or whatever the hell else she’s claiming to do. Everyone acts like doomsday is coming, and if it is, I can tell you right now I don’t want to die on this land.”

“Doomsday! Really?”

Beverly shrugged, realizing that she might have been talking too much to a stranger.

Maurice felt her pulling away and he pounced. “What would you do if you had a half a million dollars in your hand? Right now. Today.”

Her lips parted. She looked at him, then past him into her dreams.

“I would leave here.”

“Where would you and your family like to be?”

Her eyes filled with tears, but she blinked them away. “Leland wouldn’t come, and he wouldn’t let me take the kids. They’re being raised in the old ways, you know.”

“Oh. Too bad.”

She frowned. “Why on earth would you ask such a thing?”

“Because that’s what I’m offering for Layla Birdsong’s location.”

She backed up in shock. “You can’t be serious.”

“As a heart attack.”

“You have that much money on you?”

“In my car back at the tourist center.”

“Oh my God! What if someone steals it?”

“I have more.”

She gasped, unable to imagine resources that deep.

“Do you know where she is?” he asked.

She shrugged.

He pressed her, sensing that she was weakening. "They have to be talking about it. What do people say?"

"I don't know," she muttered.

"You do know. I've offered you a way out of your private hell. Think about it. When we get back, I'll get in my car and drive off with a half million dollars and nothing to show for it, or I can drive off with information and you will be a half million dollars to the good."

"It's in cash?"

"In cash."

She turned around and strode toward the tour bus without commenting, but he knew the seed had been planted, and he knew how it felt to be on the outside looking in. He felt certain she would spill her guts. Despite the misery he was in, this had been a most fruitful tour.

****

Three days later: Nearing sundown

George Begay was going through his things, packing for the journey he knew lay ahead. He was taking only what would fit in a small duffle bag, knowing speed would be imperative to their escape.

He picked up his wedding photo and slipped it beneath a rolled up pair of jeans. He might be leaving, but he was taking Frances with him. He stuffed a few pairs of socks on top of the photo, and was about to add a couple of shirts when there was a knock at his door. The presence of trouble was already in his mind, and when Leland Benally strode in without waiting for an invitation, he began seeing what had happened.

Leland was bordering on panicked. He grabbed

George by his shoulders, already apologizing before he even told George what for.

"I'm sorry. I'm sorry, but you have to get word to Layla and the Windwalker that someone bad knows where they are. Beverly and I have been having problems, but I had no idea she would do something like this."

George stifled an urge to panic. He could not help Layla, and Layla knew it. Right now, the Windwalker was all that stood between her and disaster.

"Leland, sit down and tell me what happened."

Leland sat, and the moment George sat down, Leland was back on his feet, pacing.

"A few days ago my mother fell and broke her leg. Beverly knew I had tours that day and found me at the lookout where the tourists were taking pictures. I left in our truck and she finished the tour for me. No big deal, you know? We've done stuff like that before."

George nodded. "Yes, that's what family does, right? I hope your mother is okay. I had not heard."

"She will be," Leland said. "But that's not why I'm here. There was a strange man on the tour. Weird looking albino guy all covered up to protect himself from the sun and light, but too friendly, you know? He didn't feel sincere, but hey, he paid his money for the tour so he came with the rest of them. Only he and Beverly got to talking. He figured out she was unhappy. Offered her a way out of her misery."

George frowned. "I don't understand."

Leland's voice began to shake. "Beverly left me this morning. Didn't even try and take the kids. She told me that if the world was going to come to an end, she didn't want to die out here in this god-forsaken place. She said she was going to Las Vegas. I was shocked. I asked her what she thought she was going to do for money. She opened up her suitcase. It was full of hundred dollar bills. I don't know how much. I asked her if she'd stolen it. She said no, that a man gave it to her for a little information."

Leland wiped his eyes, unashamed of the tears as he continued.

"I knew. I knew before she opened her mouth that the only information of value on the entire reservation was the whereabouts of Layla."

George felt sick. "So she told?"

Leland nodded.

"She couldn't have known the exact location because none of us do," George said.

"She heard you talking the other night when we were all at the meeting, remember? Someone asked you if Layla was safe and you said you saw her drinking water near the cave with the little pool. Everyone knows that's in the Canyon del Muerto. And any Navajo could tell you exactly how to find it."

George's hands were shaking, but what was done was done.

"Is Beverly gone?" George asked.

"Yes, and I'll be honest. If it hadn't been for the fact that our children were standing there crying and watching her leave, I would have broken her damn neck."

"It's good you don't have her blood on your hands," George said.

Leland ducked his head. "She has brought much shame to me. I am sorry."

"We have to trust that the Windwalker will know things we cannot understand. Somehow he will protect her. I believe this and you have to believe this, too."

"What about Beverly?" Leland asked.

George shrugged. "I doubt she will live long

enough to spend all her money."

Leland didn't bother to hide his shock. "This is happening soon?"

"Very soon," George said. "There will be a sign in the sky. When it comes, native people will come from all corners of this continent. There will be thousands here waiting."

Leland frowned. "Waiting for what?"

"For Layla. She will save us. Maybe not all, but all who believe and are here when she comes." George stood up. "Say nothing of this to any of the others. Only say that your wife left you. Mention nothing of her betrayal, because in the long run, it will not matter."

"This is true?" Leland asked.

George nodded. "This is true."

****

"One more round and then we'll call it a day," Niyol said, watching carefully as Layla notched another arrow into the bow and took aim at a target a good distance away.

Her arm was aching, both from the unaccustomed use of the bow and her healing arm, but the more she practiced, the more her skill was returning.

She had bow-hunted with her father from the age of thirteen, and at one time had been quite good. It had been years since she'd practiced, but some things are never forgotten.

At his nod, she took a deep breath then swung the bow up, and with nothing but a quick glance at the target, let fly. Her father had called it instinctive shooting. Her aim was better when she just looked at the tree briefly, which was the target, then by taking specific aim at the mark on it.

The arrow hit with a solid thump. She smiled.

Niyol took the bow out of her hands, laid it aside and then reached for her. Layla started to walk into his embrace then ducked and hit him in the back with a quick jab of her elbow before falling to the ground and rolling away. He was laughing when he dodged it, but he was also proud. She was paying attention.

"So, little Singing Bird, you are finally paying attention."

She eyed him curiously as she dusted herself off.

"Why did you call me that?"

He shrugged. "One day you will know."

Layla frowned. "Don't go all mystic on me again. What aren't you telling me now?"

He pointed to the bow. "You get the bow. I'll get the arrows and meet you back at the camp."

He loped off toward the trees, but Layla didn't leave. She was mesmerized by the fluidity of his body as he ran and how the sunlight caught and held in the sheen of his hair. When the pain in her heart became too intense, she walked away. Turning into a masochist would get her nowhere. She would not belittle this thing between them by wasting a single second of their time together, and reminded herself she should be storing up memories. They were going to have to last her a lifetime after he was gone.

She was already inside the cave and wiping the sweat from her face when she saw him stop and look up. Her heart skipped. He was standing too still.

She stood up.

All of a sudden he was running and the wind was rising up behind him, whipping everything in sight. He was flying by the time he got inside the cave and began throwing their gear farther back away from the opening and yelling.

"Get back! All the way back!"

Layla didn't wait to ask why as adrenaline gave speed to her steps.

The wind blew all the way to the front of the cave, but no farther, methodically wiping away the outer trace of their presence. Niyol had pushed the motorcycle to the back of the cave the first night they were here, and now she knew why.

He stood without moving, like a sentry keeping watch. She couldn't see his face, but she could hear him chanting, and felt the vibration from the air around her.

Then just as suddenly as the wind started, it stopped. Not a blade of grass, not a leaf on the distant trees was moving. It was like the earth was holding its breath. All of a sudden, she heard the high-pitched drone of a small-aircraft engine, and from the sound, it was flying low.

She was so scared that she forgot to breathe, then as before, heard his voice inside her head.

Breathe. It will pass.

She exhaled slowly then buried her head on her knees. When she heard his footsteps coming toward her, she bolted to her feet and leaped sideways, pulling the knife from her belt just as he pounced.

He caught her arm. His eyes were dark, his expression impossible to read as she held the knife to his wrist. One good slash and he would have bled out before her eyes.

Their gazes locked.

"Only you do not die," Layla whispered.

He turned her loose, lifted a finger toward her face, but then stopped when she followed it with the knife. But it was the expression in his eyes that told her she was safe.

She put the knife back in the scabbard and wrapped her arms around herself to keep from shaking.

"Bad people?"

He nodded.

"How did they find us?"

He thought a moment then frowned. "Someone told. It was a woman."

She gasped. "The only people who know where I am are Dineh."

"This one is not."

Layla groaned. "But she lives on the rez?"

He nodded. "You have enemies?"

She shrugged. "Not enemies."

"But also not friends."

"I need to tell Grandfather. What if she does something that would impact the evacuation?"

"He will know," Niyol said, then turned and began packing up their things.

"We're moving?"

"Yes, now, before they have time to send in others."

She ran to her things and began packing them up, then scattered the rocks around the fire and poured water on the embers.

She turned around to grab the weapons and they were gone.

"What happened to the weapons?"

"They are in a safe place."

"We can get them back?"

"Yes. We will get them back."

He fastened the bedrolls on the back of the bike as Layla grabbed her backpack. He gave the cave one last glance and then pushed the bike out into the light and handed her the helmet. He swung his leg over the seat as she got on behind him. The engine rumbled then roared to life. They rode out of the campsite without looking back.

Chapter Seven

Once again, Layla and Niyol were speeding through the gorge, racing against time for a safe place to hide. All of a sudden, Niyol turned the motorcycle into a spin and braked, nearly throwing her off.

"What are you doing?" she screamed.

He pointed up.

The plane was just a tiny speck in the sky, but it was visible and coming their way.

"Oh no, no, no."

She grabbed Niyol's shoulders and shook him. "Don't stop! Go! Go!"

The engine was still idling as he dropped the kickstand and got off the bike. He yanked off one of the bedrolls and when he untied it, the bow and the quiver of arrows fell out.

Layla jumped off the bike. "Are you crazy? You can't shoot down a plane with a bow and arrow?"

"But you can," Niyol said.

Layla stared at him. "I'm not the one with magic," she muttered.

"But you are. You just haven't accepted it yet," he said, and handed her the bow. "Get your arrows, Singing Bird. It's time to step into your own."

Layla was shaking so hard she was sick to her stomach.

"I can't shoot down a plane. You turn the wind into a storm and knock it out of the sky."

Niyol stopped. "No. This is your task. Look at me!"

She looked straight into his eyes. She tried to look

away, but she could not. Something was happening inside her head. She was seeing things and hearing voices chanting, and once again, in words she didn't understand.

They stopped as suddenly as they began. As always when she felt his magic, she staggered, like someone had almost pulled a rug out from under her feet. She dropped the backpack from her shoulders and replaced it with the quiver of arrows.

"Move out into that open space," Niyol said, pointing to the widest part of the gorge. "He will come low to verify it is you. Aim at the bottom where you think he would be sitting."

"I can't shoot an arrow that hard or that far," she said.

"You can now," Niyol said. "Go now, and hurry. He is already descending."

"Whatever," she muttered, and held tight to the bow as she moved in long, angry strides, pissed that this was happening, and beyond pissed that she'd become the target for a variety of fools.

****

Maurice was smiling as he came in low. This was exactly what he'd hoped would happen. The first pass had scared them out of hiding, and the second pass would be a verification of target. After that, all he had to do was follow overhead until they got to a place in the gorge wide enough for him to land. The plane was rigged for crop dusting. He would spray them with a little of his special concoction and they would be flat on their ass unconscious in seconds. Then he could land, load up the woman, and fly out the same way he'd come in. Her guard, whoever he was, would wake up with a headache, but by then they'd be gone, and he would be five million dollars to the good and ready to begin a well-deserved retirement.

When he saw the motorcycle go into a spin, he thought they were about to wreck. He cursed anxiously. His fee depended on a living breathing woman, not a body. But to his surprise, they dismounted on the run.

"What the hell?" he muttered, watching as they suddenly separated.

The woman was running out into the middle of the gorge, and the closer he got, the clearer it became what she was about to do. He had to give it to her. She wasn't going down without a fight, but she damn sure needed to update her arsenal with some twenty-first century weapons, not the wild-west bow and arrow he saw in her hands.

He waggled his wings at her as he swooped down. He knew it was a taunt, but even from up this high he could see she was a tasty piece of tail. She was stripped down to what looked like a bra and long pants and had her hair in a braid. All she needed was a horse between her legs and a feather in her hair.

He was less than a hundred yards from where she stood when he saw her notch the arrow. He laughed as he swooped down, intending to knock her on her pretty ass.

"Give it your best shot, Pocahontas, because you're already mine. You just don't know it yet."

He didn't see the arrow fly, but he heard a scrunch of metal as it tore through the plane's belly. When it shot up through the floor into his thigh, he was so startled by the sight that for a second, he didn't feel the pain. And then it hit him in a hot, searing jolt, ripping through his brain and out his mouth in a high-pitched scream.

He was reaching for the arrow when the plane went into a dive. He'd fallen forward on the controls, and by the time he saw it, he was only seconds away from impact.

"Well fuck."

****

Layla saw the arrow pierce the shell of the plane as he flew over her head, and spun on her heel to see what happened next.

The plane wobbled, then went into a dive so fast that she didn't have time to run. She knew it was going to explode and she was going to get burned. In a frantic effort to save herself she fell down on her belly with her arms over her head, and prayed for a miracle.

The plane went nose first into the narrow ribbon of water running through the gorge, shaking the ground beneath on impact. The air above her turned into an inferno as the plane exploded, and yet Layla never felt the heat.

When she looked up, Niyol was at her side and pulling her to her feet. She looked over his shoulder in disbelief.

The fifty-foot flames still burning had incinerated the plane and pilot upon impact.

"What happened?"

"You happened," he said.

"But how?"

"Your aim is true. Your heart is pure. You have work yet to be done."

"What did you do to me?" she whispered.

"It does not matter. Just know that your arrow will never miss a target again, your life will not be taken, and your journey has just begun."

Layla wanted to cry. This was happening too fast. She was losing herself and she didn't know how to stop it. Fear choked any words she might have spoken as she picked up the bow and quiver of arrows, but by the time they were in her grasp, the emotion had passed.

"Is this all that will come?" she asked.

"No."

A muscle jerked at the side of her jaw. "Then take me somewhere safe, at least for tonight."

He led her back to the still idling motorcycle. She handed him the weapons, which he rolled up in the blanket, picked up her backpack as he handed her the helmet. She tossed it right back out into the sand.

"I do not need it. I cannot die."

He laughed. Humans were funny, even at the strangest of times.

"That's not exactly true."

"As long as you're with me, it is. I thought that I would die and I didn't. I need to feel the wind on my face."

He toed the kickstand up and revved the engine. They raced past the burning plane without a glance and rode until sunset was only minutes away.

Layla was worrying about camping out in the open in the dark when he heard her thoughts.

Not in the open. With the Old Ones.

She couldn't see over his shoulders and had to bide her time to see where he was taking her. When she began hearing drums again and saw ruins up against the canyon walls, she realized where they were. The Anasazi ruins – where an entire civilization had disappeared without a trace.

They are not lost.

Then where did they go?

He didn't answer, but the drums were loud in her ears as the bike rolled to a stop. She got off, and then helped him push it up against the wall of the canyon.

"We make camp here," he said, and began carrying their bedrolls inside the nearest crumbling structure.

"Why go inside? There are only two crumbling walls left and no roof."

He sighed. "Come inside before the last light is gone. They are waiting."

"Who's waiting?" she asked, but he didn't answer.

She trailed him past the broken doorway without comment, and dropped her backpack into the dirt.

"I'll see if I can find some wood," she said.

He stopped her with a look. "There will be fire. There will be food." He pointed. "We are their guests tonight."

Layla stifled the scream at the back of her throat. They hadn't been there before, but now there were two men standing but a few feet away, watching. One beckoned her to sit. Layla dropped where she stood, too shocked to do less than was asked.

All of a sudden there was a fire between them, and then Niyol was sitting cross-legged on the ground beside her.

"They have food. Eat what they give you."

One man came toward her and yet his feet never moved. When he stopped to lay food in her hands, she looked up to say thank you, only to realize she could see stars where his eyes should have been.

He wasn't real, and yet the food in her hands was hot. She looked at Niyol for answers, but he was already eating, scooping up a big bite with his fingers. She did the same, and although she didn't recognize the dish, the taste was familiar. Something made of masa... ground corn... and something stirred in it, something small and sweet.

It is a berry. They do not grow here.

Layla ate until the bowl was empty. The other man came toward them, carrying tortoise shells filled with water. She didn't look up, but said thank you when he put it in her hands, and felt the night wind suddenly surround her in a circular breeze.

"Am I dreaming?" she whispered.

Niyol looked at her. "Do you want to?"

"Will I get answers?"

"You have asked no questions."

She sighed.

Niyol took the shell from her hands and laid it by the fire, then led her over to her bedroll.

"Go to sleep without worry. They will stand watch."

Layla looked toward the broken doorway again. A half dozen armed warriors stood between them and the night, and the drums were still beating in rhythm to her heartbeat. She rolled over into Niyol's arms, laid her head on his chest and closed her eyes.

When she opened them next, it was morning.

****

Washington D.C.

Emile Harper had a location, and thanks to an earth orbiting military satellite, he also had a photo of Layla Birdsong and the man with her that was clear and suitable for framing.

He was getting pressure to escalate this and didn't understand why. It was making him antsy, like the people in the White House inner circle knew something he didn't. With his security clearance, he should be briefed on whatever they knew. It was time to get serious with his superiors. Make them understand that the only way they were going to get to this woman was by flying onto the reservation and taking her by force, which would cause an incident of epic proportions between Uncle Sam and the BIA.

He wanted to talk to Lydia Foster one more time and see if there was anything she could add to the situation that might help, and was pouring another cup of coffee as he made the call.

"Professor Foster's office, Becky speaking."

"I need to speak with Lydia. Could you put me through? Tell her Emile Harper is calling."

"I'm sorry Mr. Harper, but Professor Foster has taken a leave of absence."

He frowned. "We spoke just the other day and she said nothing about this."

"It was a surprise to everyone. She came in the other morning, turned in her request to the Administrator and left. She didn't even wait to see if he would grant it. We had to scramble some to find a substitute for her classes at the university, as well."

"Do you have a number where she can be reached?" he asked.

"Only her cell phone, but she wasn't answering. We didn't realize until yesterday that it's here in her desk. She didn't even take it with her."

The hair rose on the back of Harper's neck. "I see. Well, thank you for the information."

"You're welcome. Have a nice day," she said, and disconnected.

Emile heard the click and felt like someone had pulled down the shades, as well. What the fuck was happening here?

He hung up and strode out of his office. He knew everything the CIA knew, but there was one person more informed in international info than he was and that was the President. He needed a one-on-one and he needed it now.

****

Emile missed lunch and he wasn't so sure but what he was going to miss dinner tonight as well. Not only had the President ordered him to find Layla Birdsong and bring her in for questioning, but had also okayed the mission to send in a Blackhawk. They were referring to the soldiers as a retrieval team, but they were going in with assault weapons, which was insane.

Without actually saying the words, Harper realized the President was acting on something less than factual information. He believed there was an imminent physical threat to the country, and he believed Layla Birdsong had information pertaining to their safety. This puzzled Harper, because he was the head of Foreign Intelligence and was unaware of any such issue. It wasn't until the President's Chief of Staff was walking him out that he began to understand what was going on.

****

"Hey, Will, thanks for getting me in to the see the President in such a pinch," Emile said.

William Schulter's position as Chief of Staff was an honored one, and one he'd been proud to hold. But there was something going on with the President that was freaking him out and anything he said could be construed as criticism – even treason. However, at the moment, it was his honest opinion that the President had lost his fucking mind and he needed to tell someone. Harper was the nearest man he thought he could trust.

"So, Harper... what's your read on this Birdsong woman? Do you think something paranormal is going on with her?"

Harper frowned. "Personally, no, because I don't believe in that stuff, but I know people who do and they're convinced that whatever saved her from the gang is not of this world."

Harper laughed then; slightly embarrassed he'd even said that aloud. It took a few moments for him to realize Schulter wasn't laughing with him.

"What?" Harper asked.

Will took him by the arm and walked him out onto a terrace, then far away from the building and any security equipment that might pick up their conversation.

"If you repeat a word of this, I will swear on my mother's life that you lie," Will hissed.

Harper's heart skipped a beat. "What the fuck, Will?"

"Remember when the President was running for office and was calling attention to his Native American roots in all the places that mattered?"

Harper's eyes narrowed. "I do now."

"So the President has been talking to the Cheyenne elders of his grandmother's tribe. They told him there is an impending apocalypse of world-wide proportions on the horizon, and that the Birdsong woman is the key to the Native American people's salvation. The reason he's so insistent in wanting to talk to her is because he's bought into this bullshit. He thinks he can talk to her, blood to blood, so to speak, and get her to help save everyone, not just the indigenous populations."

"Fucking A," Harper muttered. "Have you tried to talk to him? Doesn't he realize how crazy this sounds?"

Will Schulter nodded. "We've spoken, but he is the president and I'm not. He gave you orders. It's your job to follow them." At that point, Schulter's posture slumped. "What I told you could get me sent to prison. I've never divulged private conversation before."

For the first time in his adult life, Emile Harper wasn't sure what to do next. It was also the first time in the entire history of his career that he wanted to quit. He looked at the stress on Schulter's face, then took a deep breath, pulled his phone out of his pocket and ordered the strike, just as he'd been instructed to do. It was not lost on him that if this all went sour, he would be taking the fall. No one had said the words aloud, but it was understood.

****

Binini Island – West Indies

Landan Prince was in his library having an aperitif as he waited for cook to serve dinner. He was near the window, admiring the latest blooms on one of his orchids when he saw Madame ReeRee running up the drive. Not only did she appear upset, but it struck him that she'd never come to his house before. He set his drink aside and went out to meet her.

She was wild-eyed and gasping for breath when he stopped her on the steps, then took her by the arm and led her to a chair on the verandah.

She wouldn't sit down and was clutching at his arm, too winded to talk, but unwilling to let go. It was seriously irksome.

"Take a breath. What on earth has happened?"

"I had a vision! I saw a ghost man. I saw the Indian woman from your video. She killed him. She is powerful and cannot be stopped. He is gone! Burned up in a fire."

Prince felt the blood draining from his face. He was so shocked he couldn't speak, but it didn't matter. ReeRee wasn't through.

She pointed up to the sky. "Death comes." Then she threw herself at his feet, screaming and clawing at his legs. "We will die! We will die!"

Prince pushed her aside, then dragged her to her feet and shook her.

"Stop it! Stop it, I say! What are you talking about? What is this death?"

ReeRee's eyes were wide open, but it was obvious to Prince that she didn't see him. Was she seeing into the future?

"Tell me what you see!" he demanded.

She blinked, and then once again pointed up at the sky.

"A ball of fire is coming that cannot be stopped. They will try, but they will fail and we will die. Earth will be no more."

Prince was speechless. The cataclysm that brought the Windwalker was already upon them. He hadn't expected this. Knowing Tenet had failed and ReeRee's claim that the woman could not be stopped was something he had not expected. It occurred this might be the first time in his life he would be unable to buy his way out of a mess. He'd always expected to die one day, but not like this. Not like this.

He watched ReeRee running back into the jungle and then went back into the library just as the twins, Adam and Evan, and their nursemaid come in.

"Are we too early for dinner, Mr. Prince?"

He shook off his concerns for the moment and waved them to a seat.

"No, not at all. Would you care for an aperitif?"

She frowned. "I'm on duty."

"Yes, yes of course," he said, then poured a very large one for him, as he eyed the boys. They were such beautiful children – with their mother's dark curly hair and fine features. The strange amber color of their eyes was slightly mesmerizing, which had always given him hope they would, one day, come into their own. It was unfortunate that he might not live to see if the boys ever measured up to their potential. He felt sick. He didn't want to die.

Adam and Evan were accustomed to pretending not to know what was going on, but when they heard 'didn't want to die' run through Landan's head, they looked at each other in shock.

Neither did they.

****

U.S. Naval Observatory:

The place was in chaos. Phone calls were going out to observatories all over the world for verification of an unknown meteor that had appeared out of nowhere in the sky. But it wasn't the sudden appearance that had everyone at the Naval Observatory worried. It was the very small margin of space there would be between it and earth when it passed. Unless something changed, it would be the closest call in recorded meteoric history.

As the observatory was in chaos, a young scientist came running with a frantic look on her face.

"Has anyone seen Dr. Runyon? The President is on the phone."

Someone shouted at her from across the room. "He was on the observatory platform."

As she turned to go look, she spied him entering the room.

"Oh thank goodness, there he is," she muttered, and bolted. "Dr. Runyon! Dr. Runyon! The President is on the phone in your office."

Runyon had been expecting this, but didn't really know what to say. He shut the door behind him as he entered and picked up the phone.

"This is Dr. Runyon."

"Please hold for the President of the United States."

He circled his desk and sat down as he waited for the call to connect. Moments later, he recognized the voice on the other end of the line.

"Dr. Runyon, President Farley here. Thank you for taking the time to talk to me."

"Yes sir. It's a pleasure to speak with you. How may I help?"

Farley went straight to the issue at hand. "What can you tell me about this meteor? Why did we not know about it sooner?"

Runyon sighed. "I can tell you that initial computations have it measuring about twice the size of our sun."

Farley gasped. "That's huge. How could you not see that before?"

"We don't know why, but we do know that it did

not show up on any telescope, in any country, until three hours ago."

"How can that be?"

"Sir, we have no idea. It wasn't there, and then it was. It's like it popped out of a black hole or something. In all my years of looking at the universe, I've never seen anything like it. The only thing we can find in written history that could relate to this appearance is a vague reference to some prediction back in the 13th century."

There was a long awkward silence as Runyon waited for the President to continue, and then finally, he did.

"Just how worried should we be?" Farley asked.

"With regard to the possibility of it hitting earth... unless it takes a drastic change in course, not worried at all. It will be a spectacular sight to behold, and it might affect the gravitational flow of tides and the earth's temperature, but only temporarily. Someone here introduced a theory that there could be the possibility of a Tsunami, but that's just speculation."

"You don't think it will, in any way, damage the ozone layer that protects us now? You can't be more specific than that?" Farley asked.

"I'm sorry, Sir, but without prior data to back it up, we don't know what it will affect."

"Yes, well, thank you, and of course, if there is any change whatsoever, I expect an immediate notification," Farley said.

"You have my word," Runyon said.

"Thank you for your help," Farley said.

Runyon waited until he heard a click and a dial tone before he replaced the receiver, then went back to the telescope. Unless one knew where to look, it wasn't yet visible in daylight, but it would be by dark. And in three days time, it was going to pass so damn close between the earth and the sun that everyone was going to feel the heat.

****

Layla woke abruptly as the first rays of sun came over the eastern horizon to find she was alone. She glanced behind her. The Anasazi spirits were gone, although last night's fire was burning again. She had a brief moment of panic, fearing that Niyol had already left her before she heard footsteps, and recognized the stride. Panic settled as she peered over what was left of the pueblo wall. He was carrying the carcass of some kind of bird already ready for the fire. When she realized he hadn't seen her, she slipped over the other side of the wall and hid, still determined to catch him off guard.

When he entered their camp, she heard his footsteps stop; obviously taking in the fact that her bedroll was empty. She heard him move again, and guessed he'd just put the bird near the fire to start cooking. She heard him moving around and knew he was looking for her. When he finally started to where she was hiding, she tensed. Just as his shadow grew large on the wall behind her, she leaped up and took him tumbling to the ground.

The shock in his eyes was evident.

Layla was grinning. "It's a good thing you cannot die."

For Niyol, it felt as if a door had just shut in his face, and at the same time, he knew a sense of satisfaction. She had learned her task well. But instead of laughing with her, he wrapped his arms around her and rolled until she was lying beneath him. Their time together was coming to an end and it was painful beyond understanding. A very human emotion washed through him. He wanted to cry.

"What's wrong?" Layla asked.

"You have learned well."

And just like that, she got it. When she learned what he'd come to teach her, he would be gone. Fear shot through her so fast she struggled to breathe.

"Are you going to leave me now?"

"Not yet, but soon."

Layla choked on a sob, and fisted her hands in his hair.

"Is this a time to make love?"

Niyol leaned forward until their foreheads were touching.

"It is a time to make love."

When he got up to strip, she also stood; tearing off her clothes in short jerky movements until she was standing naked in the sunlight, wearing nothing but her necklace with the little silver bird.

He laid his hand on the small charm, feeling the swell of her breasts against his palm.

"Singing Bird."

Despair rolled through every fiber of her being. She had never loved a man like she loved Niyol, and resented having it yanked out from under her in the name of fate. Her lips twisted bitterly.

"Windwalker, make love to me now before I die from need."

"You cannot die," he said softly, and then picked her up in his arms.

She locked her legs around his waist as he walked her toward the motorcycle, dropped her backward onto the seat; and with the handlebars pillowing her head and her legs still locked around his waist, he mounted her without hesitation.

Chapter Eight

The sun was in her eyes, so she closed them, concentrating instead of the stroke of his taut erection inside her womb. She felt a sense of desperation in him as well, as he took her harder and faster than they'd ever gone before. She lost conscious thought as the first orgasm shot through her. It rolled up her body like fire burning across a prairie, then ebbed back to her core and burned all over again. Just when she thought it was finally over, he laid her down on her bedroll and took her there, again and again.

Their bodies were bathed in sweat as they moved toward an ever-growing madness. For Layla, it was storing memories of this man for the years to come, while Niyol was dealing with pain of losing all physical connection with her. To never touch her like this again – to never kiss her lips, or sink himself into the wet depths of her sex – to never feel the warmth of her breath on the back of his neck as they slept – it was a grief he did not want to bear. They chased the lust until it pulled them under, but it was love that bound them there.

The sun rose a little higher into the sky.

The scent of the cooking bird was in the air.

Once, for a brief second Layla caught a glimpse of an eagle circling far above their heads before yet another orgasm shot through her.

She had lost count of how many, and was weak, spent, and crying when he finally let go and gave up his control.

This time when she felt the orgasm rip through him, she knew the madness of his physical pleasure, but also his sorrow and resolve.

****

George Begay woke up with a gasp and ran out of the house in his shorts. The sun was just coming up as he looked to the East, then above the mountain. His heart began to pound. It was there, just like in his dream.

He dashed back inside, made a quick trip to the bathroom to wash the sleep from his eyes then began to dress. A few minutes later he was in the kitchen making coffee when his phone rang. A little early for conversation, but he was up, so he answered.

"Hello."

"George, this is Montford Johnston. Did I wake you?"

"No. I was making coffee."

"Have you been outside yet?" Montford asked.

George felt a sense of despair. So he wasn't the only one who'd seen it. It was beginning.

"Yes."

"There is a fire in the sky."

"Yes, I saw it in my dream."

"Is that the sign? Does this signal the beginning of our exodus?"

"Yes."

There was a moment of silence, and then Montford's voice was a little softer. "Are you afraid?"

"Yes," George said.

Montford sighed. "So am I. What do we do?"

George thought back to the dream, and what he

saw happening.

"Tell the chiefs. Beat our drums, say the prayers, and don't stop. The drums will call Layla to us, and the prayers will call the Old Ones."

"Will other tribes come here to the reservation?"

"Yes."

"Will the white man come with them?" he asked.

George thought of all the intermarried families. "No. They won't believe until it is too late."

****

Layla practiced her archery because it kept her from weeping. Her heart was breaking and there was nothing to be done. She shot one arrow after another into different targets then trudged, with lagging steps, through the heat to retrieve them.

Niyol was on a rock standing lookout a short distance away, but she felt his gaze. She'd seen his eyes fill with tears as he'd handed her some of the cooked meat to eat. She'd taken it without hunger, and chewed without tasting, knowing she would need all of her body strength in the days to come.

Twice in the afternoon the wind had come up without warning and swept through the gorge like a massive leaf blower, blasting waste and dead leaves from the path. It was as if the earth also knew change was coming, and was ridding itself of the chaff.

It was dusk before Layla saw the fireball in the sky. The moment she did, she ran to Niyol, who was busy re-packing the bike. After their last hasty exit, they only unpacked what they needed at the moment should the need for another swift getaway arise.

"Niyol! There's something coming in the sky. Did you see it?"

He looked up, judging the distance still left between it and earth.

"I saw it."

Layla grabbed his arm. "What is it, a comet?"

"Firewalker," he said, tying the last of their things onto the bike.

Layla pulled him around until they were standing face to face.

"Stop! I don't need vague. I need specific. Does this have anything to do with me and what I'm supposed to do?"

He felt her panic. It was to be expected.

"It signals the beginning of the end."

Layla's stomach knotted. "Of the world?"

He shrugged. "Of this world. There are many others."

She began shaking him in anger, because she was afraid if she started crying, she would never stop.

"I'm asking you! Is this world, this earth, and every living thing on it going to come to an end?"

"It will burn and crumble and nothing will survive."

Her voice was trembling. "Then how will we?"

"You will already be somewhere else."

"How will we know what to do?" she whispered.

"There are others there. They will show you. They have been waiting for you for a very long time now."

"Waiting for me?"

He put his hand on the bird charm hanging between her breasts.

"They have been waiting for Singing Bird and what she brings with her," Niyol said, and when she would have asked more, he stopped her. "We will rest now. The men will come from the sky at daylight, but they must not step foot here. They don't belong."

She lay down beside him, even though it was still light, because she was too shocked to do anything other than what he'd told her to do. She was thinking about her Muscogee kinsmen in Oklahoma, and the other native tribes all across the country. Were they aware? Were they coming? Would she ever see them again?

Niyol's chest was a wall against her back. The wind kept blowing strands of his hair across the bend of her elbow. The even rhythm of his breathing was the calm before the storm. But when she closed her eyes and tried to rest, instead, she saw the deep creeks and shady woods of her Oklahoma childhood – remembered the feel of hot sand beneath her bare feet as she ran up the rows in their watermelon patch; of crawling into a warm bed on a cold night while the snowfall blanketed everything outside in an icy white comforter.

Tears rolled. She took a deep breath, trying to still the wave of despair welling up inside her, but it was no use. There was a catch in her next breath, and then she was choking on sobs, grieving for a world already lost.

Niyol felt her pain as if it was his own. He'd seen into her mind and her heart and knew her sorrow. She carried a great burden – one she'd known and chosen long before her birth as this woman – one that ensured the lineage of their great nations did not end when this place became dust.

He held her tighter and closed his eyes. He could see her grandfather's face. They knew. He could hear the drums and the singing – they were calling out the Old Ones.

He looked deeper – farther – to the others who were scattered across this continent. Many had accepted what was coming and were preparing to die. It was their choice. It was their way. But some were coming here as fast as their rides would take them – some by bus – by car and motorcycle – and even by plane. They knew the time was short. If they were not already gathered on the reservation when Layla Birdsong went back for them, it would be too late.

****

Lydia Foster was standing out on the balcony of her hotel room, sipping a glass of wine. Considering she was a fifty-something woman with a little too much wear and tear, she still felt attractive.

Athens was stunning, both by daylight and dark. The local women were beautiful, the men as dark-eyed and sexy as she'd imagined. Her blonde hair, curvy body, and near six-foot height had been the subject of comments several times today. She hadn't expected it to be such a turn-on; being looked upon as something other than the nerd who studied legends and myths, but she liked it.

The majestic ruins that she'd toured today were now backlit on the hills beyond the city by a myriad of lights. From this distance, you could almost believe they were still in their former glory.

She took another sip of her wine, admiring the beauty of the stars strewn across the night sky. It took a few moments for her to realize one of the stars was not only red, but it was moving.

Her pulse leaped. Was this going to be her first UFO sighting? She'd never seen any, but she believed that they existed. But after watching a few moments more, decided it was most likely a man-made satellite of some kind.

All of a sudden there was a commotion in the street below. She leaned over and looked down. People were spilling out of doorways onto the sidewalks, pointing up and talking in loud, frenetic tones. She didn't understand enough of the language to know what they were saying, but she caught the words, television and newscast. It was obvious they were all talking about the same thing – the big red star.

Curious, she walked back into her room and turned on the TV. It took a few moments for her to find the station that broadcast in English. After a quick view of the broadcast, it became obvious what she'd seen was a meteor. When they switched programming to an interview with a man named Runyon; head of the U.S. Naval Observatory who was tracking the trajectory, she turned up the volume.

She sat down on the end of her bed and took another sip of her wine as she began to listen, and within moments of what he was saying it suddenly hit her.

This was the cataclysm.

This was what the Mayans had known - what the Gypsy Chronicles had predicted – why the Windwalker had appeared and spirited Layla Birdsong away.

A sudden feeling of dizziness swept through her as all the blood drained from her face.

So she'd waited too long to take her dream vacation. Such was life. She'd been missing the boat ever since the day she'd been born. A huge sadness washed over her as she emptied her wine glass. If this was the beginning of the end, she didn't plan to die in bed. She dropped her room key in her pocket, picked up her purse, and left the room.

****

The traffic on the highways and interstates was always busy, which continued to surprise economists considering the price of gas it took to travel. But for the past twelve hours, it had been increasingly worse.

Florida highway patrol reported long convoys of vehicles coming out of the Everglades with luggage tied on top. Obviously, the Seminole nation was on the move.

Texas and Oklahoma reported long lines of vehicles, all bearing license plates from local tribes driving both lanes of Interstate 35, heading north.

Lines of cars, motorcycles and motor homes had traffic so backed up on both the east and westbound lanes of Interstate 40 that truckers were bitching on their radios, wondering where the big powwow was, and wishing they'd all get the hell off the roads so people could do their jobs.

The convoys came out of Canada, crossing the borders into the Dakotas where they joined up with the Indians going south.

The media picked up on the chatter and sent their news helicopters to check it out. When the first live feeds were broadcast on CNN, theories abounded. But the Indians didn't care and had no comment when they stopped for food and fuel. No matter where their trips originated, their destination was the same – the northeast corner of Arizona to the Navajo reservation.

****

Emile Harper's phone rang before daylight, but he was already awake. In fact, he had yet to go to bed. He'd been up all night trying to get through to the President, and when he finally did, was admonished for questioning the order he'd been given. At that point, he began making coffee. It was going to be a long-ass day. The phone call was to let him know that the Blackhawk helicopter and the retrieval team had been deployed.

They knew their target. They knew the timeline they had to retrieve it. It never occurred to them to worry about a failed attempt. It was only one woman and a male companion. Their biggest threat was doing it without being made and giving the Bureau of Indian Affairs a reason to point a finger at the President.

****

Niyol had been watching Layla sleep since just after midnight. He'd seen coyotes sniff around the outside of the ruins without coming too close, watched a rattlesnake give him and their camp a wide berth, and watched the fire in the sky coming closer, knowing it was also bringing his time with her an end. He had already decided it was too painful to be human. Right now, he felt he might die from this pain in his heart, although he knew that was not so. Windwalkers did not die.

The day was dawning. The Firewalker was coming closer. The bad men were coming to take her away. They would be here soon, and as much as he wanted to decimate them the way he had the gang who'd tried to kill her, he could not. This time it was going to be her war to fight. He could help, but she had to prove her worth to the Old Ones. They had to be convinced that she would stand her ground; that she would not run if she became afraid. She had to be worthy to lead, or they would not open the gates between this world and theirs to let her pass.

She was waking up. He heard her thoughts returning, along with the realization of what lay ahead. All of a sudden her eyes flew open and she was looking straight into his gaze. She sat up, kissed him long and hard, as if she was committing the feel and the taste of him to memory, then combed her fingers through her hair and got up to relieve herself. When she returned there was a hard look on her face and she wouldn't look at him. She was gearing up for battle and had yet to say hello.

****

Cars had been arriving since midnight to the place where George Begay and his neighbors lived, and they kept on coming.

The drumming was so loud now that the air felt like it was vibrating. The more that arrived, the more that joined in the drumming and singing. The numbers grew until the sound could be heard for miles in any direction.

The children were silent, subdued; their gazes locked to the sky and the fireball that came closer with every passing hour. They heard the elders talking. They knew they were leaving but didn't fully understand why, and stayed close to their parents, afraid if they went too far that they might be left behind.

By morning, thousands of Indians, from many different tribes were spread out around the village, manning their own small cooking fires and feeding their young as they waited. They, too, kept an eye on the sky, but for a different reason. Layla Birdsong had yet to make an appearance, while the fire in the sky kept coming closer.

It was just before sunrise when George Begay walked out of his house and headed for the fire and the drums. His granddaughter was in danger. In his head, he'd seen the helicopter flying low over the canyons, across the mesas, all the way to the old ruins, and the soldiers coming out of its belly, being lowered down on ropes like spiders spinning down a web. It would do no good to tell the others. Either she would survive it, or she would not.

****

The sun was only minutes away from coming over the horizon when Layla walked out of the ruins into the open. The quiver of metal-tipped arrows was on her shoulder, the high-powered hunting bow in her hand. Her father's hunting knife was in its scabbard and strapped around her right leg just above the knee; within hands reach should the need arise.

Her hair was tied at the back of her neck and her shirt was unbuttoned and flapping open in the wind, revealing her hard, bare midriff, the silver necklace dangling between her breasts, and the sports bra beneath. She was wearing the last pair of jeans she'd brought with her that would still stay on her hips, and she was watching the skies.

Something was coming. She could feel it. The birds that usually rode the morning wind were suspiciously absent, as was the nearby herd of sheep she'd become accustomed to hearing. A part of her was still anxious, knowing she would be facing twenty-first century technology with ancient weapons and Windwalker magic for backup.

Niyol heard her thoughts. "It will not matter what they carry or how they come. It will be the strength in your heart and the sacrifices you are making that will protect you."

Layla flinched, startled by the sound of his voice so near her ear. Then she relaxed. He had told her the truth right from the start. All she had to do was believe and it would be so.

Niyol stood behind her. When it mattered, he would stand beside her, but not now. Not when she was still mentally preparing herself for the battle to come.

Wind lifted the hair from her back, blowing it lightly across Niyol's body. He wanted to bury his face against the back of her neck and lay her down in the sand and make love to her just one more time before-

His muscles tensed at the faint sound the wind brought to him. It was too late. They were already here.

"Layla-"

"I hear it," she said.

"They cannot set foot on the Anasazi's land. You must not allow it. It is sacred. Do you understand?"

She nodded as she notched an arrow into the bow and held it loosely, waiting.

The sound grew louder. Layla's heart began to race as she turned to the East. The wind rose before her, barreling through the canyon walls like a speeding train coming down a track.

Niyol was chanting.

Every muscle in Layla's body was tensed, ready to react. Her gaze was fixed on the mesa before her and the clear blue sky above her, when all of a sudden a large black chopper came over it, heading straight for her like a dragonfly to water. There was no more waiting.

The wind that had been sweeping through the

canyon was now centered and spinning above her like icing between two layers of cake. She saw the pilot adjust the chopper as the wind bucked it out of hover mode, and as he did, the wind spun faster.

The drums were loud now, beating, beating, keeping time with her heartbeat and drowning out the thunder of the rotors.

When the ropes began dropping from both sides of the chopper's open doors and she saw fully armed soldiers coming down around her, she sent her first arrow in flight. It flew straight through the body armor of one soldier's chest. She couldn't hear the sound, but she saw his mouth wide open in a silent scream. And then he was lifeless on the rope, a deadly warning to the others of what lay ahead.

She was already running as she reached for another arrow, desperate to get a different angle before the soldiers came any lower. It was in the bow before they realized a man was down.

They'd been ordered to bring her in alive, but when they saw their lifeless comrade swinging on the rope like a puppet on a string, they began firing all around her, expecting her to run, which would give them time to get down.

But the bullets couldn't go through the wind below them. Instead, they ricocheted back into the underside of the chopper, and into the men on the ropes below. Two more men went down, this time by friendly fire.

The pilot was frantic. He was losing oil pressure and men at a rapid rate as he began shouting into the radio.

"Abort! Abort!"

But the men were deaf to everything but the wind tearing through the air, slamming them into each other and tossing them about.

Layla sent another arrow into the sky, and then another, picking off the spinning soldiers one by one, until the air above her was filled with hanging bodies.

The pilot was taking evasive action, trying to move beyond her range and the maelstrom. And even as he did, the woman and the wind moved with them. She kept launching arrow after arrow through a storm their bullets could not pierce.

The panel gauges were going haywire, like they'd flown into some kind of magnetic storm. They tried to raise the bodies up, but nothing was working as it should. If he had not been absolutely certain that he was looking at the horizon, the instrument panel was indicating they were flying upside down. Blackhawks were the pride of the military – the powerhouse of helicopters, but even they could not accomplish the impossible.

The panic in his voice was unmistakable as he began a rapid relay of intel to home base. His last message was frantic.

"We're taking fire. Casualty is near one hundred percent. I'm losing power. Request rescue retrieval, ASAP."

Then he took the chopper up fast and flew off toward the mesa on the other side of the canyon while the macabre dance of bodies dangled below.

There were three live souls on board with their gazes fixed on the flat-top mesa less than a half a mile away. All they needed was to get there, but they were losing power faster than gaining ground.

Within seconds, the pilot knew they were going to crash.

"MAYDAY! MAYDAY!"

He was sending coordinates right up to the

moment they flew into the canyon wall. The spinning wind dissipated as abruptly as it had come.

Chapter Nine

Emile Harper was like the rest of the nation reeling from the news of the approaching meteor, but he didn't trust the prediction that it wouldn't do any harm. After learning Lydia Foster walked out on her job in the middle of the week, and then this speeding monolith appearing out of nowhere and hurtling toward the earth at an unprecedented speed, her warnings and subsequent behavior were beginning to get to him.

He was enroute to his office when his phone beeped, signaling a text. His driver was slowing down for a red light as he read it with a mixture of disbelief and fear - yet another sign that the impossible had happened again.

Retrieval failure. Blackhawk down. No survivors.

He needed to let the President know, but not until he got more details. But he could do neither right now. He needed to gather his emotions before he opened his mouth. He swallowed past the lump in his throat and looked out the window. The nation's capitol was beautiful this time of year – on the verge of fall. He wanted to remember it this way.

****

The moment the Blackhawk veered away from the rim of the canyon, Layla dropped to her knees in exhaustion then rocked back on her heels and screamed. She'd killed men - so many men. She wouldn't let herself think about the families who had loved them. She couldn't go there. This was no longer about herself.

There was one arrow left in her quiver and her hands were trembling so hard she would never have been able to notch it to the bow. Niyol was nowhere in sight and she was trying to catch her breath when she heard the explosion.

Her gut knotted.

They were as guilty as the gang who attacked you.

He was right. It had been a shock knowing her own government had sent soldiers, like she was an enemy of the State. She shook off the guilt and got up. When she turned around, Niyol was coming toward her.

She looked up at the sky. The fireball was larger now. She thought of her grandfather and all the people she'd grown to love on the rez. They must be terrified. When she looked back, Niyol was standing before her with tears on his face.

Breath caught in the back of her throat. He didn't have to say it. She could feel the withdrawal.

"No, please... not yet."

He put his arms around her, pulling her so close she could barely breathe.

She buried her face against his chest, but he already felt different – as if he was losing substance and warmth.

Layla looked up in sudden panic. He was disappearing before her eyes.

"No... Niyol, no." She grabbed hold of his shirt with both hands, as if she could hold him with her, solely by the strength of her love. "How will I live the rest of my life without you?"

He was shaking, both in anger that he could no longer stay, and from the pain ripping him apart. Even though he refused to let go, his grip on his earthbound body was lessening.

"Singing Bird," he whispered, and put his palm on the silver bird hanging between her breasts.

Layla was sobbing now. Despite the heat of the sun, the charm on her father's necklace was suddenly cold. She could see him, but he was air between her fingers.

"Don't leave me. I will die from this pain."

You will not die.

And then he was gone.

The wind rose abruptly, tearing through the canyon in fierce angry gusts - whining through the standing spires, whipping past brush and trees, sliding past the canyon walls in ever-increasing speed until she could hear the scream within.

She opened her arms wide, trying to absorb the wild wind because it was all she had left of him; standing against the storm as it tore the tie from her hair and the shirt from her body. By the time it passed, Singing Bird had been forged by the blast. Her emotions were as hard as the look on her face. She picked up her weapons and walked back to camp with purpose in every step.

She didn't question the appearance of more metal-tipped arrows in the quiver, or that the gas gauge on the motorcycle was still on full. She packed her weapons, and though she'd never driven a motorcycle in her life, mounted it as ably as if she'd done it all her life, toed up the kickstand and started the engine. The familiar rumble reminded her of the ride ahead. When she revved the engine and put it into gear, the ride jumped beneath her, but her legs were tightly clamped and her grip was strong. Seconds later, she was gone.

****

Dr. Runyon was in panic mode, reordering more calculations even as he was waiting for the President to come on the line. Despite the news, he was almost relieved when the call was finally answered. Now someone else was going to share the burden of what he knew.

"Dr. Runyon! How goes it?" Farley said, and waved at Will Schulter, his Chief of Staff, to hold his next appointment a few moments more.

Runyon took a deep breath and blurted it out. "There's no good way to say this, but you need to know the meteor is going to be caught in the earth's gravitational pull."

Farley blinked.

"Exactly what does that mean? Is the heat going to increase to a serious degree or what are we talking about?"

Runyon cleared his throat. "We're talking about total annihilation of every living thing on the planet. Sir."

Farley turned to the window. It wasn't visible from this side of the White House, but his gaze still went up, as if there would be answers as to how to fix it.

"There has to be something we can do. What about launching nuclear missiles and blowing it apart?" he asked.

Runyon was scanning his notes as he spoke. "The mass is twice the size of our sun and it's on fire. Not only is it burning, but it is not burning up. It is the same size now as it was when we first saw it. No matter what we kind of missile or bomb we tried to send up, it would disintegrate long before impact."

Farley's stomach rolled. "Put your best people on it," he ordered. "There has to be something we can do. I refuse to accept this."

Runyon was crying now and didn't know it. "If you come up with any ideas, Mr. President, do let us know. We're all pretty much in shock down here, ourselves."

Farley disconnected that call and buzzed his secretary.

"Amelia, get Emile Harper on the phone. Whatever he's doing, interrupt him, and send Will in here."

"Yes sir," she said, and the line went dead.

Will Schulter entered quickly. "What do you need, Mr. President?"

Farley braced his hands on the top of his desk and leaned forward. "A miracle. I need a miracle."

Will frowned. "I'm sorry, sir? I don't understand."

"The latest consensus from the U.S. Naval Observatory is that the meteor is going to be caught in the earth's gravitational pull and we're all going to die."

Will's legs suddenly went weak as he reached for the back of a chair to steady himself.

"Sir? Are you serious?"

"Yes. I need a meeting. Contact the DOD. I don't care what the generals are doing or where they are, I need a meeting with them, STAT."

"Yes sir. Right away, Sir," Will said, and bolted out of the office to put in a call to the Department of Defense.

Farley was scared, but he was also angry. This wasn't happening. With all the technology on this planet, it was ridiculous to give up without a fight.

And, he had Layla Birdsong on the back burner. As soon as the retrieval team returned, he was confident she'd have the answers they needed.

He was pacing the floor when his secretary buzzed.

"Yes, Amelia?"

"Emile Harper on line one for you, Sir."

Farley's hopes rose as he picked up the phone. "Good morning, Harper. Do we have any news?"

"Yes, Mr. President, we have news, but you're not going to like it."

Farley froze. "What do you mean?"

"We have a Blackhawk down and no survivors."

"That's terrible. What happened? How did they crash?"

"During a fire fight. She took it down and disappeared."

"She?"

"Layla Birdsong."

Farley was struggling to maintain his composure. "How did this happen? Why didn't we know she had surface to air weaponry."

Harper shoved a shaky hand through his hair. "I just got off the phone with the base. They have the pilot's radio transmissions recorded so there's no misunderstanding. She took them down with a bow and arrows; picked the men off one at a time as they were coming down on ropes. They fired back at her, trying to distract her enough to land the men, but the bullets ricocheted off some crazy wind blowing underneath the chopper, bounced back up into the belly, and took out a couple of their own men out as well. She finished off the rest."

Farley couldn't believe what he was hearing. He kept remembering that video of her being attacked, and the wind that had killed all the men before whisking her away.

"That's not possible?"

He didn't realize he'd asked a question instead of stating a fact, but Harper heard it.

"Yes, well, it happened. And she's gone. The rescue chopper did a quick recon of the area, ascertained no survivors, and no one at the camp. The military satellites are down. Base said it has to do with the passing meteor and as soon as it is out of earth's atmosphere, they'll be back up, but in the meantime we don't know where she is."

Farley dropped. "I'll call you back," he muttered, and hung up.

When he tried to put in a call to the Cheyenne Tribal headquarters, no one answered. He tried calling a couple of his cousins, but no one answered at their homes, either. Then he called the nursing home where his great-uncle was living, and to his relief, someone answered.

"May I speak to your manager, please?"

"One moment sir."

He'd been put on hold. It had been a while since that had happened to him, but it was his own fault for not identifying himself.

"This is Steve. How can I help you?"

"Good morning, Steve. This is President James Farley."

The man laughed. "Yeah right. Who is this really?"

Farley frowned. He should have had Amelia do this.

"I'm sorry. I didn't go through the usual channels, but this *is* James Farley. I have a great-uncle residing in your home, and I'd like to speak with him."

The manager sucked air like he couldn't get enough down to breathe, and finally found his voice.

"Mr. President, I'm sorry. I'm so sorry. You just

took me by surprise. Yes, we knew Maxwell Little Horse was a relative of yours."

Once again, Farley felt his world spinning farther out of control.

"Was? Are you telling me that he passed and I knew nothing about it?"

"No sir, not at all. I didn't mean to frighten you. It's just that I would have assumed you already knew about the exodus."

Farley's head was beginning to pound. "What exodus?"

"The one to the Navajo reservation in Arizona, Sir."

"And what's happening there?"

"I'm not sure what they are doing, but I know why they went. It has to do with some sign they've been waiting for. Once that meteor showed up, they began some kind of pilgrimage to the reservation."

He remembered catching something about a big powwow on the news, but assumed it had to do with Layla Birdsong's brush with the spirit world. He didn't know the People had begun some kind of exodus. This was bad. He cleared his throat and spoke again.

"When you say, they, are you referring to the Cheyenne?"

"Oh no, sir. All kinds of Indians... I mean, Native Americans from all over the place. They're clogging up the highways and interstates with all their vehicles."

"I see, well, thank you for the information, and you have a nice day," Farley said.

"Yes sir. You, too, sir. And may I say it was an honor-"

Farley hung up. He was officially scared shitless and didn't feel honorable at all.

****

Someone from the Naval Observatory leaked the latest news about the impending doom. Farley's press secretary was frantically fending off the media and the White House press, while the president was on the way to the DOD.

The news went worldwide, and people began trying to leave the cities, as if hiding in the country side would protect them from what was to come. It didn't take long for the media to link impending doom to the Native American exodus and Layla Birdsong.

People close to the Native American community were telling all they knew about a Windwalker appearance, and that it often signified world catastrophe. They were claiming the rescue of the Birdsong woman was proof, and that she'd been rescued because she was the key to their salvation.

Cities all over the world were in chaos. People began gathering in numbers, building bonfires two stories high and painting their faces in blood, as if they could conjure up the same Windwalker from the video for themselves. And through it all, the fireball got closer as earth's lifespan grew shorter.

****

Hours has passed since Layla left the Anasazi ruins. The day was exceptionally hot, but the wind blowing on her body kept her cool. She rode past the Navajo ranches with their flocks of sheep, but saw no people. Their cars were gone, the animals scattered. She passed the occasional Hogan, but there were no cooking fires burning - just a goat or two grazing, and a dog now and then, lying silently at the doorway.

She stopped by one of the shallow rivers running through a canyon to refill her canteen. As she knelt by the bank and leaned down to let the clear water flow in, she was struck by the silence. She rocked back on her heels and looked up. There were no birds, no animal sounds, not even the wind had bothered to come here. Earth was already dying. The quiet made her uneasy and sent her running back to the bike.

It wasn't long before sundown, and even though the urgency to get back to her grandfather was uppermost, she could not do it in the dark. She started the engine and rode away with the wind in her hair and the light of the dying sun in her eyes. She knew where she was, and where she intended to spend the night – back in their cave in the Canyon del Muerto.

With only minutes of light left to spare, she rode up to the cave, quickly dismounted and pushed the motorcycle inside as Niyol had done before. The ashes had blown away, leaving nothing to mark their passing but the dark marks from their fires on the floor. The pile of wood they had not burned had been scattered by animals, and she set to gathering it back up.

After she started a fire against the chill of the night, she stripped and walked out to the small pool at the mouth of the cave. There was sand in her hair and eyes, and in her clothes. She had no soap left, but she could remove the grit from her skin. As soon as she refilled her canteen, she dropped to her knees by the pool and began to wash.

The scar on the back of her arm was no longer tender, nor was the one on her belly, or the one on her cheek. Her body was hard and thin and burned even darker than before. She'd lost the last tie for her hair and it was loose down her back and windblown. She pulled it all to one side then over her shoulder as she leaned down to wash her face. Little by little, she began removing the grime from her body, wishing it would be that easy to wash away the pain in her heart.

When she had finished, she walked back to the fire and sat naked on her bedroll, eating jerky from her pack as she added wood to the fire when the need arose. Once she was warm and dry, she shook out her clothes and dressed again, then took a rifle from the bike, made sure it was loaded, and walked out to the front of the cave, searching the moon-bathed gorge for signs of danger. All was quiet.

The fireball had come a very long ways in a very short time. It was larger now than the moon. She wondered how long they had left, and how many were waiting for her arrival back at home.

There was anger in her voice when she suddenly raised the rifle over her head and shouted out at the night.

"Niyol! Windwalker! You told me I would lead them, but you never told me where to go."

The silence was like a weight on her heart as she went back into the cave. She added more wood to the fire, then rolled up in her bedroll and closed her eyes.

Within seconds, there was a voice.

The Anasazi wait. Follow their drums.

Niyol, my heart is broken.

I said that you would love me.

As always, Windwalker, you spoke the truth.

She reached out from beneath her blankets, searching for the rifle until her fingers curled around the barrel. It was all the comfort she had left.

****

Binini Island – West Indies

Landan Prince had a telescope set to watch the fireball's approach, but eventually quit looking. He wouldn't accept the prognosis of going out in blaze of glory, and was busy trying to figure out how to escape. After all the years he'd spent accumulating artifacts from other civilizations, he was convinced there had to be an answer somewhere. Madame ReeRee was useless. The spirits she'd tried to conjure were suspiciously absent, which made him wonder if they'd ever been there.

He'd skipped lunch and was digging through some papers when he accidentally knocked the paperweight off the desk. He bent down to pick it up and then realized what he was holding and looked at it anew.

He'd spent thirteen months of wasted expeditions and two and a half million dollars before he'd found the yellow crystal in the cornerstone of an Egyptian pyramid. Technically it belonged to the country of Egypt, but like everything else he'd acquired, he considered possession as nine tenths of the law.

Yes, it was beautiful and he'd found a treasure some historians didn't even believe existed, but the downside of his acquisition was that he'd never learned how to make it work. Pity, considering it was purported to be a portal to other dimensions. If ever he needed a way out of this one, now was the time.

He took it out into the sunlight as he had so many times before, convinced that the key to its power was hiding somewhere within. At that point he heard chatter and looked up.

The nursemaid had the twins out on the upstairs balcony and, as usual, they were talking between themselves without making a bit of sense.

They saw him and waved. He waved back and smiled, thinking to himself that they were the lucky ones. They had no concept of the world, or that it was about to come to an end.

But he was wrong. Adam and Evan Prince knew exactly what was happening. They also knew a way out of this world, if they could find a way to make that portal key work. Only this was not the time for experimentation.

Chapter Ten

Get up Singing Bird. He is a friend.

Layla opened her eyes to see an old man wrapped up in a blanket, sitting cross-legged on the floor near the front of the cave with a basket by his knee.

Her first thought was he was another Anasazi spirit who'd stood watch for them in the ruins, and then he spoke and she realized he was real.

"I bring food for Singing Bird," he said softly.

Layla threw back the covers from her bedroll.

The old man stood, but when Layla walked toward him, he backed up.

It was a shock, knowing he was afraid of her. Moving slowly, she picked up the basket and uncovered the food.

"This looks good. Thank you."

"It was my honor," he said.

"How did you know I was here?" she asked, as she pushed aside the red cloth in the basket and tore off a piece of the roasted meat; eating hungrily.

"They told me where to come," he said.

"They who?"

"The Old Ones. In my sleep. Eat well, Singing Bird. You must be strong for what is to come."

His words were tinged with sorrow.

"Are you coming on the journey?" she asked.

He shook his head. "No. I am done in this life. I will walk another one soon."

While she was eating, he slipped away.

She ate quickly, packing what was left on her bike, then on impulse, twisted the red cloth into a band and tied it around her head to keep the sweat from her eyes. It was barely daybreak, and already the air felt too hot to breathe.

She glanced up, her eyes widening. The fireball was visibly larger than when she'd gone to bed last night.

Firewalker comes. Make haste.

The knot in her belly tightened as she pushed the bike out of the cave and mounted it. The engine rumbled to life and then she was gone.

****

George Begay was ready and waiting.

His granddaughter would come home today. He'd seen her in his dreams, riding back into their midst. But the Layla who'd ridden away with the Windwalker was gone. The woman coming back was another. Singing Bird, they would call her. It didn't matter. He just needed to see her face.

He walked out of his house into the heat carrying the bag he had packed. It wasn't yet sunrise and already too hot for comfort.

The drums had been beating for so long now that he'd forgotten what silence felt like and the beat was so strong he felt the vibration in his body day and night.

More people had come while he slept. Their number was so large now he could no longer see where they ended. He glanced toward the council fire then looked up, judging the height of the smoke - wondering if she would be able to see it – if she would hear their drums calling her home.

The People were anxious and ready to leave. They felt the heat. They knew the signs. They, too, were waiting for Singing Bird.

George crawled up into the back of Leland Benally's pickup truck, then up onto the top of the cab. She would come from the north. He would sit watch.

****

The wind no longer cooled the skin on Layla's body and the rumble of the engine was loud inside her head. The air was hot, so hot it was almost painful to breathe. No one had given her a timetable, but the urgency was obvious. She finally rode up out of the canyon back onto an actual roadway, and even though it was not paved, she accelerated.

The rumble became a roar – the scenery a blur.

Somewhere along the way she began hearing drums over the sound of the engine, but not the ones inside her head. The farther she rode, the louder they became.

She recognized the sounds.

It was the Dineh- calling her to them - guiding her home.

****

George had been sitting on Leland's truck so long that the metal was hot against his skin - his eyes were dry and burning from the heat and the wind. It was only ten a.m. and already the thermometer on the front of the little grocery store registered 115 degrees.

"George, come down. The sun is too hot," Leland said, and handed him water to drink.

George took the water and downed it gratefully but wouldn't give up his perch. There were so many people here now that he was afraid she'd never find him in their midst. He took a deep breath and then closed his eyes, but there was too much noise to concentrate and it was too hot.

Frustrated, he stood up on the top of the truck cab and then reeled from the sight before him. He had not realized how many were actually here. How would they ever get them moved to safety in time? He didn't know where Layla would take them, but the desert was a harsh place to live. They could only go so far before the vehicles would have to be abandoned. Some people were too old. They would die along the way, and yet they would die anyway if they did not try. It was a nightmare to consider.

His gaze shifted a little to the north east as he focused on a trailing cloud of dust. Maybe more people coming. His frown deepened, and then in his head he heard her.

Grandfather. Stop the drums.

George yelled. "Stop the drums! Stop the drums!" and began waving toward the crowd of drummers sitting hundreds deep around the fire.

Word spread quickly, and when the drums suddenly silenced, the singers also stopped.

The sudden negative of noise was abrupt and unexpected.

Everyone stopped - looking first to the sky, then to the tall, gray-haired man standing atop the cab of an old pickup truck. When he threw his arms up into the air and then pointed north, all eyes turned to look.

At first all they saw was the dust trail and then they heard the faint but unmistakable sound of a motorcycle with the engine running at full throttle.

There was a collective gasp, and then the people began to move of their own accord, parting a near-perfect path from the truck on which George was standing, to the dust trail hanging in mid-air.

She came over a rise with her dark hair flying, a blur of might and metal, running with the power of eighty horses between her legs. When the drums stopped, she knew her grandfather had heard her. A wind rose up at her back, pushing her forward even faster.

Do not tarry. Others are coming who do not belong. You will have to stop them. They cannot pass through the gate.

How long do I have?

Twelve hours to disappear.

Her path was set. Then she came over the last rise before home and gasped at the sight before her.

Thousands, there had to be thousands.

If it had wheels, they'd driven it here.

Windwalker! This is not possible.

Then they die and so do you.

All of a sudden she saw the crowd begin to move in an unspoken, coordinated shift that created a path for her all the way to the little town beyond. It gave her hope. If they could do that so quickly to allow her access, then maybe they would follow her without question, as well.

All eyes were on her as she reached the farthest edge. No one moved. No one waved. But when she passed in a cloud of dust, they stared.

The silence was unnerving. Except for the roar of the engine, there was nothing. About halfway through the crowd, she saw a man standing high atop a truck, and he was holding up one arm, as if hailing her return.

Grandfather!

She sped past them, riding full throttle to the council fire burning hot in an already scorching land. By the time she reached the truck, he was coming toward her with tears on his face.

She let up on the gas, hit the brakes, and slid sideways in yet another cloud of dust. When she killed the engine, the silence was unexpected and eerie. Not even the babies cried. She got off, unaware how fierce she appeared as she strode to him and threw her arms around his neck.

"Grandfather," she whispered.

He hugged her to him then stepped back for a better look.

The gray sports bra she was wearing was stained with dust and what looked like old blood. The silver chain around her neck gleamed bright against skin two shades darker than when he'd last seen her. The scars on her cheek and belly were noticeable, as was the one he could feel on the back of her arm. Her hair was loose and blowing wild around her face and the red cloth tied around her forehead, sweat-soaked. But it was the look in her eyes that shocked him. He didn't know her anymore. His dreams had been true. His Layla was gone forever. It was Singing Bird who came home.

"You came alone," he said.

The pain on her face was instantaneous, and then just as quickly gone.

"I'm sorry," he said gently. "Will you come eat? Rest?"

"There is no time. I need to talk to the people," she said.

He frowned. "We have no audio equipment, no microphone."

"They will hear me," she said, and moved past him to climb up into the pickup he'd just abandoned, then up on the cab where he'd been standing.

The crowd shifted as they watched her climb, and then instinctively moved forward.

Layla held up her hands. As she did, a soft wind began to swirl around her, then over the heads of the crowd, carrying her words to even those farthest away.

"Our world is dying, and we will die with it. The Windwalker has shown me how to save you. Will you come?"

Their answer was an unending war cry that sent a chill through Layla's body

She held up her hands again, and silence prevailed.

"In less than twelve hours, people will be here who do not belong, wanting us to take them with us. We have to be gone before they arrive. I will protect you. You will be safe. But you have to do something for me, as well. You must keep moving, and if there are some who fall by the wayside, pick them up. I will stop every four hours for fifteen minutes. You have to lose your modesty and pee where you stand."

The shock of her words was evident on all the faces, but she kept on talking.

"We will drive, and then we will walk. The Cherokee had their Trail of Tears and survived it. The Dineh had their Long Walk, and survived it. But this is for all The People. It will be our Last Walk, and we will survive it, too. You will abandon everything but what you can safely carry. Possessions mean nothing. It is The People who must be saved, but there is no need for panic. I will leave no one behind."

She pointed up at the fireball still blazing toward earth.

"We are already burning. Get in your vehicles and follow me out in single file, now!"

A last gust of wind swept across the crowd as they began putting out their cook fires and loading family up.

Layla jumped down then paused at the tailgate of the truck, searching the faces of those most familiar.

They looked at her as if she were a stranger. She felt their awe and their fear and understood. A month ago if someone had told her this would happen she would have laughed in their face. She looked at her grandfather. He was waiting for her orders, so she gave one.

"Ride with someone. The less vehicles we have to move, the better."

"You ride with me," Leland Benally said, and quickly took the duffel bags from the back seat of his truck, tossed them in the truck bed, and shifted his children into the back seat to make room for George.

George tossed his bag in with the others and got in.

The Nantay brothers were watching her. They too, were looking at her as if they'd never seen her before. It took her a few moments to notice that they were out of uniform and then realized the tribal police was a thing of the past.

"Will you and the other police watch for stragglers?"

They nodded.

"Then we go."

Her grandfather handed her a bottle of water and Johnston Nantay handed her a pair of wraparound sunglasses. She took a drink and then dropped it in the backpack, put on the glasses and got on the bike. There was a moment when her body protested then the feeling was gone. She started the engine, revved the motor and put it in gear.

The Last Walk had begun.

****

The world was in chaos. Up to date broadcasts were streaming nonstop, doomsday preachers were carrying signs to repent. The President held one news conference and then went into hibernation mode with the heads of state, desperate to make something happen.

Nuclear missiles were aimed and ready, waiting for the meteor to get into range.

President Farley had demanded a launch time, and Runyon had given up trying to explain how shooting nuclear missiles wasn't going to work and gone home. They were all going to die and he wanted to be with his wife.

Leland Benally's wife, Beverly, was in her hotel room in Las Vegas lying on the bed. It was too hot to move around outside. The motor in the air conditioner was on high as it grudgingly emitted little farts of cool air.

She'd been watching the news for days, and given up hoping Leland was ever going to return her calls. She knew he and her children were no longer home. It was not lost upon her that she'd sold her soul for money she would never get to spend, and that she'd run away from the only place that might still be safe.

She'd thought about seeing how long it would take her to gamble away a half million dollars, but her heart was no longer in it. She knew she should be on her knees praying for forgiveness, but was too heartsick to care.

A few hours later when the air conditioner burned up from trying to cool a dying planet, she stripped off her clothes, threw her money all over the bed, swallowed an entire bottle of sleeping pills and then lay down on that which she'd sold her soul to keep, and closed her eyes. Even now, she was still choosing the easy way out.

****

Lydia Foster was sitting in a small café, drinking Ouzo and eating bread and cheese with the man she'd picked up last night. The sex had been good, but the Ouzo was better. She'd lose him sometime today before dark, This morning she realized she would rather face dying the same way she'd faced her life – alone.

There were things she regretted, but it no longer mattered.

The man recognized the forlorn expression, understood the cause, topped off her glass, and then lifted his for a toast.

"To the beautiful Lydia. *Stin Iyiamus.*"

She raised her glass.

"To our health," she echoed, and downed it in one gulp.

****

Airport radar was going crazy, resulting in the cancellation of flights and the grounding of all planes. Anything to do with magnetic resonance or imaging was either giving false readings or no readings at all. Communication was spotty and television signals were all but gone.

A scientific opinion offered the possibility that the

meteor had metal properties that, in effect, turned it into a giant magnet, impacting everything magnetic down on earth.

President Farley was torn. He knew his elected duty was to stand with the people of this country, but at the same time, he wanted to abandon it all and make a run for Arizona. He was part Cheyenne. Granted it wasn't something he'd ever bragged about until he wanted the Native American vote to get elected. But if they had a way out of this hell, he wanted to go with them. But since Layla Birdsong had refused to come to him, he was going to have to go to her.

Only how did he make this exit without having it appear as if he was abandoning the nation to its fate alone? As it turned out, it was his Chief of Staff, Will Schulter, who he decided to leave in charge.

****

Farley was standing at the windows of the Oval Office, his heart in turmoil as he struggled with his choices.

Will Schulter knew the man as well as anyone on earth, and knew his heart was in the right place, even if he thought he was mad for believing some Indian woman could save the world. But the situation was now so dire that it didn't really matter what he thought. When he was called, he entered the office, saw him at the windows and walked up beside him.

"You wanted to see me, Sir?'

Farley didn't have to fake a serious expression.

"I need you to help me. I'm going to take a squadron of soldiers with me to Arizona. If I can find that woman, we may still have a chance to save the nation, but I can't let anyone know I'm gone. They will think I've abandoned them to their own fate."

"Yes, Mr. President, I know."

Farley put a hand on Will's shoulder.

"While I'm gone, I need you to keep up the pretense that I'm still on the premises. Can you do that for me? Of course we'll stay connected by phone."

"I can do anything you ask of me, Sir. Do what you have to do, Mr. President and Godspeed."

"With any luck, I'll be back by this time tomorrow. Take care Will, and if anything happens to me while I'm gone, you have the Vice President's number. You know what to do."

Will was too shocked to say more as the President left the office.

Farley dressed incognito, wearing rough clothing for a rough climate, and left for the military base without a single sense of guilt that he was abandoning the people who had put him in office.

Planes weren't flying, but he was the President and he had resources. He left D.C. in a parade of cars carrying CIA, met up with a convoy from a military base along the way, and headed for Arizona, unprepared for the up-close and personal view of the growing devastation.

****

All things plastic were melting. Mailboxes, decorative fencing, car bumpers, shades on street lights, children's shoes, toys – there was no end, and it was only getting worse.

Highways were bumper to bumper with people trying to get to other family members – some going back to their places of birth to be with loved ones. The military was on alert, but there were soldiers going AWOL to get home to their families. The growing public opinion was that the earth was doomed. No one wanted to die alone.

And there were the others who were trying to get to Arizona, convinced that if all those Indians had gone there, then they knew something the rest of the world didn't. It was an 'every man for himself mad dash to salvation', regardless of who they had to walk over to get there.

Farley and his entourage were halfway to Arizona when the computers in the country went down. Which meant the ATMs and gas pumps quit working, and it turned fear into full-blown panic.

He got the news when they stopped to fuel up, and found out it was no longer possible. He was trying to call Will when a bodyguard relayed the message that cell phone service was gone. The satellites were either out of orbit or burning up. He felt like someone had just yanked the rug out from under him.

"Then how do we communicate?" he asked.

"We sent some of the soldiers up ahead to recon. There's a military base not far from here. They should have enough supplies to get us to Arizona, sir. Don't worry. We'll get you there."

"Yes, well done," Farley said, and got back in.

He was used to people solving his problems, but the increasing fail of technology was unnerving. All he needed was a little more time. To assuage his conscience, he envisioned finding Layla Birdsong, and finding a way to stop the impending disaster. So while the military began setting up checkpoints along the way to furnish fuel to get their President to his destination, the rest of the world was coming undone.

****

When Emile Harper got the intel that Farley was on his way to Arizona, he lost it. If the President of the United States was looking for a woman and some legendary Navajo spirit to save them, then they were fucked. Economically, the country had ground to a halt. Food and water were at a premium. People were streaming out of cities in droves, highways were bumper to bumper with cars running out of fuel, and he was going home. He had a bottle of Dom he'd been saving for New Year's Eve and a tin of his favorite caviar. He walked out of his office and stopped at his secretary's desk.

"Go home, Phyllis."

"Sir?"

"Go home. There's nothing left for us here. Whatever you need to do to make your peace with God and family, now is the time to do it."

She went pale. "Are you saying-"

"That we're toast? Yes, that's what I'm saying. Thank you for your years of service. It was much appreciated."

She was sobbing as he left the office.

The sun was brutal as he exited the building. He put on his sunglasses, took off his suit coat and dropped it where he stood, removed his tie, unbuttoned the top three buttons of his dress shirt, and started walking. His apartment wasn't far, and he'd been meaning to take some time off for quite a while now. He thought of the champagne again, then looked up, gave the meteor the finger, and kept on walking.

One way or another, he was going out in style.

****

Farley was in the front seat of the SUV with one of his bodyguards when they finally reached tribal headquarters on the Navajo reservation. Except for a jail cell full of men who looked like mercenaries; screaming to be let out, it didn't take long to realize it was deserted.

They freed the jailbirds and sent the soldiers out on a recon mission, looking for someone who could tell them where to find Layla Birdsong. He was concerned, but at this point nowhere near panic.

They finally found an old woman sitting outside on a bench on the shady side of her tiny house, and brought Farley to her. He got out with his political face on, expecting, at the least, to be recognized.

As he approached, he watched her stand, bracing herself with a thick walking stick. Her long gray hair was in two braids hanging down her shoulders – her skirt was a brown the color of the dust, and the blue long-sleeved shirt she wore over it went halfway to her knees. The ornate belt at her waist was silver Conchos, but her feet were bare.

As hot as the earth was, he thought it strange.

"Good morning, ma'am. I'm President James Farley and I was wondering if-"

She interrupted him. "What do you want?"

"I was wondering if I might talk to someone in charge."

"They're gone," she said.

She said it with such finality that his heart skipped.

"Gone where?"

She shrugged and sat down.

So he started over. "I see you aren't wearing

shoes. Isn't the earth hot to your feet?"

"I am too old to make the Last Walk so my daughter is wearing my shoes. She said it would be her way of taking me with her."

Farley felt like crying, but showing weakness wouldn't help and so he started over.

"Do you know who I am?"

She looked up, squinting against the light. "Is there something wrong with you?"

He frowned. "No. Why do you ask that?"

"You already told me your name, so why would you ask me if I knew you?"

"Let me rephrase my question." He pointed to the other end of her bench. "May I?"

She laid her walking stick across it. "I sit alone."

This was getting them nowhere and Farley didn't have time to waste. He glanced up. The meteor was too close and he was so damned scared it was all he could do to form words.

"Old woman, what is your name?"

She pointed her stick at the others with him. "You take your men and leave now. I don't want to talk to you. I am waiting to die."

He grabbed her by the arm. It was a mistake, but desperate times called for desperate measures.

"You don't understand! I'm trying to save people's lives. I need to find Layla Birdsong. I need her to tell me what to do to stay safe."

"She is not here and she will tell you nothing. She belongs to the Dineh. She belongs to our People, not to you."

"But I'm Indian. I'm part Cheyenne."

"You smell like a white man," she said. "Go away. I am waiting to die."

Frustrated, Farley turned her loose, and as he

did, a tiny mouse shot out from beneath the house only inches ahead of a rattler.

The snake struck. The mouse's shriek was high-pitched and brief, but seeing that life and death moment so unexpectedly was shocking.

"Oh my God! Did you see that?" Farley cried.

"Everything dies," she muttered, and closed her eyes.

At that point, two of the soldiers came running toward him with a pair of binoculars.

"Mr. President. You need to see this."

He looked where they were pointing – far to the north to what looked like a long line of smoke above the surrounding mesas.

"What is that?" he asked.

"Best guess I'd say that's how much dust a nation of people on the move might stir up."

Farley didn't have to be told twice. He tossed them the binoculars. "Let's go. The soldiers will lead the way," he said, and ran for his car.

About thirty minutes out, they began seeing people on foot, some dragging bags, others barely dragging themselves. And the farther they went, the more people they passed, and none of them were Native American. So, there were others looking for Birdsong. It didn't make him happy, but he was the President. He would certainly get first dibs on a free pass to safety.

****

The air was so hot it felt thick, and the dust cloud from the Last Walk was a tracking device for anyone close enough to see it. Between the sun and the fireball, the sky was not only white-hot, but almost too bright to bear.

Layla was grateful for the sunglasses, but she wouldn't look back. Her focus had to be on where they were going, not where they'd been.

But for the People, the expressions on their faces said it all. They were not only leaving behind everything they knew, but people they would never see again. Their spirits were nearly broken and there was nothing she could say to make it better.

They drove for four hours without stopping, and when she finally did, it was for fifteen minutes only. Layla dropped the kickstand and squatted down behind the bike without shame. It was a bodily function that must be obeyed. When she stood, she drank another mouthful of water, tore off another piece of the meat the old man had given her, and went to find her grandfather.

He looked old. It startled her. She'd never really seen that before, and then realized she was seeing sadness, more than age.

"Are you okay?" she asked.

"I am okay," George said.

She handed him a piece of meat and bread, and moved back to the bike, chewing as she went. She washed it down with another quick drink, packed the bottle, and threw her leg over the bike. People climbed hastily back in their vehicles, anxious not to be left behind. When she put the bike in gear and rode off, they eased back into line behind her.

Do not stop for dark.

Layla frowned. *It will be more dangerous.*

No. The danger is if you do.

She accelerated, and so did the others. The dust cloud rose until the only car any driver could see was the one directly in front. Then cars began dropping out of line from overheating or flat tires. Some ran out of gas. Some just quit.

The tribal police kept moving people from one vehicle to another – even discarding personal belongings to make room for live bodies; telling them to keep only the tools and the knives.

The second time they stopped was just before dark, and she knew they were all expecting to make camp. But when she got back on the bike and started it up, they reacted in kind. They drove down into the canyon following the tourist trails, and then onto the more narrow trails the locals drove.

Because of the dark, they were moving slower, which lessened the dust, but now they only saw the red taillights of the cars in front of them.

The fireball was a big bloody moon.

The stars were gone.

The night was at half-light.

They drove in silence. Children had fallen asleep, but the others could not – too afraid of what was above them.

The elders rode in silence, thinking back to the stories of their ancestors, remembering how time and again they had been hunted down like animals and moved from their own lands, and wondering if the ancestors had been as scared as the marchers were now. Their ancestors' world came to an end with the arrival of the white man, and now the world was truly coming to an end, and as before, the white man was on their trail.

****

Layla was so tired she felt drunk. She ate a little more of the chicken and bread as she rode, then drank water, thinking if she fed her body it might revive it, but it only made it worse. It was like wanting to sleep after a big family dinner.

She screamed just to hear something beside the rumble of engines, knowing no one would hear it but her, then began reciting some of the stories she used to read to her students, but it made her sad because that life was gone.

When she started to cry it didn't matter, because there was no one ahead of her to see the tears. And when she began talking to the Windwalker, it was because he also knew her pain.

She cried aloud, angry that she was facing this alone.

"I ache for the sound of your voice."

I said that you would love me.

"You should have just taught me how to kill and not bothered my heart."

You chose me just as I chose you, long before you ever set foot in this life.

Tears were running down both cheeks, leaving tracks in the dust on her face. The pain in her chest was so strong that it felt like she was dying. She couldn't stop sobbing.

"But you left me behind."

You are a red feather warrior, Singing Bird. It is your path to walk. It is your time.

Physical and mental exhaustion was taking its toll.

"I don't know how much farther I can keep moving."

The Firewalker comes no matter how tired you are. When you begin hearing the drums, they will pull you, like a magnet. Then you must run.

The warning sent chills up Layla's spine,

wondering what unknown dangers they had yet to face.

Chapter Eleven

Daylight came before the sun came up, and with it a heat like they'd never endured. It was with shock that Layla realized it was Firewalker and not the sun that lit the earth. The only good thing about morning was realizing they had already passed through the Canyon del Muerto. She was farther along than she'd thought.

But as soon as the heat really set in, more cars began to quit - some due to heat, but more often from lack of fuel. They were losing cars faster than they could redistribute the people, and the roads were becoming impassable to anything but motorcycles or ATVs.

At that point, Layla was forced to stop again, and that's when she began hearing drums, which exacerbated the need to hurry.

She dug a long sleeve shirt out of her pack and put it on, then tied the tail of it around her waist for some protection from the sun. As others began climbing out of their vehicles, they followed suit, putting on hats and sunglasses, changing t-shirts for those with long sleeves and changing shorts for long pants, knowing they would now be walking without shelter from the sun.

She began issuing orders.

"Everyone walks but the elders. Find people with motorcycles and ATVS, and load them up any way you can. Pass the message down and follow as soon as you can. Time is short."

As she turned to walk away, she glanced down and saw that she was standing on scorpions. Two were trying to crawl up her pant legs and the others were writhing on the ground, dying from the excessive heat of the earth on which they moved.

"Oooh, dang it, I hate these things," she muttered, and knocked them off, then stomped the others until they were dead.

"Watch where you walk!" she yelled. "We aren't the only ones trying to find a place to hide."

It was another addition to the horror of what they were facing, but there was nothing she could do. She looked around for Leland Benally's truck, then ran to it and pulled her grandfather out. The gas was gone and there was steam coming out from under the hood. It had gone its last mile.

"Granddaughter, I hear drums," George said.

"It's the Old Ones, Grandfather. They are guiding us.

You will ride with me. Leland and his children will walk."

George didn't argue, which said a lot for his state of being, and even staggered a little as they moved back to her bike. She gave him a quick drink of water, handed him the last of her bread and then got him seated on the back of the bike as the drumbeat echoed in her ears.

"Chew and swallow, Grandfather. I need you to hold onto me with both hands."

When his arms went around her waist, she started the engine, and they were once again, on the move. The line was less orderly with people on foot, but they moved as quickly as they could, while giving way for the transports carrying their elders.

As they rode, Layla was ever conscious of her

grandfather's health and safety. The heat had become a blast furnace. Her lips were cracked, and every time she licked them, she tasted blood. Everyone was suffering. There was no way around it.

The small ribbon of water that had run through the gorge was gone, evaporated from the all-consuming heat. The only water left was what they carried.

The groves of small trees that had been so green only a week earlier were completely devoid of leaves. And now that they were on foot, the odor of decomposing animals was more evident. The only sheep she saw now were bloated carcasses.

They rode past a grove of trees where she and Niyol had once stopped for water, and it made her ache all over again for the sight of his face – for the sound of his voice.

She was still thinking of Niyol when she became conscious of two things. Her grandfather's arms were suddenly tightening around her waist, and she could hear a woman's scream. She hit the brakes as she put the bike in a one-eighty turn and was off the bike and running with the bow and arrows before her grandfather could dismount.

Layla had seen the cougar come out from behind rocky ledge even before she'd dismounted. By the time she was armed and running, it was in a full-out dash toward a half-grown boy who'd stopped to shake the sand out of his shoe. He saw the cougar too late to get away.

Men closest to the boy were reacting, as well. One was already pulling his knife as he ran, but they would be too late.

Layla let the arrow fly just as the cat was leaping. In those few brief seconds, everything seemed to happen in slow motion.

She saw the cat in mid-air.

The arrow slicing through blood and muscle.

The cat's scream, only an octave higher than the child's mother.

Then it dropped.

Shot through the heart; dead before it hit the ground.

The silence that came afterward was broken by the mother's sobs as she gathered the boy into her arms.

Layla's heart was pounding as she scanned the area, wondering what would cause an animal naturally reluctant to be around humans, to attack them in such number. Then she saw another cougar lying dead a short distance away, and one more unable to walk without staggering. Whether it was the heat or something poisonous they'd ingested trying to find water, it was obvious the animal population was as desperate as the humans.

She jogged over to the boy. His face was ashen, his eyes burned red from the wind and heat. His skin was dotted with raising blisters and he was still shaking from the shock.

"Are you okay?" Layla asked.

He nodded as he buried his face against his mother's breast.

"Thank you, Layla Birdsong, thank you," the woman said.

Layla touched the child lightly, admonishing him as she might have a student – with a gentle voice, but a stern message.

"Stay closer to your family, okay?"

He nodded.

The People gathered around her, murmuring their gratitude, looking at her with awe. Somehow, the

Windwalker had turned her into a superwoman. Even though she was still riding, she had strength and speed that the others did not.

"I said that I would protect you. Have faith that we can do this together," she said, then waved down the line, signaling they were ready to move.

****

Originally, it was Beamer Paulson's idea to go find the Indians to keep from dying. He got the notion after his sixth beer at the Roadrunner Bar in Farmington, New Mexico.

The men who frequented the bar were mostly loners. No family ties. No responsibilities; the kind of men who often picked up and moved from one place to another with little more than the clothes on their backs.

They considered themselves tough and didn't think much about crossing into the Navajo reservation. It wasn't far from Farmington to the Northern-most corner of Arizona, and they weren't ready to go toes up to the meteor without a fight.

Two of the men in the bar were too drunk to notice what was going on, but once Beamer voiced the idea, it didn't take long for the notion to spread.

Sometime before midnight, the bartender and fourteen others walked out with several cases of beer and a drunken plan to escape. With no way to pump new gas, they siphoned off the gas from the other cars in the parking lot, divided it equally between the three newest pickup trucks, and started driving due West.

Even at night, riding in the back of the truck beds and with beer to drink, the heat was oppressing. Every time they opened their mouths to take another swig, it felt as if the wind was sucking oxygen from their lungs. Within an hour they'd crossed the Arizona border, straight onto reservation land.

Their bravado was fueled by the beer, but the lack of real roads and rough landscape began to take the starch out of their half-assed plan. It quickly dawned on the drivers that they didn't know where to go. The reservation was huge. The Indians could be anywhere. They stopped the trucks, had a little meeting and a lot more beer, and decided to sit it out until morning so they could see where they were going.

Most of them were sound asleep or passed out when a man named Darryl got out of the truck to take a crap. He got the job over with, but passed out behind some brush and never made it back to the truck. He was still there when it got light enough to see, and no one knew he was missing. They drove off without him.

One down, fourteen to go.

Once the vehicles started moving, the motion of the vehicles only added to the misery of their hangovers. Men were hanging over the sides of the truck beds throwing up, and just when they thought it was over, another surge would boil up their throat and they'd throw up again.

One man leaned too far out of the pickup bed and fell out on his head, splattering brain matter and blood on the scorching ground, but no one told the driver to stop. There was no need.

Two down, thirteen to go.

When the first truck ran out of gas, they stopped and re-distributed their load between two trucks instead of three.

The elation of the trip had disappeared with the beer. With no shade, no water, and still no direction in which to go, their brains were cooking on high heat.

When the second truck ran out of gas, the other truck kept rolling. There was no room for six more passengers. It had become an 'every man for himself ride'.

Eight down, seven to go.

It was the driver who first noticed the giant dust trail due southwest from their location.

"Hey ya'll look at the size of that dust cloud! That's got to be them Indians on the move. Hang on."

He turned the wheel sharply to the left, and as he did, the bartender, who was standing up in the back of the truck bed taking a piss fell out.

He was holding onto his dick when he fell and had not braced for the fall. He went face first into the rocky ground and died from a broken neck.

Nine down, six to go.

The fireball rolled closer as the sun moved higher, and just when they thought things couldn't get worse, they ran out of gas, stranding the men who were left. Now they were lost *and* afoot without water or food.

The group was silent as they struck out, keeping an eye on the dust cloud. Within a few minutes, the heat and the hangovers began to take a toll.

Roscoe Aldridge watched his drinking buddy stagger, then grab his chest and fall to his knees. Roscoe stopped to help him up, but Fred was beyond help. His face was turning purple and when his eyes rolled back in his head, just like that, old Fred was gone.

Roscoe jumped back, his eyes wide with shock. They'd started out fifteen in number and had been dropping like flies ever since the sun came up. He was scared. He didn't want to die.

The others never slowed down or looked back. Roscoe took Fred's pistol, stuffed it in the waistband of his pants and ran to catch up, wiping snot and tears from his face.

Ten down, five to go.

The fireball was like the bad relative who wouldn't leave. Their skin was on fire. Blisters were popping and breaking on their arms, and without sunglasses, they were slowly going blind from the glare.

A man named Stan stumbled over an uneven patch of ground and reached out toward a rocky ledge to keep from falling.

The rattlesnake lying in the shade on that ledge was barely moving, but not so close to death that its instincts were gone. It struck Stan's arm just above the wrist, sinking fangs so deep it was still hanging on when Stan began to flail.

"Oh Jesus! Oh no! Somebody help me!" he screamed.

He finally managed to yank the snake from his wrist and beat it to a bloody pulp against the rocks.

His hands were shaking as he dropped to his knees, pulled out his knife and quickly slashed the puncture marks where the fangs had gone in. He began sucking blood and spitting it as fast as he could, hoping he could suck out enough poison to stay alive.

The men stared for a few moments.

Roscoe even empathized. He'd just lost old Fred, but this man was a goner too, and there was nothing to be done. He shook his head in commiseration.

"That's damn hard luck, Stan."

He aimed for the dust cloud and kept moving.

The others followed, unwilling to watch what would be a slow, painful death, walking faster than they wanted to, just so they wouldn't have to hear Stan's cries for help as he fell farther and farther behind.

Eleven down, four to go.

There was a long line of mountains between them and the dust cloud, and no way to judge the distance between. The canyon ahead gave them a hope of shade and water and they kept moving toward it.

Beamer Paulson was a relative newcomer to Farmington, and was cursing himself for ever opening his mouth about going to look for Indians, but it was far too late for regrets. He focused on the dust in the sky, and kept putting one foot in front of the other.

Chuy Garza had been born and raised in Guadalajara, and wished to God and the Holy Mother that he'd gone home to Mexico die, instead being here in the fucking desert with a bunch of men that he barely knew.

The man beside him was struggling. He didn't even know his name and felt guilty that he wanted the bastard to hurry up and die so he wouldn't have to listen to him cry anymore.

Suddenly, the man stopped.

The other three paused and looked back. The man was just standing there with his shoulders slumped, staring blankly at the ground.

"Hey, Walter," Roscoe yelled. "Aren't you coming?"

Chuy watched the man's face for a sign that he'd even heard, but there was nothing. At least now he knew his name.

Roscoe waved toward the Mesa. "Come on, Walter. You can do it. There'll be some shade and maybe some water up in that canyon."

"If there is a canyon," Beamer muttered.

Roscoe glared. "Shut the fuck up, Beamer."

Beamer started walking and Chuy followed.

Unwilling to be left behind, Roscoe struggled to

catch up. The last time he looked back, Walter was still standing there staring at the ground. He swallowed past the knot in his throat and kept on moving.

Twelve down, three to go.

It was Chuy who led them straight into the canyon, but their elation swiftly died when they realized the riverbed was dry.

Beamer cursed.

Chuy thought about it, but didn't waste his breath.

Roscoe had a different outlook on their situation. He pointed at the dust cloud.

"I'm thinking we just got lucky. From the looks of that dust, I think they're in this canyon and coming toward us. All we gotta do is keep moving. They're bound to have food and water."

"What if they don't want to share," Beamer asked.

Chuy pulled a knife out of his boot. "I always carry a little persuasion."

Roscoe had the gun, but he wasn't talking.

Beamer wouldn't let it go. "From the looks of that dust, there's got to be hundreds, maybe thousands of them. We can't force them to do anything."

"If they won't give us water and won't let us go with them, then either way, we'll die," Chuy said. "I'm thinking to take some with me when I go."

****

The drums were so loud now that when Layla's bike began sputtering, she almost didn't hear it die in time to keep it from falling over. She dropped the kickstand and quickly dismounted before helping her grandfather off.

She was trying not to panic, but she didn't understand. Everything the Windwalker left with her had been in endless supply. She squatted down to check to see if a wire had come loose, but saw nothing that would explain it. What she did see though made her belly roll.

The ground was cracking from the heat. She could see cracks a good two inches wide beneath the bike, spreading out across the canyon floor like a giant spider's web. Within moments, she heard more engines sputtering, and looked back. Whatever was going on had nothing to do with fuel.

Firewalker stole the power. Make haste Singing Bird. There is danger ahead and behind.

She saw nothing that would explain the warning, but knew not to ignore it. Every muscle in her body was protesting as she pulled herself upright.

"We walk from here," she said, touching her grandfather's arm. "Can you do this?"

"Is it far?"

Layla recognized the landmarks. They were less than two miles from the Anasazi ruins.

"Less than two miles I think, but we must hurry. I think now we have to run."

She saw the shock on his face, and then the determination.

"I will run until I cannot, and then you will leave me."

Layla frowned. "No. I'll carry you if I have to. I-"

George grabbed her by both arms. "Stop. This is Layla talking, and you are no longer Layla. You are Singing Bird. You have a nation to save. It is your destiny. I am one old man who longs to see his wife's face once more."

Layla wouldn't answer. She couldn't let herself

think about making that choice. She turned toward the marchers. They were silent and swaying on their feet. Their skin was raw from wind and sun burn, their lips cracked and bleeding. There was so much white dust on their hair and faces that they all looked like ghosts – an analogy too eerie to ignore. She couldn't let them die. She'd promised she would save them, and she still had their trust.

"Listen to me! We are very near. I think less than two miles, but there is danger and time is running out. We have to run the rest of the way. Drop whatever you are carrying. Nothing matters but your lives. Pass the word."

The murmur of their voices as word spread along the march was like a breeze tickling her face, but the noise grew as it rolled back, until the sound was a distant roar.

People began dropping their bags as she took the water bottle out of her backpack. There was less than an inch of water left. She took one small sip then handed it to George. While he drank, she shouldered the quiver of arrows and her bow, and felt for the hasp of her father's hunting knife strapped around her knee. It was all the protection she could carry, and was hoping it was enough to handle whatever they had yet to face.

George handed the bottle back, but there was water left.

"Drink it Grandfather, and don't make me ask you twice."

He downed it without shame.

It wasn't until she tossed the empty bottle onto the ground that the drumbeats began to get faster. When the bottle suddenly flattened and began curling inward, she realized the heat had intensified.

"Run," she screamed, and took her grandfather by the hand.

The thunder of the footsteps behind her was quickly muffled by the drumbeats and the singers chanting in her head. They were calling her to hurry.

They ran until they were too winded to run another step, then they jogged until lapsing into long, staggering steps. She kept hearing cries of dismay and wails of disbelief behind her. Some were falling who would not be getting up.

She had not let go of her grandfather's hand and was afraid to look at him for fear she'd see quit in his eyes. They were close now. Maybe a mile, maybe less.

Her lungs felt like they were on fire and it hurt to draw breath. At first she'd been sweating, but when she realized that had stopped, she knew her body was shutting down. She sent a desperate message to the Windwalker.

Help us. You do not bring us this far to let us fail.

You are Singing Bird. You lead. You do not fail.

She looked up just as three men walked out from behind a twin pair of spires standing sentinel in the middle of the gorge.

Now she understood Windwalker's warning.

White men! And they looked as bad as she felt. Despite their condition, she knew why they were here and they didn't belong.

"Get back!" she yelled, but they kept coming toward her.

One called out. "We need food and water."

"We have nothing," she said, and gave her grandfather's hand a little squeeze before turning it loose.

It was Chuy who took the lead. He was crazy desperate and wanted this over with. He palmed his knife and started toward her.

"I know who you are," he yelled, carrying the knife close against his leg.

Layla tensed. The drums were thundering - the singers chanting at fever pitch. This man's threat was obvious. If they didn't get what they wanted, they were willing to die for the chance to take it.

"You have to help us, Layla Birdsong. It is your duty," Chuy yelled.

Moving sideways to draw danger away from the ones behind her, Layla notched an arrow.

"Get back now. Go away or you will die," she yelled.

Then a second man started toward her, only this one had a gun.

"We're gonna die either way," Roscoe yelled. "I ain't got nothin' left to lose."

She didn't have time to think. He was already aiming for her when she swung the bow. His shot went off, but her arrow was true. It pierced his chest, then all the way through his back.

Roscoe's screams were bouncing from rim to rim inside the canyon as he dropped the gun. He fell to his knees; still trying to pull the arrow out as he died.

Thirteen down, two to go.

Roscoe's death galvanized Beamer.

He grabbed the gun Roscoe dropped, but took aim too late. He heard the thud of the arrow, but still hadn't felt the pain as he looked down at his chest in disbelief.

Sonofabitch! He was gonna die just like in the old cowboy and Indian movies he used to watch when he was a kid. Only in those movies, it was the cowboys who always won.

"What the fuck," he mumbled, and dropped.

Fourteen down, one to go.

While his two companions had been trying to play shoot-out with the woman, Chuy Garza had been getting closer. Now he was so close he could see the scar on her cheek and another on her belly. He made his move.

Layla heard men behind her coming to her aid as the last man rushed her, but they would be too late. Without time to get off another shot, she dropped the bow and palmed her knife just as he jumped.

One moment she was on her feet, and the next thing she knew she was on her back and fighting for her life.

Chuy was ready to die. He knew it was going to happen. He couldn't fight them all, but he was taking her with him. He was swinging his knife in an arc toward her when he realized she'd gotten her knees drawn up between them. Her feet were on his chest as he suddenly went airborne; landing so hard on his back that he lost his breath and the knife. He was still scrambling for air and a weapon when the woman leaned down and slit his throat.

Chuy's last sight of life was the fire in her eyes, and a small silver charm swinging from a necklace around her neck.

Fifteen down - none to go.

Layla kicked the knife out of his reach without bothering to watch him die. She picked up her bow, shouldered the quiver of arrows, and was turning to look for her grandfather when she saw him lying on the ground. A crowd of people were kneeling around him.

The pain that rolled through her was as visceral as the day she had buried her father.

She ran screaming, "Grandfather! Grandfather!

But it was already too late. Roscoe's first shot had hit him right between the eyes, and the blood that had spilled into the earth beneath him was already dry and blowing away like dust.

The pain of his loss was overwhelming. She couldn't think. She couldn't focus. And there were no tears left in her body to cry.

Run, Singing Bird. There are others coming from behind. Run now. Tomorrow you weep.

It was as if Windwalker had grabbed her by the arm and yanked her to her feet.

"Run now!" she screamed. "Run for your lives."

She turned toward the steady drumbeat and began running, lengthening her stride with every step.

The singing was in her head, in her heart, in her gut. She felt their power as if they'd tied a rope to her waist to pull her home. When she rounded the curve in the canyon wall and saw the ruins, she shouted aloud in a cry that matched what she heard in her head.

Although they had yet to cross over, they had reached the destination, which reminded her that she didn't know where to go from here. As she ran, a large part of the canyon wall appeared to be melting. The air between them was dancing from the heat waves coming up from the ground and she feared the rock was melting from the Firewalker's heat.

Then where there had been rock, came a burst of light, and inside she could see the silhouettes of the Old Ones coming toward them, spilling out into the canyon, waving them in.

Relief overwhelmed her. That was it! They'd done it! Now all she had to get them through.

The footsteps behind her were like thunder, the ground shook beneath her feet as they came running.

They'd seen it, too.

"Keep moving! Don't stop! Your brothers and sisters are behind you," she shouted, waving them on, pushing them forward.

She saw their faces as they ran past her; heard their voices shouting her name – shouting "Layla, Layla, Layla," until she was reeling from the sound.

She didn't move from where she was standing, still keeping guard as she lifted up those who had fallen. One hour ran into the second, and they were still staggering past her with bloody lips and sunburned skin; red eyes in ghost faces passing her by. She didn't know their names, but she felt their joy.

The line seemed unending, the sky was white-hot, the fireball looming larger, and the ground was burning her feet through the soles of her boots. The world was only degrees away from exploding into a ball of fire as big as the one in the sky.

Chapter Twelve

President Farley lost focus about the same time the last vehicles quit. They'd been on foot for hours and somewhere along the way they joined up with another group, and then another, until they were walking thousands strong. Some recognized him, but were too miserable to care. In the grand scheme of things, a president no longer mattered. Not when they were all on the verge of incineration.

Another hour had come and gone when they began seeing the bodies of people who'd been ahead of them. The stench was only slightly less shocking than their black and bloated carcasses.

Farley thought about his Chief of Staff, and the generals in the DOD. It wasn't the first time he'd wondered why they were still waiting to fire the missiles? What the hell could have gone wrong?

He would have known the answer sooner if his brain wasn't frying as he walked. When the answer finally hit him, he actually cried out in despair. Had it now been for one of his bodyguards, he would have fallen.

Without power, they could not launch. Without a launch, they didn't have a devil's chance of salvation. There was no way, even if Layla Birdsong was standing before him, that he could make everything happen fast enough to save a nation. At that point, he abdicated what was left of his conscience and started running, desperate to get closer to the front, leaving his entourage and responsibilities behind.

And then like a miracle, word began passing down through the hikers that the Indians had been sighted. As they approached an overlook a short time later, the march of Indians down in the canyon below was plainly visible.

As the crow flies, the Indians were only two, maybe three miles ahead of them. Walking, it would be longer, but it was enough that they'd been sighted. Someone shouted down at them to wait, and then others began screaming and yelling until their voices became a roar.

The sound carried down into the gorge. The People looked back and then up. When they saw the horde on the ridge above them, they broke out in a run.

And just like that, the ones above them gave chase.

The race was on.

****

Binini Islands – West Indies

The ocean was boiling. Whatever had been alive below was now floating dead upon the surface of the water. The sight was horrifying, and Leland Prince had finally come to the realization that he would die.

He'd always thought he'd be philosophical about his passing, imagining he would be clean and comfortable in his own bed, surrounded by servants tending to his every need until his last breath had come and gone.

He'd never given a thought to an end like this,

and believed it a most inglorious and disturbing way for such an interesting man as he to be snuffed.

He'd gathered the servants around him for company rather than comfort, although several of them were closer to death than he. The twins' nursemaid had gone into a swoon from the heat, leaving the boys in the house to fend for themselves.

Prince had been shocked by the sight of them pilfering through his treasures, but was so overcome by ennui that it took a few moments for him to accept that when they were all blown to bits, it wouldn't matter what broke or what didn't.

His head was spinning as he gazed around his library, past the books and maps, the diaries and oddities that he'd collected throughout his life, and remembered how the children had come to be. They were interesting children, but a failed and disappointing experiment. When he realized they had his crystal paperweight – the precious portal key - he started to tell them to put it down then let it go and sat in a stupor watching them play.

Even in this most miserable state of heat and starvation, they seemed oblivious. They were jabbering between themselves in manic fashion, turning the crystal over and over from point to point, rather than flat side to flat side. Then one of them stood it on a point, and to Prince's shock, it balanced perfectly upright. The other one crowed, then spun it like a top.

He expected it to spin until it ran out of momentum, but instead of falling, it continued to spin, faster and faster until he began to hear a hum, and the air around him was beginning to vibrate. When he saw a small pinpoint of light forming on the wall behind the twins' backs, he nearly fainted.

"Fuck me blind!" he shouted, and stood up.

The twins threw themselves into each other's arms. When Prince moved toward the desk, they moved in unison, like Siamese twins bound together for life, backing up as fast as he was approaching.

The cube was spinning so fast it had virtually disappeared, and the light behind the boys' heads was the size of a window.

Prince's heart was pounding as he leaped, but the boys were faster. They went backwards into the light and disappeared, taking the light and the crystal with them.

The portal closed.

The crystal was gone.

Prince screamed, and began hammering on the wall with both fists until his hands were shredded and his heart was pounding so hard he thought his head would explode.

He'd been shown salvation, only to be dropped back into hell. How bloody unfair of fate to have done that.

He turned around, looking past the people in the room through the windows behind them, to see a moving wall of water higher than the house.

The wait was over.

****

It was nearing two hours since the portal had opened, and still the people kept coming. Layla was standing at the edge of the light, but the tempo of drumming had changed to a drumbeat for war, and the Anasazi spirits were no longer singing. All Layla could hear was a continuous war cry. It was no longer a beacon. It was a warning, and her wait was almost over.

The people who'd been the farthest behind were now running toward her at a more frantic pace. She saw fear on their faces, when before she'd seen relief. Had they been afraid the portal would close before they arrived, or was that danger from behind coming closer?

"Hurry!" she screamed, urging them on, pulling them in, pushing them through until a woman's frantic warning told her all she needed to know.

"Thousands behind us."

"What? Who?" Layla shouted, as the woman ran past her.

"White men... soldiers with guns."

Before she could panic, she heard the Windwalker's voice.

Leave none behind.

Layla would obey, even if it meant sacrificing herself to make it happen. Within a few moments, she saw the last of the line. It was a miracle. They were going to make it after all.

They were going into the light in twos and in threes, even carrying those they'd refused to leave behind.

Her legs were trembling as she watched the last one go, and still she watched. Leave none behind.

There was a huge cloud of dust rising in the air beyond the twin spires. The enemy was too close.

She looked over her shoulder. The Anasazi who'd come out to greet her were now standing in her way.

Her heart nearly stopped. What did this mean? Was she supposed to stay back and die? Windwalker said she would sacrifice. Did he mean give up her life or were the people making that dust meant to pass through?

She looked back toward the spires, and to her

horror, the top of one began to crumble. As it began, it reminded her of watching the twin towers of the New York Trade Center falling the day the world was forever changed.

When the first chunk of rock hit the ground, it sent up a dust cloud so large that it momentarily blotted out the earth below, giving the spires the appearance of hovering.

Then a small boy came out of the dust, staggering and falling, and then getting up only to stagger and fall again.

The war cry in her head became a scream.

Leave no one behind!

Layla bolted, running with a sudden wind at her back, carrying her faster than her weary legs would have ever been able to move. The heat from the sky now was like standing in fire, but the child was in it and still moving, and so must she.

The farther she ran from the portal, the more panicked she became. The ground was shaking beneath her feet.

Then the boy went down and didn't get up.

She had no memory of running those last yards to get to him – only that he was still breathing when she picked him up.

And that was when she saw the runaway horde, less than a football field away. They saw her at the same time and it felt as if they leaped forward *enmasse*. There were soldiers with guns, and people screaming, and others crying out for mercy – crying out her name.

She turned to run, and when she did, the drums suddenly stopped, and her heart nearly stopped with them.

All she could hear now was the scream.

The Anasazi were moving into the light.

She wouldn't believe that they would leave her.

She wouldn't believe and kept on running; the child held fast against her heart.

The light was fading.

The portal was growing smaller.

The horde behind her was closing the gap.

Just when she thought she was going to be too late, the last Anasazi stopped, then turned and held out his hand.

He was holding the gate!

If only she had enough strength left to make it.

She leaped, felt a hand on her arm pulling her forward and fell into the light.

****

The portal disappeared and with that realization there came a wail of great despair, echoing down the gorge. But the wail quickly turned into shrieks of horror.

The earth was in death throes.

The ground on which they were standing burst into flames, while rock exploded all around them; raining down boulders and shards of rocky shrapnel. The air was vibrating at a terrible speed and when they looked up, the sky above them was no more.

Firewalker's journey was at an end.

People dropped where they stood, some with mouths agape in a scream that never surfaced - others catching fire like tissue paper; their skin going up in flames.

The woman next to Farley swelled and burst before his eyes. The only blessing he took with him was going blind before he died.

Chapter Thirteen

The New World: Naaki Chava

Water.

First it was the sound - then the taste – then the silken feel of it on her feet, up her thighs, to her belly, then her breasts - soaking into skin raw and burned.

Layla moaned.

"She wakes! She wakes! Singing Bird wakes!"

The voice was female, as were the hands putting something cool and silky on her eyes, then her face, soothing, whispering in her ear, calming, reassuring. The language was stilted, but she understood the words.

"You are well, Singing Bird. You are safe."

The news was welcome, but Layla didn't feel well. She felt like she was still dying. A part of her wanted to go there. Then she remembered how hard they'd all fought to stay alive and the option of dying was no longer a consideration.

She heard footsteps. The stride was long, bringing with it a scent reminiscent of the earth after a rain.

"Open your eyes, Singing Bird. See my face."

The voice was male and demanding. Layla shook her head. Too much had already been demanded of her. She wanted nothing to do with anymore.

"Sssh, Cayetano. You are too hasty. Her eyes are burned. They need to heal. She will know you when it is time."

She heard a sigh, then shuffling, then a splash, then that same male voice.

"Give her to me."

Suddenly she was floating from the arms of one person, into the arms of another. She didn't need eyes to know that a man was holding her now. The hands beneath her breasts were callused. The muscles in the arms cradling her neck were hard.

But the touch was gentle and his patience unflinching as he kept her afloat.

She licked her lips, and within seconds, she heard a sigh as one callused finger lightly rubbed more of that cool, silky liquid on her lips.

"Not food, Singing Bird. Medicine."

Something about his voice made her think of Niyol, and the pain of that loss was raw beyond measure. She sank back into the safety of unconsciousness – because it was easier – and because she was suddenly afraid to see his face.

****

The next time Layla woke she thought it was night. Everything around her was silent, save for the occasional sound of an intermittent snore. She needed to go to the bathroom, which became an issue. Not only did she not know where she was, but she couldn't see. And, she quickly realized she was still naked. She touched her skin. It was tender to the touch, but the pain was less. Whatever they were putting on her was healing, but it didn't change the fact that she still needed to pee. She reached out to feel for the side of the bed, realized she was on the floor, and she wasn't alone.

What the hell? Hard muscles. Long arms and a callused hand. Definitely a man.

She felt him stir, then sit up.

"You are awake, Singing Bird. Do you thirst or have a wish to pass water?"

The phrasing was odd and she knew it was the man from the pool, but he was correct.

"Yes, both."

He rolled off the other side of the mat then picked her up and carried her outside.

The moment the soft air hit her skin, she realized he was carrying her away from the house.

"I'm naked," she said.

"You are too burned to cover your body."

"But other people will see me."

She heard him chuckle.

"It is dark now, but when you can see, then you will also see them."

"Are you saying that none of you wear clothes?"

"We cover parts. Not all. There is no need."

He stopped and gently stood her on her feet.

"We are here now. You are safe to do what you need."

"Are you going to watch?"

"I won't be far, but I will not look. When you have finished, call my name. I will take you back."

"You sleep in my bed, but I don't know your name," she muttered.

"My name is Cayetano, and you sleep in my bed because you are mine."

Shock mingled with anger. She'd lost the man she loved. She didn't want another.

"I do not belong to you. I belong to no one but myself."

"You belong to me. You have always belonged to

me. You have yet to remember, but you will love me."

She heard him walking away, but was so shocked that for a few moments, forgot what she'd come here to do. That was what the Windwalker had told her – the same words that Niyol had used. She shuddered.

The night was still, but she could hear rustling all around her. She reached out and felt leaves in front of her, bushes behind her, vines hanging above her. She could hear what sounded like frogs, and some night birds, but nothing threatening.

By the time she had finished her business, she was even more confused. She called his name.

"Cayetano."

"I come, Singing Bird."

And in that moment, standing in the dark, in this place with the wind blowing on her bare skin waiting for him to arrive, there was a feeling of deja'vu so strong that by the time he got to her, she was crying.

He swung her up in his arms, and in the moonlight saw her tears. He laid his cheek against the crown of her head.

"My heart hurts that you are sad."

"What happened in my world was very bad. Everyone I love is gone. I came to this place with thousands of others, and yet I came alone."

"You came to this place to return to me, Singing Bird. This is Naaki Chava. It is home."

His breath was on her cheek. She knew he was close to her face, to her lips. If she let herself go there, she could almost believe it was Niyol, and they were holding each other as they had in the Canyon del Muerto – in the cave with the little spring.

When he began to move, she knew he was carrying her back to where they slept. What was it he'd called this place? Naaki Chava? Two Earth? Or, maybe he was saying Earth Two. The second home? Wherever she was, it was far better than the place from which they'd come.

****

One moment Adam and Evan Prince had been in the plantation house waiting to die, and the next thing they knew they'd been dropped into a strange land, in a busy marketplace, and half-naked people were running and screaming from the explosion of light that had dumped the boys into their midst.

The crystal was on the ground at their feet and they grabbed it. It had gotten them here. They would need it to get back. They didn't know where they were, but it was hot, it smelled bad, and there was too much noise.

Before they could move, the crowd parted to reveal two large, brown-skinned men running at them with spears.

"Run Evan!" Adam shrieked, and turned, only to fall headlong into the arms of more guards coming up from behind.

As the guards grabbed them by the napes' of their necks, they launched into twin speak, cautioning each other not to give away their secrets.

They were dragged through winding streets, past a large temple-like structure in the middle of the city, to what could only be called a palace set into the side of a mountain. There, they went up countless more steps, down long dark halls, into a large great room in the center of the building.

They had little time to notice the architecture, the decorations, or the tables filled with bowls and platters piled high with fruits and breads as they were dumped, rather unceremoniously, at the foot of a very large throne.

A guard handed their crystal to a servant, who quickly carried it up the steps to the man sitting on it.

Another servant kicked at the boys.

“Stand in the presence of Bazat!” he shouted.

The boys rose, their arms around each other as if they were connected at the chest and looked up.

Adam and Evan Prince had read many books and many minds. They knew things about the human race that only God should know. From the time they were tiny children they heard vile thoughts they were too young to understand, and seen past outward behaviors to the hearts beneath. They learned the hard way to trust none but each other.

And when they looked into the heart of the squat little man sitting on the throne, they saw that he was not kingly at all. He looked Native American, but the breechclout he was wearing was of cloth, not of skin, with both silver and gold threads woven into the fabric. The big collar-like jewelry around his neck looked to be made of gold with turquoise fastened about. There were small curved bones in the piercings of his nose and ears, with small pieces of turquoise hanging from the bones.

His hair was in red, muddy hunks, not unlike dreadlocks the boys had seen on the islanders back home. There were dozens of green and red feathers fastened throughout the crown of his head, giving him the appearance of plumage. Despite his looks, Adam knew he was but a brute and a criminal in royal clothing.

And he had their crystal. He leaned forward, resting an elbow on his knee as he yelled down.

“Look at me!”

They didn't understand the language and immediately shifted into reading his mind to understand the words.

He frowned. "You have the same face."

Now they were faced with trying to communicate with a man who would not understand their language. They'd never tried it before, but wondered if they sent their thoughts into his head without saying them aloud if he would understand. So they tried it.

We are twins.

Bazat stood up. "How is it that I heard your words yet your lips did not move?"

We do not speak your language, but we can hear your thoughts. We are sending our answers to you in the same way.

Bazat was immediately afraid. Witchcraft was a danger.

One of his servants standing beside the throne leaned down and whispered in Bazat's ear. He listened, then looked up and addressed them again.

"It is said that you fell out of the sky in a flash of light. Is that so?"

They nodded.

Bazat's thoughts were spinning. The sons of Sun and Earth Mother were twins – Little War-Gods. Gods would be able to read human thoughts. Maybe this wasn't witchcraft. If the Little War-Gods had been sent to this place, they would have come out of the sky. He was nervous. He didn't want to anger Sun or Mother Earth, or go to war with these Gods, even if they were small.

"Speak your names!" he demanded.

I am Adam Prince. I am Evan Prince.

Their voices were as interchangeable as their faces. They intrigued Khan, but he didn't trust outsiders and this could still be a trick.

"Prince. What name is this?"

Evan had already picked up on the fact that Bazat thought they might be Gods.

"A prince is the son of a king...like a God, he added.

Bazat did not like that at all. He was the ruler here, God or not God.

"You cannot rule here. This is my land. I am Bazat and you are trespassers!" He rolled the crystal between his hands then held it up to the light. "What is this thing you have with you? Is it an amulet? Does it work magic?

"You talk," Evan whispered.

Adam was reading Bazat's mind as fast as he could think, figuring out how to word his answer to their best advantage. He'd already guessed they had gone back in time. He used to hear Landan Prince talk about such things, and they were young enough to still believe anything was possible.

And, Adam thought the man was Mayan. He picked up on the fact that he was very superstitious, and was thinking he and Evan were some kind of War Gods. He thought back to the Harry Potter movies he and his brother had loved so much, and went for the magic angle.

We were cast out of our land for divination. We are shamans. We know secrets.

Evan's eyes widened. He knew the meaning of divination. It was straight out of Harry Potter!

Bazat believed his own Shamans had power, and for him, this added to the possibility that they could be the sons of Sun and Mother Earth, especially if they knew magic.

"Where is this land of which you speak?" Khan

asked.

Adam waved his hand. *On the far side of the world.*

Khan frowned. "You lie. The world is flat. Everyone knows that."

No, it is round, like your belly, Evan said.

Adam gave his brother a frantic look.

"You tell me no! You tell me the world is round like my belly?" Bazat yelled.

The great hall went silent. Servants held their breaths, waiting to see which head was chopped off first. But to their surprise, Bazat threw back his head and laughed. The sound echoed within the great room and then out into the halls. And when he laughed, the servants laughed also.

Adam clutched Evan's hand and waited.

Bazat's laughter was over. He looked back at the boys. The smile was still on his face, but there was murder in his eyes.

"If you two are truly shamans and you know secrets, then tell me something only I would know is true. Tell me now, or I will cut out your hearts to the Sun God and chop off both your heads."

Adam straightened his shoulders.

You made your first kill when you were nine. It was the man who ravaged your mother.

Your spear has a name. You call it Heart-eater, Evan added.

Bazat hid his shock well. He'd asked, never believing their claims to be true. But this was another thing altogether. No one knew this but him. He waved to a servant.

"These little princes were cast out of their land. Let it be known that they are now mine."

Adam was afraid to show the relief he was feeling.

He grabbed Evan's hand and gave it a quick squeeze, as if to say stay silent. Evan got the message.

We are honored, Adam said.

Bazat squinted at them so long that his small slanted eyes seemed to disappear.

Adam could hear Bazat's thoughts. He wasn't sure whether they were going to be an asset or a liability, but he was intrigued enough to keep them alive – at least for the time being. And they were twins. There was something about their beliefs that had to do with twins, but he couldn't pick up on all of it. He'd have to ask Evan. Evan liked ancient history better.

"You will eat with me each morning. I will ask you questions. You will keep me informed in a way that will ensure my rule, and protect me from my enemies," Bazat announced.

Evan nodded. Adam did the same.

Bazat waved them away.

****

The woman with the soft voice and gentle hands was combing Layla's hair and coaxing her to eat.

"You eat, Singing Bird. It will make you strong."

Layla took a bite that was in the bowl and recognized the masa and berries. She'd eaten it before, in the Anasazi ruins with Niyol. It brought back so many sad memories that it was hard to swallow past the lump in her throat.

The woman seemed satisfied with the effort and kept combing.

Layla ate another few bites and then countered with a question.

"What's your name?"

"I am called Acat."

"So, Acat, tell me something. How did you know I would be coming here, and why does everyone here call me Singing Bird?"

Before Little Bird had time to answer, Layla heard footsteps and a very familiar stride. Even though he made her nervous, her heart quickened.

It was Cayetano.

"You are Singing Bird, because it is your name," he said. "I have come to take you to the healing waters again. Soon your skin will be smooth as it was before."

She frowned. He kept speaking as if he'd known her. If only her eyes would get well. She needed to see where fate had taken her.

"I'm not going outside again naked."

Acat giggled, then reached out and took Layla's hand and put it on her own shoulder. "You touch me. You see."

Within seconds Layla could tell she wore nothing above the waist but what felt like large braided bib, and a swath of fabric tied around her waist.

"Does everybody dress this way?" Layla asked.

"Only women. Enough talk," Cayetano said.

She felt him wrapping something around her waist and then he was scooping her up into his arms.

"Her eyes, her eyes!" Acat said, grabbed a tiny pot with the cooling medicine, lifted the bandages on Layla's eyes and swiped it across her eyelids before pulling the bandages back down.

Moments later, Layla felt the sun on her body and cringed.

"The sun... is it bright?" she asked.

"Yes. It makes the crops grow and the babies healthy."

"Babies? You have children?"

She heard a catch in his breathing. "I am

speaking of the babies in Naaki Chava."

"You don't have children?"

"I have no other woman. I want no other woman. I have been waiting for Singing Bird."

Layla was stunned. She needed to see his face and this place.

"I don't understand. How could you be waiting for a woman who didn't even live in this world?"

He didn't answer and she didn't push it.

As they walked, she began to hear voices now – lots of voices, people laughing and talking, some passing them closely enough she could hear their footsteps, then their voices, speaking directly to her as if they knew her.

"Singing Bird has returned."

"Singing Bird... it is good that you are here."

"Singing Bird, it is good you are home."

It was one little comment after another that still made no sense, and Cayetano had not spoken to them or to her. She didn't know what was wrong, but his silence was telling.

When they reached the water, he set her on her feet only long enough to unwind the cloth from her waist and then picked her up again and walked into the water, easing her in little bit at a time so as not to shock the sensitive skin. As soon as he was chest-high in the water, he laid her down to float as if he was putting her to bed, still cradling her head on his arm for a pillow.

It was soothing, and a habit Layla was learning to appreciate.

"Cayetano?"

"I am listening."

"There were many others who came with me. They had injuries and burns, too."

"We were prepared. They have shelter and food. They are all being cared for."

"There was a little boy. He fell just beyond the portal and I went back to get him. We were the last to come through. Did he live?"

"He lives. Acat cares for him."

She was silent only for a few seconds. There were so many things she wanted to know.

"You said that you'd prepared for our arrival, but how did you know we were coming? Why did you already know my name?"

He was silent for a few moments, and Layla wondered if he would answer. It was hard to concentrate with the cooling waters lapping her breasts and between her thighs. Just when he had almost lulled her to sleep, he began to speak.

"There are people who can see things from the past and things that have not yet happened."

"Like my grandfather," Layla said, and then immediately flashed on his bloody body turning into dust before her on the ground. A rush of sadness swept through her, spilling out in a burst of anger that quickly turned to pain. "They shot him. I never got to say goodbye. One minute I was holding his hand, then fighting, and when it was over he was dead." Even though her eyes were covered, she put her hands over her face and began to sob. "He was all I had left."

Cayetano pulled her close, cradling her against his chest.

"No, Singing Bird, no. You have me. You have always had me."

He cradled her like a baby, letting her cry while his own heart ached for the time when she would know him again.

Layla cried until her head hurt, her heart hurt.

She cried until the bandages fell off her eyes and the healing medicine was gone.

"Let me stand," she said, and when he would have hesitated, she insisted. "I'm strong enough. I won't fall."

He moved his arms from beneath her back and head. When she dropped her feet to the bottom, the water rose to her shoulders, but it felt good to be upright.

She heard a catch in his breathing as he touched the scar on her cheek. The urge to see him was overwhelming, to see for herself that this man was not Niyol. She was convinced that she wanted Niyol back so badly that she was only imagining this odd connection to Cayetano.

She began cupping water in her hands and splashing it on her face, rubbing the gel-like medicine from her eyes until it was all gone from her skin.

"Is this place in the shade?" she asked.

"Yes. Why do you ask?"

"I want to see your face."

Suddenly he was afraid that she would reject him. He grabbed her hands.

"The healer said your eyes were not well."

She held onto his hand and then slowly opened her eyes – just a little – just a test.

At first the light burned, and she blinked several times in rapid succession until it eased. Her first sight of him was blurry, and then as it adjusted, she found herself staring at the span of his chest.

It was brown like hers, which she expected. He was taller than her, which she already knew. His neck, rising up from his shoulders was strong and muscled. His face was broad at the cheeks, slanting down to a more angular jaw and chin. His forehead was broad, with a nose that jutted proudly from the middle of his face. His ears were pierced, and there were small chunks of turquoise laced through cord, dangling from the lobes. Both sides of his hair had been pulled back from his face and tied together at the crown of his head in a topknot. The eyebrows and lashes were as black as his hair, and arched over eyes as dark as a night without stars.

When her gaze slid to his mouth, she started to shake.

His lips were full, with a most beautiful curve, but it was the scar at the corner of his mouth that nearly stopped her heart. It wasn't a big scar, and it certainly wasn't ugly. But it was familiar. Her pulse kicked out of rhythm as she reached toward him. He flinched and then sighed, as if accepting the inevitability of the moment.

Layla lifted her hands, and when she began to trace the shape of his lips, she closed her eyes too soon to see his tears.

All she could think was that she knew this shape, and the scar – dear God, she knew this scar - angling very slightly down, giving him the appearance that he was about to grimace.

"I am losing my mind," she whispered.

"Why?"

"Because I know this, and I should not."

She heard a swift intake of breath, and then his hands were beneath her backside and his voice was rough and thick with tears.

"Do you remember this, Singing Bird? Do you remember me?"

He lifted her up.

One second she was floating in the water and then he stepped between her legs. She made way for him without thought, and when he eased her down onto his erection, she wrapped her legs around his waist and held on.

He shuddered as he settled deep within her. It had been so long since he'd known this. He had to pace himself or it would be over far too soon. He had to accept that she was real and would not go away like she did every night in his dreams.

He buried his nose against her hair and smelled the cleansing root Acat washed into her hair. He could feel the scar down the back of her arm. All of this was real, so she must be, too.

He began to move his body within her, and as she rocked against it, his heart was full. This was real! This was true! He was thrusting up - then again - then again - and again - until the water was slapping against their bodies to the same rhythm as the ride they were on.

Layla's arms were around his neck, her forehead pressed hard against his chest, her legs locked around his waist. When he shifted his stance and pushed her down harder on his erection she knew he was going to groan.

And he did.

His fingers were splayed wide beneath her backside, and when he began to dig them slightly into her flesh, she knew he would groan again.

And he did.

It was frightening that she knew that, but also a turn-on that she could do this to him - that she set him on fire - that it was her he claimed. The elemental need that shot through her was unrecognizable. In the few brief moments between one thrust and the next, she became a woman she did not know.

She remembered everything that pleased him -

how to move, what to touch, how long to wait between each stroke. When the climax finally rolled through her, it came in a mind-bending wave.

Cayetano's blood was on fire. He couldn't think beyond how she made him feel. When she leaned back within his arms, he knew she was pushing him deeper into her womb. And when she braced herself against his chest, her fingers digging into his flesh, her eyes closed and lips parted in building ecstasy, he knew she was going to come.

And she did.

And because he'd been alone too long to be without her again, he went with her.

****

Seven sleeps later:

Layla accepted her place in Cayetano's life. She didn't fully understand it, but she couldn't deny what she felt. He was Cayetano, and although their faces weren't quite the same, there was something of Niyol in him, as well. And when he wrapped her in his arms at night, he was the Windwalker, sweeping her up into the wind and carrying her away from danger.

The blisters on her skin were nearly healed, and as soon as the sun no longer made her eyes weep, she would be officially welcomed back by the people of Naaki Chava.

With the bandages off, she finally saw the world into which they'd come.

****

The city sprawled out across a great valley

between jungle-covered mountains. It was tropical in appearance, but while the foliage was somewhat familiar, it was much larger and more colorful than anything she'd ever seen in books. There were enormous trees that looked like palms gone wild, and ferns higher than a two-story house. It made her think of artists renderings of earth during prehistoric times.

Color was everywhere - in the mountains surrounding Naaki Chava, in the fabric of their skirts, in the designs on their handmade pottery, and most especially in the bird-life.

There were all sizes of parrots, in colors of the rainbow, as well as birds that she'd never seen. Large, royal-blue birds with massive wingspans and tails as long as her grandfather's braids, red and green birds with topknots that fanned out across their heads when they were angry; like a hand-carved comb stuck in a woman's hair. And their calls were just as colorful as their plumage. It was, without doubt, the most stunning sight she'd ever seen, and at the same time made her sad, wondering if their earth had looked this way in the beginning. The monkeys high up in the trees were of every hue and size. At night, the sounds of big cats on the hunt could be heard coming out of the jungle around them.

The streets were paved with a kind of limestone that made them so white that they glistened in the light of day. Nearly all of the dwellings were square, like the old pueblos, but larger, and with ornate carvings above doorways and on roofs. Everything started with a square and if it was more than one room, it went up in graduated sizes of the same shape. There were no round corners anywhere that she could see except in art, or in the carvings.

Despite the numbers of newcomers she'd brought

with her, they had somehow made room for them to live. She didn't know whether they'd built new dwellings in preparation for their coming, or if they were living with the residents.

During the Last Walk, before their earth died, Layla and the others had moved through vast desert-like areas with sparse growth and trees stunted from a shortage of water. Here, everything was in abundance, from the river running through the valley, to the lush abundance of the fields where food was grown. It looked like paradise, and yet Layla sensed an undercurrent of secrets she had yet to learn.

As Acat had shown her, the women wore a length of hand-woven fabric around their waists that hung just to below their knees, and ornate bib-like collars that lay on the front of their chests like a breast-plate on a piece of armor. Some of the bibs were braided cloth or woven reeds, some were formed by connecting different sized pieces of hammered silver. The more ornate bibs had tiny shells fastened within the silver. But the collar Acat put on Singing Bird was nothing like the others. It was all different sizes of turquoise; the sky stones signifying status.

The mens' breechclouts were made of hand-woven fabric and hung to their knees. Their hair was cut straight across at the ends, pulled back from the sides of their faces, and fastened at the tops of their heads.

Cayetano's dwelling was what she would consider a palace of its time. It had been built on a rise overlooking the valley below. Adobe-like brick and natural stone had been laid in colorful geometric shapes to form the floors. The openings between the rooms were tall and arched, and most without doors. There was a natural water flow from the mountain behind the dwelling that flowed into an aqueduct beneath it, furnishing water directly to the cooking area and to a room where a sunken bath had been built. It channeled the water in such a way that it was always running a trickle of fresh water through it, like a self-aerating pool.

She was continually surprised at what she would have called advance technology for the times, and wondered how it had all been lost.

The servants treated her with deference, which furthered her belief that Cayetano held some high office, but it was the large open room in the middle of the palace that proved her suspicions correct. He was obviously their chief and that great room was where he ruled. Even though it was nothing like the tribal council she'd been used to, she had to keep reminding herself that wherever they were now, old rules no longer applied.

There was a raised section at one end of the great room where the throne had been placed. The back and arms of the chair were made of elaborately carved wood with large, equally over-sized spears fastened in a crossed position behind it. The walls were painted in fresco-like fashion with pictographs telling centuries' worth of history she had yet to understand.

A Jaguar skin with a fully attached head hung on the back of the throne. The head was positioned so that whoever sat beneath it appeared to be its next prey, its mouth open in an eternal snarl with two large amber-colored stones set where they eyes used to be. The big cat's legs were draped over the arms of the throne, so that whoever sat in the seat took on the persona of the cat, claws and all.

Servants came and went throughout the palace all day, some bringing food, carrying water, cleaning behind the constant stomp of the footsteps of those who came and went.

One did nothing but work a loom weaving cloth, and the steady thump as the woman worked it was, at first disturbing, then after a time no longer noticeable.

The room that concerned her the most looked like a war closet, rather than storage. It was filled with feathered headdresses, and what looked suspiciously like body armor. There were hundreds of spears and bone knives and axe-like weapons. The axe blades fastened to the handles appeared to be the fangs of the same kind of cat as the one on Cayetano's throne and guessed them to be ceremonial rather than useful.

But seeing the weapons was a reminder that the aspect of war had begun when from the start of human existence. She started to worry about what kind of world she'd led her people into then cast aside the worry. Whatever was here was still far better than what they'd left behind.

The only building higher than the palace, was the temple; a towering four-sided pyramid in the middle of the city. From a distance, it looked a little like a square layer cake with a single stairway on every side. The top of the pyramid was yet another small room and she wondered what happened in there.

In her mind's eye, she already knew the vista from the highest point of the temple - from the rooftops of the city, to the marketplace, to the river, to the acres and acres of growing crops, and the jungle beyond. It was yet another unsettling memory that had no explanation.

Cayetano ruled it like the chief he was, but she had no idea how that would impact her until the day she made her first public appearance.

Chapter Fourteen

Cayetano walked into their rooms as Singing Bird was being dressed. Acat and two other servants were trying to help, but she was balking despite their insistence of certain garments.

Although the women of Naaki Chava wore their hair in elaborate hairstyles, looping the lengths into big fat rolls both at the sides and the tops of their heads, Layla wanted hers down, and so it was; glistening like sunlight on dark water. The silver necklace she'd worn around her neck was now threaded through her hair in such a way that the little bird charm was hanging in the space between her brows; a private homage to her father and her past.

The bib of turquoise around her neck rested on the swell of her breasts, and the soft fabric of her multicolored skirt clung to her shape like another skin. She was still thinner than she'd ever been, but Cayetano understood why. It was at great cost that his Singing Bird had returned from the dead.

He eyed her proudly, thinking to himself what a magnificent woman she had become and discarded the tiny changes. Besides the lack of weight, the only other differences were the scars on her body, which she wore proudly, and the occasional glimpse he would get of how fierce she had become. She'd died a woman beloved of her people, and returned a warrior for their race.

He walked up behind her and despite the women

giggling around them, kissed the back of her neck.

Layla shivered with longing. Just a touch and she melted before him.

"You like these best," he said, and put them in her hand.

She looked down at the chunks of turquoise marbled with thin threads of gold, obviously meant to hang from her ears. But they were hardly metal studs and she didn't have any holes big enough in her earlobes for the cords to fit through.

"They're beautiful, but they won't fit in my ears."

Acat giggled and took them out of her hands. "Yes, they will fit. I will do it for you."

When Layla felt the weight of them on her ear lobes she was stunned.

"But how?" she muttered, running her fingertips along the sides of her face and then along her ears. Without warning, she abruptly stopped. In her mind, she'd been touching a stranger's face.

"I need to see. I need to see!" she muttered, and began moving from table to table, looking for something that would give off a reflection.

"What is wrong?" Cayetano asked.

She was beginning to panic.

"It doesn't feel like me. It is the face of a stranger."

He smiled, pulling the scar at the corner of his mouth upward.

"You came home, that is all."

But she wasn't satisfied. Of all the things that she'd lost from one world to the next, at that moment she would have wished for a mirror. When she saw the large platter of fruit on a nearby table she grabbed it. The fruit went flying as she carried the silver platter to the light. If it was shiny enough, it just might give off enough reflection to satisfy her panic.

Cayetano had known this day would come, and quickly sent the servants away.

Acat was in tears as she left, thinking she'd done something wrong.

Layla tilted the platter slightly to catch the most light. For a few moments all she could see were shadows. And then she moved it again and there was an image, but she didn't recognize the woman she saw.

Her hands began to shake. How had this happened? She was still Layla inside, but Layla Birdsong's face was gone. This face was a little thinner and her nose had a tiny bump where before it had none. Her cheekbones were higher, her mouth wider, her lips fuller. Some parts of the face were the same, but other parts were not. It was what she'd first thought when she'd seen Niyol in Cayetano.

She turned to Cayetano with a look of disbelief.

"How did this happen?"

He took the platter from her hands and set it aside.

"You have become who you once were."

She frowned. "I don't understand. I know we have a connection. I don't dispute that. But are we talking about reincarnation? Do you say my spirit once lived in this time? And if this is so, then why is the face I came here with no longer mine?"

He sighed. "It is your face. It was always your face. I will tell you this now. I should have told you before, but today you need to understand why our people so readily accept your presence, and why you understand everything that is said to you."

He led her to a bench then pulled her down onto his knee.

"What I am going to tell you will be difficult to

hear but you must wait until I am finished before you judge."

Layla saw the fear in his eyes and wondered what would be so terrible – so frightening – that a warrior like Cayetano would be afraid to voice.

"I am listening."

He reached for her hand, threaded their fingers together then held it over his heart, then without thinking, lovingly stroked the scar on her face.

"Soon it will be the celebration of the corn. It is the celebration for a good harvest. During that celebration when you were here before, you were killed by an enemy I did not know I had. He escaped, but I went mad with grief. I tracked him for many days, and when I found him, left pieces of his body all over the jungle so that his spirit would never be whole to meet his ancestors."

Layla was still grappling from the shock of hearing him say, you were killed, when she focused back in to what he was saying.

"Your death started a terrible war between our tribes. During that time, one of our shamans began having visions, and each vision he had was worse than the one before. He saw into the future destruction of our people, and how one day we would disappear from our land, and the earth would be no more forever."

Layla's head was spinning.

"You are talking about the Firewalker, aren't you?"

He nodded.

"But if all of you disappeared when earth burned, then how are you here? I thought that this place and all of you are the children of the Anasazi who disappeared so long ago."

"No. We are not their descendants. We *are* those

people, but in a time before our culture died."

Her heart was beginning to hammer. This was about to get worse, she could tell.

"So, when we escaped Firewalker, we did not come through the portal to a new land?

"This is not new land."

"But you call this Naaki Chava. That means two, or second in the Navajo language."

He nodded. "But our people have moved many times over this earth. This is our second time."

"Where were you before?"

He shrugged. "I do not know the name. The Shamans say it was far away where mountains blew fire and the sky was always dark with smoke."

"So we are here in your time, before your people disappeared, long before the old earth was destroyed?"

"Yes. I will tell you more. After your death, the wars continued and in my grief, I turned into a warrior with no mercy. I killed everyone in my path, no matter if they were an enemy or not."

Layla was struggling with the concept of a butcher and the man who'd cried making love to her. She was almost afraid to hear more.

"And then I died," Cayetano said. "I died, and still my spirit was not at rest because I could not find you. During my journey to find you, my spirit grew stronger. I could see what was happening to The People. They still fought each other, but in doing so their numbers grew small and tribes grew weak. When the white stranger came to our land, they could not stop him, and they were weakened even more, losing land and losing hope, and finally losing a sense of our race."

Layla slid an arm around his neck.

"Firewalker became angry. But it was when our

young began dying at their own hands that his anger worsened. He felt their pain. He shared their sorrow. They were born into a time without hope. Their own ancestors had let them down."

Layla was crying now, because she'd seen it happening – on every reservation – no matter what tribe – drugs and alcohol had taken over their lives. But the shame had killed them long before their hearts quit beating, decimating the families who were left.

Cayetano continued. "My spirit was in great despair because my actions so long ago were part of what caused the wars that continued after I died. My sadness drew the wind, and the wind became power, and when I finally wept for the loss of my Singing Bird, the Windwalker was born."

"I knew it," she whispered. "The first time you held me, I felt the Windwalker's heart."

He touched her face. "In my power as Windwalker, I sent the wind to find your spirit, and you were found. But even then our joining would not happen because we were on different paths. Your spirit was pure and beautiful, while mine held rage. And yet you, who walked without me in the spirit world, still loved me enough to offer a solution. It would be dangerous for you, maybe even deadly. But in my selfish need to get you back, I willingly agreed."

Layla closed her eyes to hear him out because she could no longer bear to see the pain and shame on his face.

"Firewalker had already launched himself toward earth before Layla Birdsong was born, so we could not delay. You were born on earth as Layla, the woman who came here with the New Ones. The people there who loved you taught you all you would need to know to make the Last Walk, without truly understanding why they felt a need to do it. But you learned and learned well, and when it became necessary, you did not fail me or yourself."

Layla opened her eyes. There were tears on his face. She took his hand and held it against her heart.

"So, I knew all of this would happen before I was born, remembered nothing of it afterward living as Layla Birdsong, and still did what I was supposed to do?"

He cupped her face. "You are a red feather warrior. I knew you would not fail."

"Because I killed the man from the gang that attacked me?"

"You were a red feather warrior before. Here, before you died, you also killed one of the men who attacked you. When it happened again as Layla Birdsong, it was the signal to me that you were prepared for what lay ahead."

Layla stood abruptly. "This is crazy. I died here and now I'm back? Why? Am I to die all over again? What does this mean?"

"No. You have already sacrificed yourself for the People. You have returned to the time before your death. This is when we were happy. This is before I turned bad. You didn't just save our People from Firewalker. You have come to save me. What happened before cannot happen again. You cannot die. You must not die."

Once again he ran his thumb across the scar on her cheek, then slid his hand along the one on her arm before touching the third mark on her belly.

"These scars you bring with you... they are the same places you were stabbed the day you died in my arms. It is your proof that what you sacrificed for us will stand."

At that moment, Acat poked her head into the room.

"The people gather, Cayetano. Your guards are waiting."

"Soon," he said, and waved her away. "I tell you this so that you understand... the people here know and love you now, because they knew and loved you then. To them, you were only gone for a short time. Not many thousands of years. And the enemies I have are still real, and so is the danger to you. But you brought something with you that, one day, will ensure peace between our People."

Layla gasped and then jumped to her feet.

"No! Tell me I did not drag our people on that Last Walk just so you could turn them into warriors? They've suffered enough."

He grabbed her hand when she would have pushed him away.

"It is not the people who came with you, although our numbers are now more impressive. It is the baby you carry."

Layla spread her hands across her flat belly.

"I'm pregnant?"

"I do not know that word," Cayetano said. "But you are with child." His shoulders slumped. "And that is the price I agreed to pay to get you back."

Now she was scared all over again.

"How is a baby your price?"

"Because the child you carry is not mine. It belongs to the Windwalker – the spirit I became. But if we are able to change history and I never go the bad way, then Windwalker never exists. And the only child you ever bear will belong to something I never become." He shrugged. "It is a trick of time, and of the Old Ones justice. It is the price for my loss of mercy. I will never give you a child of our own. But the child you bear will change history."

Layla's head was spinning.

"How? I don't understand."

"The shamans tell me the knowledge you and the New Ones have will help the change. We will grow stronger faster. Our cities will prosper. New ways of doing things will make living easier. But most important, the child you carry will be a peacemaker who puts an end to our wars. By the time white men come, we will be one endless tribe, united in purpose and spread all across the lands.

Layla touched her belly again. "How can a child stop wars?"

"I do not know. I know only what the shaman said."

"Is it promised that I will bear a healthy child? What happens if I lose it?"

"Then we are doomed, and when Firewalker sweeps across the sky in the times to come, there will be no Layla Birdsong to save our people, and they will perish with all the rest."

The thought was horrifying. Her hand fell on the scar on her face. Once she'd turned her fear to rage. She could do it again – would do it again – as many times as it took to keep her and this baby alive – to keep all of them alive.

Acat poked her head around the door again.

"It is time. Do I tell the guards you are ready?"

Cayetano didn't move. His gaze was on Singing Bird's face. Was she ready?

Layla's shoulders stiffened. Her chin was up, her eyes narrowed.

"I want my bow and the quiver of arrows, and I want my father's knife."

Acat looked confused. “I do not know this.”

Cayetano wanted to argue, but knew he must trust her instincts as much as his own.

“Do you mean the weapons you had when you came back?” he asked.

“Yes.”

“I will bring them,” Acat said, and scurried away.

“What are you going to do?” Cayetano asked.

“This first step back into your world will be on my terms. I will not show fear.”

The answer surprised him, but it was the right one.

“It is good,” he said softly.

Acat came running and laid the weapons at Layla’s feet.

Layla strapped the knife and holster on her leg, just above the knee, knowing every time she took a step her skirt would part just enough for it to be visible. Then she slung the quiver over her shoulder and picked up the bow.

“I am ready,” she said.

Cayetano exhaled slowly. “Together,” he said.

A dozen guards joined then surrounded them. Layla stopped again.

“Once we begin the walk to the temple, tell them to walk behind us. Tell them we walk alone.”

He frowned. “That is not safe.”

“No. It is wise. They have not seen me in this way since we came back. I must be seen as the warrior, or they will not care what I have to say.”

Once again she was right, but the thought of losing her all over again was horrifying. Still, if his Singing Bird was brave enough to do this, then it was not his choice to make.

He gave the guards their orders, ignoring the

shocked looks on their faces as they moved toward the doorway.

Cayetano looked every inch a chief. His headdress, a spire of long pheasant feathers fastened into his headband, bobbed as he walked, and the wide leather belt at his waist was studded with gold and turquoise, as were the leather cuffs that spanned his arms from his elbows to his wrists. A chunk of turquoise the size of his fist hung from a cord to the middle of his chest, not unlike the bulls-eye on a target. It was a 'look at me' challenge that couldn't be ignored. His leather sandals laced up past his calves, accentuating the strong muscles in his legs. He was a most impressive man, but it was the pride he felt for the woman at his side that was most notable.

The moment Cayetano and Singing Bird stepped out of the doorway into the sun, a roar went up in the city below that sent a chill up her spine. She paused, not for effect, but because she was so shocked. They were saying her name.

Singing Bird. Singing Bird.

Cayetano was watching her, gauging her reaction.

She lifted her chin and took the first step down with him at her side.

It was immediately evident to the crowd that something was happening. Cayetano and his woman came down the steps alone, with the guards flanking them instead of leading the way.

Before, the guards would have surrounded them, and Cayetano would have held her hand as they moved through the crowds. Singing Bird's demeanor would have been affectionate and happy, both with him and with those around her.

This woman was still Singing Bird, but she had changed. She was no longer smiling and the only thing she was holding was the bow in her hand.

As they came down the steps of the temple, the more clearly the people saw her. They remembered the condition of Singing Bird's near-lifeless body they had carried into the palace, and saw hard muscles where soft curves had been. They saw scars on her body and anger on her face that they didn't understand. As they began noticing the weapon strapped to her leg and the bow and arrows she was carrying, they didn't know what to think. Was she going to the temple or going to war?

Layla eyed the crowd closely as they moved past the throng, looking for familiar faces, but now that everyone was dressed the same, it was difficult to single anyone out who'd come with her from before.

Finally, it was a man with short hair that caught her eye; Montford Nantay, one of the officers of the tribal police. Then she saw his brother, Johnston standing beside him. The shock on their faces as they saw her was understandable. She hadn't recognized herself. How could they? She had a sudden urge to connect and shouted out.

"Nantays!"

A slow smile of relief spread across their faces as they raised a hand in greeting.

Layla felt their disbelief and knew she was being judged. She wasn't the same. They had yet to decide if they liked that or not.

As they kept moving toward the temple, the hot sun put a knot in her belly. Even though she knew this heat would not grow worse, the memories of Firewalker were still with her, but she couldn't show fear. She walked with her shoulders back, meeting gaze after gaze with her chin up and her fingers curled around the bow.

The walk was a long one, through the marketplace, beyond the river, then into the brick-paved playa surrounding the temple. But Cayetano was at her side, and the longer they walked the easier she began to feel.

The quiet in the crowd began to shift, first to a murmur, then once again to many voices saying her name. By the time they started up the steps of the temple, it was an ongoing cheer.

Cayetano was so proud of her he could hardly maintain his stride. Her instincts had been right. Show no fear. She had their attention in a big way.

The guards stopped at the base of the temple and then turned to face the crowd as Layla and Cayetano climbed the steps. As they reached the top, four elders came out of the small room.

Layla arched an eyebrow questioningly.

"Shamans."

She greeted each of them with a nod, and just as she turned to face the crowd, saw an expression on one of the men's faces that surprised her. He didn't like her, and without a memory of the past, she didn't know why.

But that was for another time. Today was about setting the stage for what was to come. As she turned around, she immediately thought of the day she'd climbed on top of Leland Benally's truck and spoke to the thousands about what was ahead. Somehow, she had to make that happen again.

She stood at Cayetano's side, waiting - wishing for the wind to carry her words, but in this world, Windwalker did not exist.

Cayetano lifted his arms and the crowd was instantly silent. When he began to speak, Layla was surprised how easily his voice carried to the crowd below.

"By now you have seen the strangers who came among us. You know Singing Bird brought them, and this is true. You saw their burns. You saw their pain. She too, suffered greatly. You have seen her scars. You have seen her burns. She protected them with her life, and killed their enemies to keep them safe. She left us as the woman at my side. She comes back to us a red feather warrior."

Cayetano caught her eye as he took a step back.

She moved forward without hesitation, unaware that she stood with the majesty and assurance of a queen.

"I have a story to tell you. I had a journey to take that none of you knew... a warning from our own shamans that could not be ignored. It is about the people who came back with me... the New Ones who stand among us today."

The crowd shifted as they scanned the area for strangers' faces.

Layla shouted. "Look at them. Do you see them? Now, do you see yourselves in their faces? You should, because your hearts beat as their hearts. Your blood runs in their veins. My journey was a journey of the spirit. I walked through a portal that took me many thousands of years into our future, to a time where Naaki Chava was dying, and so were our people. So were all people."

The gasp from the crowd was one of disbelief. How could this massive empire cease to exist? They didn't believe her and she knew it.

"This is true, I tell you! And it is what will happen to us if nothing changes. In the times to come, we become weak and sick, and we lose our land to a race of people without color on their skin who will despise us because ours is brown. As time passes, our people become sad because our way of life will be gone. Our language will no longer be spoken, and our lives have been damaged by the white men's ways. It becomes so bad that our young will take their own lives."

She felt the crowd shifting, but she couldn't tell in which direction.

"When Firewalker saw this he became very angry."

They gasped again, but this time in understanding. They knew Firewalker. There were legends about him throwing pieces of fire from the sky that would burn up trees and leave big holes in the earth.

Layla felt the empathy and kept pushing.

"Firewalker became so angry that he launched himself toward earth to destroy it. The People had not taken care of their great gift. They were fighting among themselves to gain power over others. Greed abounded."

The crowd was so silent it was as if they were breathing as one. Now she had to find a way to explain the rest.

"The Old Ones saw Firewalker coming and took pity on The People. They told me to find as many of the tribes as I could find, and before it was too late I must bring them away from harm. My spirit went into this place. I lived there and loved those people as I love you. They did not deserve to die. I began calling them together, and every day as we waited for more to come, bad people came after me." She touched her scars to accentuate the point. "I fought them and they died."

A roar rose into the air... it was a war cry of approval.

Layla knew they were hearing her. It was going to be okay.

"Yet as we waited, even more bad people came and I fought them, too." She held the bow up over her head to illustrate the point. "Firewalker was upon us, even as we were running through land without trees, without water, running through fire in the sky to escape. Look at these strangers among you now and know that they did this with me. They are strong. They, too, are warriors, but of a different kind. These people come with much knowledge. They know everything we did wrong and can show us how to make it right. And..." She paused for effect. "...You must also know that they are all that is left of our race."

The gasp that went up throughout the crowd was sudden shock.

Layla held up her hand and silence followed.

"This, too, you must understand. They endured terrible hardships as they ran with me. Many fell by the wayside from the fire in the sky. They lost people they loved just to come to Naaki Chava and help me save you. For them, it would have been easier to die."

She could see people weeping. Their hearts were full of understanding and empathy.

"But if you are willing to hear them, and learn from them in the many sleeps to come, their sacrifice will be what saves us from ourselves."

She felt Cayetano moving up to stand by her – using his presence as a visual statement of approval.

He began to speak.

"The future holds many wonders, but as it is now, we, as a people, will lose ourselves because, while we fight each other, the white men will see us as animals. They make promises that are lies, and kill women and babies. They take the lands that have always been our homes, and we will go because we are no match for their weapons, or their number."

The silence was telling. She could feel the shock emanating from the vast numbers. Layla took a deep breath, grateful for Cayetano's help in explaining this.

"I have seen this in my dreams," Cayetano said. "If we cease fighting among ourselves, and learn the language of the white men and learn to fight with their weapons, when the time comes for them to step onto our land, we will be ready. These brave people Singing Bird brought with her will have prepared us. We will not make the same mistakes twice. Are you willing to change? Are you willing to let old grudges die for the chance to become one people? A people so vast in numbers and so wise and strong in the ways that when we are finally challenged by this strange race of people, that we stop them where they stand?"

Another roar went up – a roar so loud and so long that it sent bird life in the nearby jungle into flight; coloring the sky like a rainbow.

Chapter Fifteen

Adam Prince was readjusting to their situation far better than his brother Evan. Evan still cried at night, and his appetite was poor. At the present, he was hanging over a brown earthen bowl, vomiting profusely. Evan was miserable on so many levels Adam was beginning to worry.

Every morning since their arrival they had eaten with Bazat as he demanded. But it was not a congenial meal as they'd been accustomed to having with Landan Prince. Even though there had been no emotional connection to Prince, he had behaved in a decent manner, while Bazat was proving himself to be a beast.

This morning had been no exception. When the servants brought in the food, Bazat stuffed it into his mouth as he talked; spewing it back on the rest they were supposed to eat.

It had been too much for Evan. He threw up at the table. Bazat sent them away, and Evan had been throwing up ever since.

Adam knew Bazat's interest in them was waning. It was just a matter of time before he had them killed. He didn't quite know what to do, but they had to do something before it was too late.

A monkey sat on the ledge outside their window, staring curiously at them. There had been monkeys on Binini Island, and when Adam looked up and saw it watching, he had a moment of deja'vu, half-expecting their nursemaid to come charging into their room with some medicine for Evan to take.

Then he remembered those days were over. Binini Island was over. The people were all gone. Earth was gone. Even if they could find the crystal that Bazat had taken from them, he would be afraid to use it again for fear of where they'd wind up. Without knowing how to control the time portal, it could prove deadly. They were in a terrible mess.

Evan choked on his last spasm and fell backward onto the mat as Adam carried the bowl away. He hurried back with a wet cloth to wipe Evan's face.

"I'm so sorry you're sick."

Slow tears rolled from the corners of Evan's eyes. "I wish we had died too, rather than be here."

"No!" Adam cried. "You don't mean that. As long as there is life there is hope."

"This isn't living," Evan said and rolled over onto his side and began to sob.

Adam threw the wet cloth aside and curled up behind his brother until their bodies were spooned one to the other. It was their safest place to be.

A few moments of silence passed as Adam comforted his twin, but Evan wasn't ready to be consoled. Adam looked over his shoulder to make sure they were alone and then whispered into Evan's ear.

"I had a dream last night."

Evan stilled. His brother's dreams were always powerful.

"Did you dream us a way out of here?"

"Maybe."

Evan rolled over so that they were now facing. "How?"

"There is a city on the other side of this mountain.

I heard one of the servants talking about it. It's called Naaki Chava."

Evan frowned. "One city will be just like another. We time-traveled, Adam. These people are uncivilized."

Adam scooted closer so that their faces were nearly touching. He could smell the sour stench of his brother's breath, but it didn't matter. Nothing that was of his brother was disgusting to him. He was the other half of himself.

"People here are uncivilized only because there is no technology like we were used to, but mentally, not much different from any good or bad man. We saw uncivilized behavior in the village on the island, remember? One beat his wife. One slept with children. Civilization, as you mean it, didn't make them better."

Evan's eyes widened. "I never thought about it like that. So what did you dream?"

"After I heard about Naaki Chava, I went to see it."

Now Evan was nervous and glanced over his shoulder, as well.

"In your sleep?" he whispered.

Adam nodded.

Evan frowned. "You know we agreed not to spirit-walk again. Remember when Madame ReeRee told us what we were doing was dangerous because we have no way to control it. What if you had not found your way back to your body?"

Adam shrugged. "I don't think she knew what she was talking about. From the time I leave my body I feel an invisible pull – like I am attached to that body no matter where I go."

Evan was intrigued. "Next time you go, I want to go with you."

Adam nodded. "There's something else we need to consider. Sometime in the future, Bazat is going to decide we're no longer useful and he'll have us killed."

Evan gasped. "What are we going to do? There are jaguars in the jungle. And there will be snakes, poisonous ones, and the big ones that squeeze their prey."

"I know, but we chance that death, or sit here and wait for a real one."

"When do we go? Where do we go?"

"I think we go to Naaki Chava."

"What if the ruler there is just as mean and crazy as this one?"

"But he's not, and neither is his wife. I saw them when I was there. I went into lots and lots of their houses as they lay sleeping. People are happy there. I could feel it."

Evan sighed. "But you said it was on the other side of the mountain."

Adam nodded.

Tears welled and rolled down Evan's face. "We will die before we get there."

"Maybe not. There's something else I haven't told you. I don't know how it happened, but there are a lot of people there who are from our time."

"So maybe they were like us, here by accident."

"No. There are thousands of them, and the woman who brought them there is the chief's wife."

Evan sat up. "Brought them? What do you mean, brought them?"

Adam sat up beside him, then took his brother's hands and pulled him so close that their foreheads were touching.

"Do you remember when we overheard Mr. Prince talking on the phone to that man with the red eyes?"

"The man who has no skin color? I remember that he came to the island once when we were small. He was scary to look at."

"Yes, Tenet. So remember not so long ago when Prince told Tenet to find a woman named Layla Birdsong because he thought she had special powers?"

Evan nodded. "Mr. Prince was always looking for things with special powers... like us."

Adam squeezed Evan's hands. "Yes, like us. So guess what?"

Evan's eyes grew wide. "What?"

"The woman who is the chief's wife is *that* Layla Birdsong. I know because I could see her dreams. I think she went back in time to save those people. That has to mean she's good, right? That means they would be good to us, don't you think?"

Evan nodded. For the first time since their arrival, he felt a glimmer of hope.

"When will we go?"

"I'm not sure. I think we should spirit walk to Naaki Chava tonight and try to talk to the woman. Maybe she would have a plan."

****

Layla rode Cayetano like she used to ride the horses in Oklahoma, straddling his hips, feeling the blood race through her body just as she used to race the wind. His hands were tight against her waist, pushing her down harder and harder upon his erection with every motion. She liked to watch his face when they made love – with his nostrils flared and the fire in his eyes burning hot for only her.

Layla fell forward, bracing her arms on either side of his head, as the need for completion rose in her. She was on her knees now, rocking against him while the sweat rolled from their bodies, increasing the friction.

She heard him groan, and she rolled her hips as she went for the next thrust. It was how he liked it, and she liked making him lose control.

All of a sudden Layla was on her back and Cayetano was between her legs, pounding himself into her body with force just short of savage. And she started to come.

One wave rolled through her, turning her body to sand. The second wave came afterward with such force that for a heartbeat, she felt as if she was being washed away. She arched her back to catch the third wave, and rode it all the way out to where it disappeared. But then the last wave came, and she threw her head back and screamed.

It was her scream that took Cayetano's breath. He grunted as if he'd been kicked, spilling his seed in a series of short, jerky thrusts.

When their lust had been sated, he rolled over onto the sleeping mat and took her with him. Their eyes closed in mutual exhaustion, and within seconds, they slept.

****

It was some hours later when the air within their room began to stir. Layla woke abruptly, thinking that a storm might be on the horizon, but when she opened her eyes, there was no storm – only two boys, standing at her feet. She saw them, but at the same time, saw through them. That was when she gasped.

Cayetano woke with a knife in his hand, his heart pounding.

"What?" he asked, looking into the darkness for signs of an intruder.

"Can you see them?" she asked.

"See who?"

"The boys standing at my feet."

Again, his heart was pounding, but this time in fear. Spirits were an enemy that could not be killed.

"I do not see them," he whispered.

All of a sudden, Layla heard voices in her head and realized it was them.

"I hear you. Why are you here?"

If we came to you, would you save us as you saved the others?

Layla gasped. "You are not from Naaki Chava. How do you know of what has happened here?"

We are from your time. We went through a different portal, but because yours was also open, I think it drew us to the same place.

Layla grabbed Cayetano's hand. "The spirits of these boys have asked if I would save them as I saved the others. They say they are from my time as Layla Birdsong. They did not come through our portal, but because it was open when they went through theirs, it drew them here."

"What if this is witchcraft?" Cayetano said.

We aren't witches. We're psychic. I am Adam and this is my twin brother Evan. We have no family, and are being held captive by a war chief on the other side of your mountain. His name is Bazat.

"Cayetano, do you know a war chief on the other side of the mountain by the name of Bazat?"

Cayetano stood abruptly, the knife gripped tightly in his fist.

"That is the name of the man who killed you... the man I tracked down into the jungle and cut up in pieces. How do they know his name?"

"They tell me that he's holding them prisoner

because they are like our Shamans. They know things other people cannot. They know how to spirit walk, which is how they got here tonight. Lots of my... lots of Layla's people knew this was possible. It was not a secret. We knew those who could do this and those who could not."

He frowned, staring hard into the darkness, but without sight of anything mystic.

Will you help us?

"How?" Layla asked.

We are going to run away. We will run toward your city, but we cannot protect ourselves for long. We are twelve years old, but have no knowledge of weapons. If we run, will you come find us?

Layla relayed what they said to Cayetano and waited for him to speak, but he was still silent. She turned to the little shadows. They appeared to be fading.

"How did you know to come to me?" she asked.

Back on earth, the man who owned us sent a man to find Layla Birdsong. He collected people with special powers. He saw you on television and wanted you, just like he wanted us because of what we can do. We have never been free. Will you help us? If you do, we will gratefully spend the rest of our lives helping you."

"Oh my God," Layla muttered.

"What God?" Cayetano whispered.

She shook her head. "No, not that. It's just a figure of speech that doesn't pertain here."

She looked back at the boys. "When you leave, can you send me a message so I'll know when to go look for you?"

In your mind, you will suddenly hear birds..., lots and lots of singing birds because your name is Birdsong. That is when we will be running.

"Then yes, when that happens, I will go into the jungle to look for you."

Cayetano grabbed her arm. "No. You cannot do this. Think about your purpose here."

"I am thinking," she said. "They are part of the solution, and I am going to get them."

Thank you, Layla Birdsong. You will never be sorry.

And just like that, they were gone.

"Are they still here," he asked.

"No."

"I don't like this, but I will find them for you. You stay here."

"No. I go, too. I have to. You can't hear them and I can."

He pulled her into his arms and then held her close.

She could feel the rapid beat of his heart against her breasts. He was afraid, and so was she, but instinct told her this was all part of the plan.

****

Three days passed and there was still no message from the boys. What if they sent the message and she had not heard it? What if Bazat killed them before they could get away? She was sick with worry, and also, beginning to be physically sick.

She had not bled since all this began, not in Layla's time or in this one, and now she was beginning to feel sick every morning when she woke up.

Morning sickness. Cayetano had been right. She was pregnant, but she wasn't going to announce it. In time, people would figure it out for themselves.

Cayetano was happy to keep this news between

them. In the eyes of all around them, they would see this as his child, and in his heart, it would always be so. Nothing else mattered.

For Layla, the thought of a baby was both exciting and frightening. Before Firewalker, it wouldn't have scared her. There had been hospitals, and doctors and nurses who knew what they were doing. Here it would be left up to her and whatever servants happened to be around. But, countless women had given birth since the world began, and countless would afterward. Any way she looked at it, it was still a blessing.

To pass the time, she thought of what she could do toward helping change the face of this lifestyle without interfering in the natural progression. Back on old earth, she'd been a school teacher. She decided that had not been an accident, either. She would need to teach these people new ways. It was good she knew how.

Excited about creating what would amount to a school here, she began planning what to use as educational tools and prayed a sign from the boys would come soon.

On the morning of the fourth day, Acat appeared with a small boy in hand. The skin on his shoulders and the bridge of his nose was not as brown as the rest of his body; obviously new skin. He was thin and listless, and his eyes welled continually, but it was his silence that had worried Acat most. He ate only what she put in his mouth and showed no interest in feeding himself. It was as if he was willing himself to die. She didn't know what to do and slipped into Layla's quarters, hoping for answers.

Layla heard the footsteps approaching, and when she saw the expression on Acat's face and the little boy at her side, her heart skipped. She knew Acat was caring for the child she'd carried into the portal and she had wanted to meet him. It appeared today was the day.

"Good morning, Acat. I see you brought me a visitor."

Acat dropped her head. "He does not eat and is too sad for a child to be. I am sorry, Singing Bird. I do not know what else to do."

"Bring him to me," Layla said, and when he stopped at her knee, she lifted him onto her lap and waved Acat away and lapsed into English.

"I am so glad to finally meet you. We came into this place together. Do you remember?"

Tears were rolling down his face. He shook his head and never looked up.

"How old are you?"

"I am eight. I was going to be in the third grade."

"Where did you live?"

"Tahlequah, Oklahoma."

"Tahlequah! That was a beautiful part of Oklahoma. Are you Cherokee?"

He nodded.

"Will you tell me your name?"

"Yuma Littlehawk."

"I'm very glad to meet you, Yuma. That's a good name. Do you know who I am?"

He shuddered; fighting back tears. "Daddy said your name was Layla Birdsong. He said we had to go with you, but I didn't want to go. I wanted to stay home," then he covered his face.

Layla felt his grief as sharply as if it was her own. She already feared the answer, but had to ask.

"Where is your daddy, Yuma?"

He began to sob. "He died in the camp when we were waiting for you to come."

The answer shocked her. She couldn't imagine how sad and afraid this child had been.

"And yet you waited alone?"

"Daddy said we had to go with you. I am eight. It was my time to be a man. Some people fed me and gave me a ride. But when we walked, I walked alone."

The pain in her own heart grew stronger as she pulled him against her chest, and began to rock back and forth in a slow, gentle motion.

"Are you all that's left of your family?"

He nodded.

"Want to know a secret?"

For a few seconds, he was silent, and then he nodded.

She put her lips against his ear. "So am I."

She watched his eyes widen as he looked at the elegance of her clothes and the luxuries in this room that were hers alone, and saw the confusion.

"Yes, I belong here, but I also belonged there where you lived. I was born to lead the Last Walk. My grandfather was all the family I had left and he was with me. But he was killed as I fought the people who tried to hurt us. And so I stood alone at the portal as everyone went through. I had no one with me, either, and then I saw you coming. You were also alone and when you fell and didn't get up, I ran to help you. We came into this place together, so that makes us a kind of family, don't you think?"

She paused, watching the expressions coming and going on his face. He was interested, that she could see.

"What do you remember of the Last Walk?"

"I wanted water and there was none," he said softly.

"I know. It was terrible, wasn't it? What else do

you remember?"

"The sun burned me even though my skin was brown. It never did that before."

"It wasn't the sun, Yuma. It was a meteor that fell from the sky we called Firewalker. Did you ever study about the stars and the planets in school?"

"Yes. I remember Ursa Major. That means Big Bear, doesn't it?"

She nodded as she smoothed down the hair on his head.

"Do you like living with Acat?"

He shrugged and looked down at his hands.

"I know she's not your family, but she was very nice to you, wasn't she?"

He nodded.

"I know no one can take your daddy's place in your heart, just like I'll never forget my grandfather. His name was George Begay. He was Navajo."

Yuma was listening again.

"Would you like to meet Cayetano? He is my husband here, and he's also the chief of Naaki Chava. He is a good man. You don't have to be afraid."

He shrugged, but slid off her knee and then waited for her to get up.

She hid a smile as she took him by the hand.

"I had a tribe and a clan, but it is gone. You had a tribe and a clan, but it's gone, too. One day, we will all be of the same tribe and clan, but for now, I think you and I need to make a new one. We are alone, like a lobo wolf. Do you know what that means?"

"A lobo is a wolf without a pack," Yuma said.

"Right, so if you don't have a clan and I don't have a clan, we could be the wolf clan, but only if we stuck together."

His eyes widened. "The wolf is a totem for the

Cherokee."

She gave his hand a slight tug. "It's up to you. What do you think?"

He nodded. "I think that would be good."

"You know that means you could live with me, if you wanted to, but first we'd have to thank Acat for all the good care and food she gave you."

He nodded.

"So, let's go talk to Cayetano. He will want to meet the newest member of our family, for sure."

Yuma Littlehawk was no longer crying. The tears were still there, but they were drying, and when he walked at Layla's side, there was just the slightest of bounce to his step.

****

The Shamans had asked for a meeting with Cayetano. The moment they started talking, it was all he could do to hide his shock.

"One at a time," he ordered.

Chac was the first to speak.

"For three sleeps, I have been dreaming about the Little War-Gods, the twins of Sun and Earth Mother."

Cayetano hid his surprise. Twins, like Singing Bird had seen.

Naum, another Shaman, spoke up. "They are among us. I know this because I saw them as I slept, standing at my feet."

"I did not see them, but I felt their passing," Ah Kin said.

Cayetano looked a Chak but, he chose to remain silent.

"What of you, Chak? Have you seen the Little War-Gods?"

He frowned. “No. I only dreamed them. I did not see them. I did not feel their passing. I don’t believe this is so. It is nothing but fear brought on by the coming of the New Ones in our midst.”

Cayetano leaned forward. “What of the New Ones? They are but more of our people. Just because you do not know their faces does not mean you should be afraid. You heard Singing Bird’s words. Do you doubt her truth?”

Chak knew any wrong words could mean losing his head.

“I do not fear them, but I don’t think they should be here. It makes more mouths for us to feed.

“We are not short of food now, and we will not be short of food in the time to come. We have been planting more for the last five seasons and storing it because two of you predicted that many strangers would come. Have you forgotten that?”

Chak refused to look at the other shamans as he continued.

“I do not doubt that your woman believes what she said. But I doubt that it is true. Firewalker only spits and fumes. Firewalker would never destroy the world.”

Cayetano frowned. “And how do you know this? Are you greater than these three? Are you wiser than a woman who has been where none of us have been? Singing Bird was not talking of next season. She was not talking of our next generation. She talks of thousands of years into a future we cannot see.”

Then Chak forgot to be cautious. “Once you were our chief and now you let your woman speak for you.”

Cayetano stood up. “She does not speak for me. She spoke for the thousands she brought with her. You saw their burns. They walked through

Firewalker's fire. You saw her scars. She came back a red feather warrior. She has killed her enemy. Are you her enemy? If you are, be warned. She does not take prisoners, and I do not take to threats against my woman."

Chak felt the blood draining from his face.

"I am the enemy of no one. I read the stars. I see the people of Naaki Chava as strong and brave."

Cayetano looked at the other three. "Do you hold his thoughts as your own?"

They shook their heads in unison and glared at Chak for being a fool.

Cayetano looked into each man's eyes, looking for signs of deception.

"I have heard your words. We will watch for the twins. If they come into our midst, then I will believe that we are being blessed by Sun and Earth Mother. It would be a great honor if they have given their twins into our care," Cayetano said.

"As do I," Ah Kin said.

"As do I, Chac said.

"As do I, Naum said.

Chak hesitated. "As do I," he said, but the hesitation was a moment too long.

He had lied and they knew it. And if a man lies about one thing, he will lie about another.

They were walking out the door as Singing Bird entered with a child.

They nodded cordially, anxious to get out of sight before Cayetano told her what had been said. If the truth be told, they were all afraid of her now; Chak more than the others, because he'd seen something in his dreams that none of the others had mentioned. She was with child, and it was going to be the ruin of their importance in Naaki Chava. That child needed to die, and if Singing Bird died with it, then that would be that.

Chapter Sixteen

The sight of Singing Bird sent the anger from Cayetano's thoughts. He smiled at her, and then at the little boy hanging onto her hand. It was the first time since her return that he saw peace on her face. He was grateful, whatever the cause.

"Welcome. It is good to see happy faces."

Layla arched an eyebrow. "Some are not happy?"

"Some are not, and it does not matter," he said abruptly.

She stored the knowledge for when they were alone, and focused on the boy instead.

"So, love of my heart, I think you should know this boy. We both came into this place alone, and so we have decided to form our own clan."

His smile widened. It was the boy Acat had been caring for. He had wondered how long it would take her to find him.

"Your own clan? Is this so?" he asked, looking down at the boy.

Yuma's grip tightened, but he faced the great chief with a nod.

"How did you come to be alone?" Cayetano asked.

Yuma looked down.

Layla answered for him. "His father died even before the Last Walk began. He told me it was his time to be a man and so he made the walk alone."

Cayetano's opinion quickly shifted. The child was

small, but he had a warrior's heart. This was a big omen. He laid a hand on the top of the little boy's head.

"That is a very brave thing," he said softly.

Yuma nodded, but wouldn't look up.

Cayetano decided it was time to change the mood.

"So, you and Singing Bird have formed a clan? What do you call it? Is there a place in it for me?"

Layla sighed. She should have known he would 'get' what was happening.

"Tell him, Yuma."

"We are lobos. That means a wolf without a pack. We came to this place without our families so we made a family of our own."

She quickly translated.

Cayetano felt a quick moment of pain knowing there was a part of Singing Bird he would never get back. She had given away a part of herself to Layla Birdsong, but he didn't care. As long as he had just a piece of her heart, it would be enough.

"So, I, too, am a lobo," he said. "My mother and my father are no more. I have no brother. I have no sister. I only have Singing Bird. Do you think I might join your clan?"

The boy's eyes widened as Layla translated the chief's words. The thought of the great chief being part of their clan was a big deal. He looked up at Layla.

She nodded her approval.

He puffed up his chest and threw back his head. "Yes, Cayetano, you can be in our clan."

"Yuma says yes," she said.

Cayetano tried hard not to smile. "I am grateful for the honor. Do you think we might walk to the marketplace and look for some sugarcane to celebrate?"

Again, Layla continued to translate for the both of them.

Yuma didn't know what to think. "What is sugarcane?"

Cayetano shook his head. "You have much to learn about things that are good. It is a sweet food, like mango and berries."

"I like berries," Yuma said.

"Then you will like this, as well. Do we go?"

Layla felt like dancing for joy. Instead, she solemnly agreed.

"We go," she said. "But with guards, I think."

He frowned. So she'd already figured out something was wrong. He should have known.

"Yes, with guards."

When the people in the marketplace realized that Cayetano and his woman were walking among them, it caused quite a stir. They had come with a child. Word began to spread that it was the boy Singing Bird had carried into Naaki Chava.

Cayetano went straight to the vendor who had chunks of the raw cane. The moment the man realized it was the chief, he puffed up with pride.

Cayetano pushed Yuma in front of him.

"See this boy. He is Yuma. He only has eight seasons, but he made the Last Walk all alone. He is a very brave boy from the wolf clan."

The man eyed the boy. "All alone! That is a feat worthy of any great warrior. May I gift him with my cane, Cayetano?"

Cayetano smiled. "That is why we came. He has never had this treat. Show him how it's done."

The man grabbed a chunk and stuffed one end into his mouth, chewing on it until it was soft, then sucking the juice from the pulverized stalk. A single drop of the sweet liquid stuck on his lip as he smiled.

"Like that," he said. "You try."

Yuma took one of the chunks and poked it in his mouth. By now, everyone in the market place was watching curiously. Yuma chewed on the end and sucked off the sweet juice; his eyes wide with delight. The people around him laughed.

Layla laughed with them. It felt good to be happy.

"You like it?" Cayetano asked.

"Yes," Yuma said.

"So, we go. Thank you," Cayetano told the vendor.

The man was still beaming as they moved away.

Cayetano continued their walk, showing him monkeys stealing fruit from the tables and the colorful macaws with wingtips trimmed, tied to perches and begging for treats.

Layla watched Yuma's face and knew this was right. Cayetano said he would never be able to give her a child, so she'd given him one, instead. They didn't know it yet, but these two would be bound at the heart by a love far stronger than the bounds of blood.

****

Acat became Yuma's nursemaid. He slept on a mat at her side each night, satisfied that he had a place to belong, and during the day, prowled the palace either with Layla or Acat, learning every alcove and every hiding place. During their times of rest, Layla taught him the language of Naaki Chava and it was good for Yuma, but she was also uneasy. The lost boys had not spirit walked to her again, and she had not received a sign. Her heart was heavy, fearing the worst.

When morning came, she woke up to find herself

alone. Cayetano had already begun his day and she had not. She dressed quickly, and was on her way to get Yuma for their first meal when she began hearing birds - all around her - above her, singing, singing, and there were no birds in sight.

It was happening! She ran for the throne room, calling Cayetano's name as she went.

****

Cayetano had begun his day settling arguments - petty squabbles that, if left undone, would cause bigger issues within the city. It tried his patience more than anything he did as their chief, but when he heard Singing Bird shouting his name, he was up and running even before she appeared.

As he met her at the door, she grabbed his arms, her fingers digging into his flesh.

"They are running. We go now!" she whispered.

He didn't pause. He pointed at one of the servants.

"Send the guards!"

Then he turned to the people who had come with complaints for him to settle. They were watching curiously.

"Go home," he shouted.

They had never seen Cayetano like this and didn't ask why. "I want my weapons," she said, and ran back to her quarters as he ran to get his own, then stopped a servant on the way down the hall. "Tell Acat she is to keep Yuma with her until we are back."

"Yes, Singing Bird," he said softly, and hurried away.

Layla was pulling off all of her jewelry as she ran. By the time she got to her room, she was naked.

Regardless of the dress code, she wasn't going topless into the jungle. She began digging through her things until she found the clothing she'd worn coming in here; the old gray sports bra and the last pair of jeans she owned that would stay over her hips. She abandoned her sandals for the hiking boots and tied her hair back from her face. She was about to go looking for Cayetano when she saw her father's necklace and put around her neck. It had served her well on the Last Walk. It would do so, again.

When Cayetano walked in and saw her weapons and what she was wearing, it took him aback, and then he saw the wisdom of it.

"The guards are waiting," he said. "Follow me. There is a way out of the palace that does not take us through the city. The fewer people who know we are gone, the better."

"I am behind you," she said, and ran to keep up with his long, hurried stride.

****

Adam and Evan knew how to get out of the palace without being seen, and they knew where they going and how to get there. They had been practicing their trip from the City of the Sun to Naaki Chava every night in a spirit walk. They knew the landmarks to look for, and the dangers they would face. They had stolen two knives days ago, and hidden them in their room, waiting for the moment when they could escape. Yet when the opportunity finally arrived, it was so unexpected they were unprepared for the hasty exit.

For the past few days, they had been giving Bazat information most pleasing to him. During the past week, they had told him of a tribe far to the east that was going to move across his territory with the intent of stealing women from the fields. They told him the right place to find the biggest tapirs he liked to hunt, that one of the women he slept with was with child, and that a Shaman in the palace was going to die.

Acting on their warnings, he set some guards in hiding near the women working in the fields, and when the warring tribe appeared as the little War-Gods had said, they not only stopped them from stealing the women, but brought them back into the city and offered them as sacrifices to the Sun God and to Mother Earth.

One after the other, the things they predicted came to pass, and Bazat's opinion of them continued to grow. He no longer thought about killing them. Instead, he was thinking daily of more ways to use their power to his advantage.

And then the old Shaman died.

Bazat received word about the death just as they were to begin their morning meal and bolted from the room before he'd taken a bite, leaving the boys alone. Even the servants who attended the meals had run after him.

The boys took one look at each other, grabbed some bread and fruit from the table, and headed for Bazat's quarters. They didn't know where he'd hidden their crystal, but they wanted it back.

They spent precious minutes digging through his things until Evan found it on a shelf behind an idol. They put it in a small bag and headed for their room to get the knives they had hidden. Adam slung the bag over his shoulder and then they slipped down a hallway into an ante-room and took a back way out of the palace.

They didn't talk, and they didn't look back. They

crept behind the dwellings, startling only the parrots tied to their perches, while sending one long frantic signal to Layla Birdsong, praying she would hear. Once they reached the jungle, they quit worrying about being caught and ran as fast as they could; headlong into a world they had seen only in their sleep.

****

It was morning in the City of the Sun and time to welcome the new day. Zotz was the oldest Shaman in the city, and the honor to welcome the sun was always his. He walked slowly up the steps, aching in every joint, but moving, nonetheless.

He paused at the top to catch his breath. The people were gathering below as they did each morning, waiting for the blessing, and so he began.

He was halfway through the ritual when the vision came to him. In his mind, he saw the Little War-Gods running through the jungle - running away. They had already usurped most of the Shamans' powers, and the Shamans were already afraid Bazat would discard them. If the twins got away, they would be blamed.

In a panic, he turned to shout the warning, and then his brain exploded. He dropped where he stood as a seizure took control of his body; rolling him too close to the edge. He fell over, rolling down the steep steps, bouncing head over heels, and flopping all the way down.

By the time he landed, his neck was broken, his head cracked open; his eyes staring sightless toward the sun. But it was his mouth, open in a scream he never voiced that caused the fuss. Convinced he'd been trying to warn them of something dire, the other

Shamans began praying for protection, which sent everyone into a panic.

The sun was directly overhead before Bazat returned to the palace. It had taken most of the morning to quell the riot that ensued. The death was a distraction but not a surprise to Bazat.

It was exactly what the Little War-Gods had predicted, and he was anxious to find out what came next. Were they in danger from some unknown enemy? Was the harvest going to fail? Would the rains come too soon? There were a dozen reasons to worry, but his were only beginning. When he sent a servant to bring the boys, he came running back in a panic.

“They are gone! They are gone! The Little War-Gods are gone!”

Bazat screamed out in disbelief, and then in rage. He slashed the servant’s throat for giving him the bad news, and then sent trackers to find the trail. When he received word they had found it, he took his warriors into the jungle, chasing little Gods and outrunning the fear he was leaving behind.

****

The boys were wet, both with sweat from the heat and from the dousing they’d taken after falling into a stream. Adam had a long scratch on the back of one arm that was stinging to the point of real pain. Anywhere they were bare, there were insects. Some were just hitching a ride, others were blood-suckers. They were so weary of swatting them that they were completely ignoring them now. Their food was gone and their bellies were hungry. They had fallen into water, tripped over exposed tree roots, and were so exhausted they were stumbling with every other step;

too tired to pick up their feet.

Their physical conditions were a setback to the wisdom of spirit-walking for information. Since they had not been in their bodies, they had taken no notice of the possibility of physical discomforts. It was a huge reminder to pay closer attention, and they were exhausted.

"Wait. My side hurts. I need to rest," Adam muttered, as he paused to catch his breath.

Evan dropped where he stood. He didn't even look for a safe place to sit. Instead, he pulled his knees up and leaned forward on them, struggling for every breath.

"Are we lost?" he asked.

Adam looked up, then all around. It was thick and green in front of them and behind them. There wasn't a path and they couldn't see the sky.

"I don't know for sure. I thought we'd see those green orchids by now."

Evan closed his eyes, remembering the fall of green flowers spilling down the sides of a tree.

"I can see them in my head," he offered.

"Yes, so can I, but I don't see with my eyes open, which is what needs to happen," Adam said, and then suddenly groaned. "I never thought, but some of that stuff might only bloom at night. We could have already passed important landmarks."

Evan wiped the sweat from his face and looked up. "So, are we lost?"

"Maybe, but we know the general direction we have to go. All we have to do is keep moving. We should be halfway there, don't you think?"

Evan's eyes welled with tears. "I can't tell. We move very fast when we are spirits. I think we should have practiced this in our bodies, too."

Adam frowned. "You can't practice running away, Evan. You just do it."

Evan nodded. "Are we rested enough?"

"Yes, I think we are," Adam said, and reached down to help his brother up when he heard a rustling in the leaves above them. He looked up just as a massive python dropped off a limb onto the ground.

One moment Evan was in front of him and then he was disappearing within the snake's giant coils.

"Adddaaammm! Help me!" Evan screamed. "I can't breathe! I can't breathe!"

Adam began stabbing and slashing at the snake with his knife - cutting it in dozens of places until both he and the snake were red with blood. He tried to stab at the head, but there was so much blood the knife slid off the bony plate. He was begging God to help him even as his brother's face was turning red, but when his eyes rolled back in his head, Adam screamed. He felt Evan's absence as surely as if it had been his own. His brother was dead!

A fear-fueled rage swept through him as he raised the knife above his head, stabbing it into the snake as far as the blade would go. When he felt it hit bone, he adjusted his grip and started pulling it through the flesh in a see-saw motion, laying the python open as he went.

Adam realized the snake was dying only after the coils began to loosen. He grabbed his brother, pulling as hard as he could, and suddenly Evan was free!

He laid him flat on his back, checked for a pulse then felt his chest, checking for broken ribs. He could do mouth to mouth, but the fear of puncturing his lungs with already broken ribs was a definite possibility. Still, he would rather take a chance than do nothing.

When they were younger, they had been fascinated by the concept of CPR, and bringing people back to life to the extent that they had play-acted saving each other's lives for the longest time. Only now it wasn't play.

Adam lost track of how long he'd been doing chest compressions and blowing air into his brother's lungs, but the sun was nearly overhead. At any second Bazat could catch up with them and it would be over.

It was difficult to do CPR when you were crying between every breath, but he wouldn't quit. He couldn't give up. Evan was the other half of himself. He had just finished a round of chest compressions and was leaning down to put his mouth on his brother's lips when he thought he noticed Evan's eyelids suddenly flutter.

He blew into his mouth one last time, and when he heard Evan choke, and then take a breath on his own, he rocked back on his heels and let out a scream that sent the birds above him into flight. Evan was back from the dead! God had heard him after all.

****

The search team had been on the move for nearly two hours. Layla was in the lead following the boys' voices, just as she'd followed the war drums on the Last Walk.

One moment she was running, and then all of a sudden she had stopped. The warriors stopped behind her, eyes wide with fright. They had never followed a woman into battle, and they'd never had an enemy they could not see. They kept their eyes trained on the jungle in fear they would be attacked at any moment.

Suddenly Layla groaned and bent double; in

obvious pain and gasping for breath.

Cayetano immediately thought of the baby she carried.

"What?" he asked, as grabbed her arm to pull her up.

The look on her face was one of horror. "One of the boys is dying. He can't breathe. It's a python, I think."

"How do you know this?" Cayetano asked.

"I don't know. Could I not do this before?"

"No. Never," he said.

"So things change," she muttered. "We need to hurry."

"Do you know how far away they are?"

"They are closer to us than they are to Bazat, but he follows."

Cayetano's eyes narrowed. The expression on his face grew grim.

"We go," he said. "Show me and I will lead."

"Straight ahead," she said. "If it changes, I will tell you."

He thought of what had happened to Singing Bird before and coming face to face with Bazat. If he killed the man again, the curse would not be broken.

"Stay behind me," he said.

She didn't argue. When they resumed their trek, Cayetano was leading the way, and she was running in the midst of the warriors who had surrounded her.

****

Bazat and his men were tireless. They ran to hunt down game. They ran when fighting their enemies. Their legs were strong, their muscles hard. The heat did not bother them and the mosquitoes fed on their blood and flew away without notice.

Bazat's strength was rage-filled. His will should be obeyed and the Little War-Gods had disobeyed him. Gods or not, they would be punished.

He pushed his men without care for their condition. Their brown bodies were slick with sweat and their arms were covered with tiny cuts and scratches from the razor sharp edges of the leaves. They needed water and they needed to rest, but he would not stop. He had no idea how long the boys had been gone, where they were going, or if they were even still alive. They would rest, and they would drink, after the Little War-Gods were found.

****

Evan woke up with the sun in his eyes and his body aching.

Adam was leaning over him crying. The first things that went through his mind were that Adam was covered in blood and that he hardly ever cried.

"What's wrong?" Evan asked, and then gasped when he tried to inhale. "My chest hurts. My stomach hurts too."

Adam covered his face with his hands and began to sob. He couldn't talk for the relief flooding through him.

Believing that Adam needed him, Evan managed to sit up but then he saw the python and screamed. It took a few seconds for him to realize it was dead. His focus shifted to the gaping wounds on the snake and the countless insects feeding from the blood.

"That's why I hurt," Evan whispered, and managed to get to his hands and knees, then crawled to Adam. "You saved my life, didn't you?"

Still sobbing, Adam tried to pull himself together.

"Thank you. You are the bravest brother, ever," Evan said.

Adam began wiping at the tears on his face. He had cried long enough. It was time to get back to business.

"Evan, do you think you can stand?"

"I don't know. It hurts to breathe."

He stood up and reached for his brother's hand.

Evan looked up to grasp it, then saw beyond his brother's shoulder to the jungle above.

"Look, Adam! It's the green orchids. They're just higher up than we thought."

"Of course," Adam cried. "I am such a dummy. When we spirit walk, we aren't actually walking. We just move. We must have been moving higher off the ground and didn't know it."

He helped Evan get up, brushing away the ants and mosquitoes from his back and legs.

"Move your legs," he ordered.

Evan took a step, but it hurt to breathe and move at the same time.

Adam knew Evan had internal injuries, but if they stopped, the worry would be moot. Bazat would kill them.

"We go slowly until you can do better, but we have to keep moving," Adam said.

Evan grabbed hold of his brother's arm to steady himself. "So now do you know which way to go?"

"Yes. That way to the waterfall and then we're almost there."

They moved slow at first, and then as they progressed from steps to a stride, began to cover more ground, but Adam could tell his brother was in trouble. He was bent nearly double, trying to walk and breathe at the same time, but it wasn't happening. Adam was so afraid of what he had done to him by giving him CPR, but if he hadn't, Evan would be lying dead beside the python.

Another hour passed as they pushed through the jungle. Sweat was pouring from Evan's hair into his eyes, but he was too weak to complain about the sting. Then suddenly he staggered and would have fallen but for Adam.

Adam slid his arm beneath Evan's shoulders, shifting the weight onto him instead, and they kept on going, putting one foot in front of the other. Adam was so tired that he didn't realize he'd been hearing the rush of water, until Evan spoke.

"I hear water. Can I have a drink?"

Adam's heart skipped a beat. The waterfall! They were almost there!

"Yes, brother, you can have a drink. Just a little bit farther."

They came out of the jungle into a small clearing. About thirty-five feet above them, a small waterfall gushed out from between rocks, forming a pool at the base that fed the stream beyond.

A mist hung halfway between the trees and the ground from the constant spray of water. Flowering vines abounded as did large green and red parrots, squawking at the arrival of strangers.

The boys gasped at the beauty of the sight.

"Look, Adam! A rainbow. That's a good sign, right?"

"Looks like it to me," Adam said. "Just a little bit farther and we can get a drink."

At that same moment they took a step, they saw movement to their right. Adam yanked them to a stop as a jaguar padded out of the jungle to get a drink.

They held their breaths, afraid to move, afraid to blink. Adam felt the weight of his knife against his thigh, but against a jaguar, this would be a far different fight.

The big cat had massive claws and huge fangs that curved downward on the outside of its mouth. It was fully capable of snapping the backs of their necks with one bite.

Suddenly, it stopped, lifting its head as to sniff the air.

Adam groaned inwardly. They must be upwind.

They watched in horror as the cat slowly turned its head until it was looking straight at them.

Don't move, Evan.

Even if I wanted to, I can't.

The cat's ears went back. Its tail began to twitch. When it fell into a crouch and began to stalk them, Adam sent a last ditch message to Layla. Even if she didn't get here in time, at least she would know what happened.

****

Cayetano stopped when they reached a stream. He wanted Singing Bird to rest, but she would not sit down. She dropped by the bank to drink and the moment her hand went in the water, she saw a waterfall, and then she saw the boys.

Cayetano was crouched in the middle of the water, drinking from the cup he'd made of his hand. The other warriors were scattered up and down through the stream, refreshing themselves as well when she suddenly sprang to her feet.

"Cayetano! Is there a waterfall that feeds this stream? We need to find it."

One of the warriors pointed. “That way. Not far,” he said.

“The boys are there and they are in danger.”

Cayetano leaped toward her, grabbing her by the hand as the others followed. They were running without caution now, feeling the urgency of the mission without understanding the need. Weapons were out. Their stride was long. They heard the rush of water only seconds before they heard the screams.

Layla dashed forward, pulling away from the warriors as she ran. When they reached the clearing, she saw that they were on one side, and the two boys were on the other side of the water. One was sitting, and the other was in a crouched position in front of him with a knife held in his hand.

Then she saw the jaguar.

Cayetano leaped past her, dashing into the water in an all-out sprint to get the boys before the cat did, with the warriors right behind him.

She didn’t hesitate. She notched an arrow into the bow and launched it just as the cat leaped. There was a moment of deja’vu as she flashed on the cougar during the Last Walk. She’d had Windwalker’s magic to guide her arrows there, but in here, Windwalker didn’t exist.

Cayetano was only steps away from the boys when the big cat left the ground.

“Now!” he shouted, and his men drew back to throw their spears when a flash of movement caught the corner of his eye. When he looked again, the cat was on the ground with an arrow through its heart.

He turned abruptly. Singing Bird was on the other side of the water, her bow hanging loosely in her hands. He grinned, then lifted his spear and sent a cry of jubilation into the air. His warriors followed suit as she jumped into the water.

She came running, bypassing the men to get to the cat and pushed it with the toe of her boot. It was lifeless. She pulled out the arrow, wiped it on the grass, and dropped it back into her quiver as ran to the boys.

They had collapsed into a heap on the ground; visibly trembling, and covered in blood. She began scanning their bodies for wounds. From the amount of blood, it could be serious.

"Which one of you did the big snake get?"

"You *do* see with your mind, just like we do," Adam said softly, and then pointed at his brother. "He's Evan. I'm Adam. The snake got him."

Cayetano knelt beside her, still struggling with the knowledge that not only had Singing Bird been right about them running away, but they had been real children after all, and not evil spirits trying to trick them.

"How did you get away from the snake?" he asked.

"I killed it with my knife," Adam said. "It was very big, larger around than my body."

Layla translated.

The warriors murmured to each other. A python was something to always be avoided, and for a young boy to kill such a snake was quite a feat.

"We need to go," Adam said. "I think Bazat is very close."

Layla translated again, and the thought of facing the man again made Cayetano's flesh crawl. He'd killed him once. He couldn't let history repeat itself. None of this was going to work unless it began with change.

He looked at his men. "We carry the boys."

Adam heard the thought and shook his head. "I will walk, but my brother can't."

"It will be all right. I will get you both to safety," Layla said.

Adam eyed her curiously as she helped him up.

"Are you a magic woman, like Madame ReeRee?" he whispered.

She shifted her bow to the other hand as Cayetano led them across the water.

"I don't know what I am," she said. "I am a different woman here than what I was before. All I know is that whatever we do from this time forward, we have to make better choices. Do you understand?"

Adam nodded. "I can see your thoughts. So can Evan."

Her eyes widened.

"I wanted to tell you now, so you would not think we were deceiving you."

She thought about what he'd said, trying to imagine how all of that would work into what needed to happen, and at the same time, he answered for her.

"We will never betray you, Layla Birdsong. We owe you our lives. When we hear trouble, you will be the first to know."

She eyed him curiously and then thought of Yuma, yet another boy without a home.

"How do you feel about wolves?" she asked.

"I have never actually seen one because they were not native to the island where we lived. I've read about them. I know that they are very loyal, and that they mate for life."

"Yes, those are true facts, I think. How would you and Evan feel about letting just one small boy into your very special world?"

He thought, and saw a boy with brown skin and a sad face.

"I think Yuma will like us," Adam said.

Layla was surprised. She hadn't said Yuma's name, and yet he'd known. So they *could* read thoughts.

"I think he will like you, too. He belongs to the wolf clan, as do Cayetano and I. It's for people who are alone in the world."

He nodded. "We have always been alone. We would fit there."

"So, we will talk to Yuma. I will let him be the one to invite you into the clan. It is his right, since he was the first."

She glanced over her shoulder as they hurried away. One day she would come face to face with this Bazat, but not today.

Chapter Seventeen

It was one of Bazat's scouts who first found the python. He led them to the site, pointing to the tracks and the blood trails leading off into the jungle.

Bazat saw the tracks, but was more concerned about how the snake had died. He lost count of the stab wounds as he circled the mutilated corpse. It was surprising that either one of the boys would have been strong enough to do this. It made him wonder if there was more to his Little War-Gods than he'd first thought.

But, a dead snake was a dead snake. It had nothing to tell them about where the boys had gone, so they followed the blood trail, although the farther they went, the fainter it became. When they began hearing the far-off rumblings of thunder, they knew it was going to rain, and when it rained, the trail would be gone.

"Run!" Bazat screamed, and they began to move faster, desperate to catch up. They had been helpful to his domination and he wanted them back.

He and his men were almost at the waterfall when the first drops of rain began to fall, hitting the leaves above their heads in loud, heavy plops.

He pushed to the front of the pack, his chest burning, his legs nearly numb. They had run for a very long time and still no sight of the boys. He didn't understand it. Someone had to have helped them, but who?

The drops turned into a downpour, blinding their vision, plastering their hair to their bodies, and still Bazat pushed them, convinced he would see them just beyond the next trees, just over the next fallen log.

Then they reached the waterfall and saw the jaguar's body. More big magic! More unanswered questions. The jaguar was a mighty hunter, and those boys had appeared weak and useless as warriors. Bazat would not believe they had killed that jaguar themselves, yet it was dead like the python and the Little War-Gods were gone.

His warriors were of the opinion the hunt was cursed. They kept finding dead animals, each one more dangerous than the other. Two normal children would never have been able to kill the great python, or take down the mighty jaguar. The boys must truly be Gods, and it was bad luck to anger the Gods. They should not be chasing them.

Bazat heard but ignored them. He was too busy trying to read the signs around the big cat's carcass. The grass had been flattened all around it, but the rain could be responsible for that. Plants had folded up their leaves for protection against the storm while the water rushed ever faster in the stream before them.

He was beginning to believe the Little War-Gods had put a curse on Zotz that led to the old Shaman's death, just so they would have time to escape. They had fallen out of the sky into his midst without explanation, and they had disappeared in similar suspicious circumstances.

"We cannot fight the Gods," he announced. "They cursed the Shaman and he died. They are gone from us as quickly as they came. We must go back and make sacrifices to purify our city from the evil they have caused."

The warriors went with him, but their hearts were heavy, fearing they would become sacrifices for their failure to find the missing boys.

When Bazat got back to the palace and realized they had taken the crystal, he accepted their absence as final. It must have been where they kept their powers, and now that they had it back, he was helpless to fight them.

****

It was almost dark by the time Layla and Cayetano got back to Naaki Chava with the twins. They went into the palace the same way they had left, wanting to control the time when the boys' presence would be announced.

Layla knew she could easily slip them into the general population as part of the New Ones. They had come in such great numbers, it was impossible to identify them all. And the fact that they would be living in the palace would not be questioned. Cayetano and Singing Bird could do as they wished in that respect. But she was concerned about the Shamans, and so was Cayetano. They would know the truth, both about the boys' powers and the reason they had suddenly appeared. It remained to be seen as how they would accept it.

They left the boys with servants who were cleaning the blood from their bodies, while Cayetano sent a guard to bring the healer, Little Mouse, to the palace, then they headed for their quarters.

Yuma was sitting in their room with Acat at his side when Cayetano and Layla entered. He leaped up and ran to them with arms outstretched.

He had been crying.

"I am sorry, Singing Bird. He would not be happy. I think he was afraid you would not come back."

"It's all right," Layla said, and picked Yuma up and carried him with her to a stool so they could sit. She was so tired she could hardly think, but the boy's needs had to come first.

He was trembling and hiding his face in the curve of her neck. She motioned to Cayetano to go get the boys. He nodded once then left the room.

"I'm sorry you were worried," she said. "But I think you will be happy for why we were gone. Would you like to know?"

"Yes," he whispered.

"Then sit here on my knee and we will talk." She wiped the tears from his eyes and then settled him against her shoulder. "We have been in the jungle looking for two boys who were lost. Like you, they came into this place just before our old earth died. Today, we learned where they were and went to get them."

"Did you take them to their parents?" he asked.

"No. They are like you. They don't have any parents."

He got very still, absorbing this information, and Layla could almost hear the questions in his head.

"They will stay here in the palace with us, like you do. They are older, so it will be like having two big brothers. Would you like that?"

"Maybe, if they liked me," Yuma whispered. "Sometimes older boys don't like little kids."

"These boys will like you," Layla said. "You know why?"

He shook his head.

"Because they *never* had a family. They were born,

but they never knew a mother or a father. They were orphans for all their lives."

"I had a mother and a father," Yuma said. "I don't really remember much about my mother. She died when I was four. But I always had my daddy until..."

He couldn't say the words and it didn't matter. Layla kept talking while watching the door. They'd be here at any moment and she wanted to prepare the way.

"I told them about our clan, and that only lobos could belong. But I also told them that you would be the one who would invite them in, because you were the first."

Yuma's eyes grew wide. The thought of having any kind of power was intriguing.

"If I didn't like them, then they wouldn't belong?" he asked.

She nodded. "But I hope that isn't so, because they are very sad. One of the brothers was hurt and the other one saved his life. I think bravery is a good thing. You were the bravest boy I ever knew, going on the Last Walk all alone. And now we have two more brave boys."

"I will probably like them just fine," Yuma said.

She hid a smile. "I'm sure that is so. Their names are Adam and Evan and they are twins. I wonder if you'll be able to tell them apart."

Yuma eyes widened. "There were twin girls in my class at school back in Tahlequah." Then his expression fell. "But they were white girls. I think they died."

Layla nodded. "Yes, they did. But this is one of the reasons we have all come here, my little man. We came back to teach the ones who are living here now about the white man. One day he will come, but when he does, our people will have learned how to be stronger. We will not be overwhelmed by their numbers and their weapons and their greed. We will teach our people not to fight between each other, so that our numbers will remain strong. They will learn how to live with the white man without losing themselves and their pride, and if we do that, Firewalker will never come and the world will not be destroyed. You can help by being the first to make friends with two boys. It will be a good thing."

"I will be the first?"

"Yes. Ah, I hear them coming now."

He grew still as he looked toward the door. Just before they walked in, he suddenly jumped off her lap and stood on his own.

She smiled to herself. He'd just remembered he was a little man and no longer a boy. It was good.

Cayetano was carrying Evan, and Adam was walking at his side. Their hair was still wet from the bath and all the blood had been washed from their bodies. She was glad. It would have been a horrifying sight for Yuma to first meet them that way.

"Evan is in pain," Cayetano said. "I have sent for the healer, but he and Adam wanted to meet Yuma first."

Layla nodded. "Boys, this is Yuma."

Adam lifted a hand in greeting. "Hi. I'm Adam. This is Evan. I hope it is okay with you that we are here. We were afraid that we would die in the jungle before someone found us."

Yuma marched forward like a little soldier and shook Adam's hand, then laid a hand on Evan's knee.

"Just call me Yuma. Nice to meet you guys. Layla said you were lobos, too."

"Yes, we have no family but each other."

Yuma nodded. "So, we have this wolf clan, and even though you're not Native like us, if you want, you can be in the wolf clan, too."

Adam saw into this little boy's heart, and he saw far into the future of his life. This gesture was just the beginning of the impact he would make.

"We would be honored, wouldn't we Evan?"

Evan nodded, and put a hand on his chest. "Yes. Sorry I feel bad right now, but a python nearly killed me. Adam saved my life."

Yuma eyed Adam with renewed respect. "A big snake? You killed it?"

"Yes. He is my brother. You would have done the same," Adam said.

"I must take Evan back. Would you like to come with us, Yuma? The healer will stay with Evan all night. If you want, you and Acat could sleep on your mats in their room. The healer might need Acat's help," Cayetano said.

Yuma looked at Layla.

"Yes, you should go. You and Acat will be needed tonight."

And just like that, the little boy who had cried for their return was all about helping out.

Cayetano glanced at Layla.

"We bathe before we sleep. I will meet you there. There will be food. You eat to stay strong."

Layla nodded, grateful for the reprieve. She was exhausted.

"Yes, I will eat and I'll wait for you."

He left carrying one boy and two chattering beside him.

Layla followed them to the door, watching them going down the hall together and thought to herself how easily Cayetano had fallen into the role of father-figure. It was a good thing, considering their family had grown from one to three in one day. And in a few months, there would be four.

Time heals many things. In this case, it would be a Windwalker's heart.

She took a wrap to use when she had finished bathing, and headed toward the bath. It was her favorite part of the palace - the water coming in from the natural spring; funneling into the sunken tub and flowing out in a gentle trickle as it moved on through the aqueduct.

A servant was waiting and when she arrived, helped Layla off with all her clothing and steadied her as she stepped down into the tub. The woman's voice was soft, her touch gentle as she picked up the dirty clothes Layla had discarded.

"Are you well, Singing Bird?"

"I will be as soon as I wash away this dirt."

"I will wash your hair for you," she offered.

Layla waved her away. "No. I can do it myself. It is late. You can wash my dirty clothes tomorrow. Cayetano will be here, soon. If I need assistance, he will help."

"It is good that you are back safely," the little woman said, and then slipped away.

Layla could tell from the few carefully chosen words the servant had used that their abrupt absence had been much discussed. But the worst was now behind them. The boys were here. Hopefully Evan would recover without harm, and all would be right in their world. At least for a while. She knew the time was coming that would mark the anniversary of her murder. They had to get past that day with her alive before there would be a way to change her past.

She ate some of the fruit then began to wash,

grateful for the quiet and the sound of trickling water. She was getting ready to wash her hair when Cayetano walked in, naked and fully erect. The lack of modesty among the People was, in a way most endearing, and at the same time, growing up as Layla Birdsong, disconcerting.

He stepped down into the tub and reached for a cloth.

"The healer came?" she asked.

Cayetano nodded. "Yes. Bones are broken here." He was touching his side. "She says they will heal. She bound his chest and gave him medicine to take away pain."

"I want to see them before we sleep."

Cayetano laid a hand on the side of her face.

"Today I saw the woman who led the Last Walk. You have a woman's soft heart, but a warrior's spirit. I am proud that you are mine."

"I am proud to be yours," she said softly. "Here, use some of this. It will make your skin feel clean."

She rubbed the crushed root onto his chest and back and then let him scrub to his heart's content as she washed the jungle out of her hair. Her eyes were closed as she ducked beneath the water to rinse and when she came up, Cayetano was waiting with a look on his face that made her heart skip a beat.

She reached down to grasp his erection and as she did, he grabbed her by the shoulders and pushed her backward.

"Like this?" she whispered, stroking up the extended length of his penis, then stroking down, squeezing ever so slightly as she did.

"Yes, like that," he whispered, as his eyes closed and his nostrils flared.

She locked her fingers around the shaft and

began to stroke it, from the base of the shaft up to the hard, swollen head; over and over until Cayetano was about to burst.

Between one breath and the next, he lifted her off her feet and pushed her down on his erection. All she managed was a grunt of surprise before he pushed her against the wall. She wrapped her legs around his waist and her arms around his neck.

"With you," he said, and began a whole other ride.

Reveling in the tight heat into which he fell, he gritted his teeth and made himself focus on her.

But Layla was already aroused. With the first thrust, he pushed her down hard and held her, and as he did, a climax hit her so fast she forgot to breathe. She clung to him even harder, afraid that she coming undone.

Unprepared for the swiftness of her release, Cayetano groaned. He was done. His seed was spilling, his head was spinning, and when it had passed, he kissed her hard and took her under.

Layla's lungs were aching for air when they shot to the surface of the pool. He came up laughing, then carried her out of the water. Ignoring the wrap she brought with her, he carried her naked through the darkened halls, following the light from the burning torches all the way to their rooms.

By the time he had put her down on her sleeping mat, he was hard all over again. But this time, he took her slower, and when the climax came back, she was ready and waiting. Layla let it roll through her all the way to her toes, and then fell asleep in Cayetano's arms.

When they next woke, it was morning and a macaw was sitting on their windowsill, scolding for a treat.

Chapter Eighteen

Layla woke abruptly and sat up, looking around in confusion. In her sleep, she'd been standing in a crowd with her arrow notched, searching desperately for sight of Cayetano's face.

Cayetano woke the moment she left his arms, and reached for her.

"What is wrong?"

"A bad dream. Nothing. I want to go check on the boys. I didn't do that last night and I feel guilty."

He smiled. "Last night was for us. If there had been trouble, they would have awakened us."

She shook her head. "No. I was a bad mother, thinking only of myself."

She began grabbing clothes, and dressing, then trying to comb out the tangles in her hair, but she'd gone to bed with it wet, and now it was a mess.

"I'll just braid it," she said, and quickly divided it into three parts.

Cayetano watched in amazement. "How do you do this when you cannot see behind you?"

"I don't know. It's just how it works," she said. "Will you tie this cord around the ends so it doesn't come undone?"

He did as she asked, and then she pointed at his naked self.

"Do you intend to go see the boys in this condition?"

He was already erect. “It is of no concern,” he said, and dressed without giving it another thought.

“What if Evan gets a fever? Does your healer know how to cool his body?” she asked, as they hurried down the hall.

“We know,” he said. “You will see.”

And he was right. By the time they neared the boys’ room, they could hear voices.

They walked in to find Adam sitting on one side of Evan’s mat, and Yuma and Acat on the other side. They’d propped Evan’s head up on some pillows and were taking turns feeding him bits of fruit. There was a monkey chattering at the boys from a limb near the window, as if begging for bites.

When they saw Cayetano and Layla enter, Yuma began talking.

Layla smiled. He sounded a lot like the scolding monkey at the window.

“Evan had a fever in the night but he’s better. He likes mango but he doesn’t like these bananas. I think they are a little green.”

“Then we will find him some riper ones,” Layla said, as she knelt beside Adam and laid her hand on Evan’s forehead. “Maybe a little warm, but not bad. How do you feel, Evan?”

“It hurts, but I will get well.”

“Good,” Layla said, and then eyed the dark circles under Adam’s eyes. “And did you sleep?”

“Some. I was glad that Yuma and Acat were here. Evan was talking out of his head. It was scary to hear.”

“Fever does that sometimes,” Layla said. “Have you never had a fever before?”

“Not like that,” he said. “Will it happen again tonight?”

Layla translated to Cayetano.

"I will ask," he said, and looked to the healer. The tiny woman was sitting in a corner, dozing.

"Little Mouse. How was the night?"

The woman jumped up, shocked that the chief had caught her dozing and quickly began to list all the instructions she had for the family.

"The heat was in his body last night, but we bathed him with water. He is eating. He should not move unless he needs to pass water and then someone must help him stand, and walk with him. He will heal."

"Good. Good. This we can do. You go now, and if we have need of you again, we will call."

She left, but they could hear her footsteps scurrying down the hall.

Layla thought the healer's name fit her behavior very well, although it was different from most of the names in Naaki Chava. "Her name is not like the others. Why is she called Little Mouse?"

"She is like me. My mother was from another tribe. She gave me a name that she knew, instead of one from my father's people, who are here. Little Mouse came to us as a child. I don't remember when, but she was always Little Mouse."

It was the first time Layla thought about different tribes intermingling and marrying.

"Do some tribes steal people from other tribes and then take them into their lives?"

Cayetano nodded. "It happens. Why?"

She sighed. "It is one of the things that we have to learn to stop. No wars between tribes. No killing. No stealing people from their families. No slaves. But, if they want to go, that is another matter."

He frowned. "It will not be easy to make this stop."

"Nothing good ever comes easy," she said.

"That is not true," he said.

She frowned. "What do you mean?"

"You are very good and also-"

"Stop talking," she said quickly, and then felt herself blush.

He laughed, pleased with his joke. "I am hungry. Acat. You will bring food. We will eat here with our sons."

Adam and Evan understood the honor he'd bestowed by referring to them as his sons and translated to Yuma.

Just as quickly as he had embarrassed her, she now had tears in her eyes. She eyed the boys to see how they had taken to the label, and to her delight they were looking at Cayetano with something akin to worship.

"Yes, with our sons," she echoed, as Acat left.

"Want some more mango?" Yuma asked, holding up a bite for Evan to eat.

He nodded, and so the day began.

****

The City of the Sun was in mourning. Bazat had called his Shamans to the temple, along with two very unhappy citizens who had become unwitting sacrifices to the Gods.

Their families were standing in the crowd below, quietly sobbing as they watched their loved ones brought to the altar. The sun was at its zenith when the first man was pushed down onto his knees; his head shoved onto the blood-stained chopping block.

The Shamans were chanting. Bazat was watching the crowd. They already knew the little War-Gods were gone. They knew their chief was sacrificing one citizen for each God to pacify their anger, for it must have been anger that caused them to leave.

They watched in horror as the axe went up, and then held their breaths as it came down. It took two more swings before the head was completely severed, but thankfully the victim never knew it. He was already gone.

The second victim was so overcome with fear that his legs would no longer work and had to be dragged to the altar. He was sobbing as the axe came down, cutting off the sound as suddenly as it cut off his head.

The crowd exhaled on a moan.

Bazat looked up just as a large bird flew overhead.

"It is a sign!" he said, pointing at a long-legged bird that often stood in water. "The Gods are happy. Go back to your tasks."

They quickly obeyed, afraid if they did not, Bazat might decide to sacrifice more. Finally, there was no one left but the families gathering up their loved ones' bodies to be buried. The fact that they would be buried with honors for their sacrifice was of no comfort to their grief.

Bazat had convinced himself that it was over. His time with the Gods had caused trouble, and he wanted nothing more to do with any of them.

****

The Shamans in Naaki Chava heard of the presence of twins in the palace through the tongues of their servants, but thought nothing of it. They had no forewarning of any problems, and chose not to make trouble for themselves.

All except for Chak. He wanted to see the boys for

himself. He would look into their eyes and know if they were a danger. He'd heard that one of them had been injured, but didn't know how or to what extent, although it didn't matter. He was taking a poison with him, and if they were bad for Naaki Chava, he would find a way to put it in their food and the problem would be over.

****

Layla was sitting on a stool watching Evan sleep. He was young. His body would heal, but both he and Adam were jumpy, and it was difficult to get a smile from either of them. She suspected they had lived in fear so long that they were afraid to let down their guard.

Yuma was nearby, making toys that were causing quite a stir among the servants. He had a fat piece of cane about five inches in length that was going to be the body of his car, then four slices of cane about two inches thick to be the tires. He cut two lengths from a hard, narrow stick long enough to go through the width of the cane to use for axles, and so the assembly began.

Layla was surprised by his ingenuity, and when she saw what he was making, knew the residents of Naaki Chava were in for their first shock.

Then Cayetano walked in, saw the cane and the pieces, the small awl Yuma was pushing through the cane, and squatted down beside him.

"What is the little wolf cub making?" he asked.

Yuma smiled. He knew enough of the language to know what Cayetano called him and he liked the name.

"I know what it is," Adam said.

"I know, too," Evan added.

Cayetano looked at Singing Bird. "Do you know?"

She smiled. "Layla Birdsong knows. Singing Bird would not."

"Ah, something from your time."

"Yeah," Yuma said. "Watch this."

His little fingers flew as he poked a hole all the way through the longer piece of cane about an inch from one end, and then did the same at the other end.

He pushed the narrow sticks through the holes to make the axles, then shoved the round slices onto the extended parts, turning them into wheels.

Cayetano stared at the object, confused as to what it could possibly represent, but when Yuma set it down and gave it a quick push, he rocked back on his heels.

"It rolls."

Layla laughed. "It's called a car."

Cayetano frowned. "What is a car?"

Adam hid a giggle.

"It is a way to go from place to place without walking," Layla said. "Real ones have seats inside and a roof on the top so you won't get wet or cold. They move because of something called an engine, and when you sit inside the car and turn on the engine, the wheels will roll and it will take you very far in a short time."

He laughed, certain that they were making a joke, but then realized they were serious.

"This is real?"

Layla sighed. "This was real. But it won't happen for a long, long time. Before this, our people will capture and tame wild animals called horses. Have you ever seen a Vicuna or a Llama in your country? They are tall animals with very long necks and small heads, and are used to carry heavy loads."

He frowned. "These I have seen, but they do not live here."

"In the Andes," Adam said. "The high mountain areas. These are the lowlands... the jungles."

"Well, anyway, a horse is a little like that animal only beautiful, and so strong. In the future, they will be tamed and we will have big herds of them. When we want to go a long distance, we get on the horse and it will take us wherever we want to go, much faster than if we walk."

The servants were staring.

Yuma saw the doubt, and pushed the car back toward Cayetano so they could watch it roll again.

The servants giggled behind their hands and then ducked out of sight.

Cayetano frowned, and then got up and walked out.

The boys were immediately upset.

"Did we make him mad? We didn't mean to hurt his feelings," Yuma said.

Layla got up. "He's not mad. I think it's a little scary, knowing you boys understand something so easily, and yet it's a thing he will not grasp. You play. I'll go talk to him."

She went out into the hall but he was nowhere in sight. She looked in their room, but he wasn't there either. It took a bit of searching before she found him standing at a window overlooking the city. She slipped her arms around his waist and laid her head in the middle of his back. The tension in his body was palpable.

"Don't be angry."

"It is not anger that I feel."

"Then what?" she asked, and slipped under his

arm to look up at his face.

"Fear. I see this city and the many people who live here. They have food and shelter and they are happy. Why is this not enough? Why do things change?"

She sighed. "Everything changes, Cayetano. Even the people we are now have changed greatly from what we once were. Once we lived beneath bushes and in caves. I guess we got tired of being hot or cold, and learned how to make better shelters. Much time has passed between then and now. The palace is beautiful, and the white streets of your city are beautiful. We walk on them and do not get muddy when it rains. But there was a time when such a thing as this place would not exist."

She could see him coming to grips with that answer, and slowly understanding dawned.

"So our people will always be changing?"

"Not just our people, all people will be changing, Cayetano. Some change faster than others. One day we will have cities so large it takes a whole day to pass through. In Layla Birdsong's world people got in cars that could fly like a bird. Before Firewalker destroyed earth, man had already walked on the moon."

His voice was shaking. "That is not possible."

"Not now, but it will happen, but when it does, this time our people will not be standing by watching, we will be making it happen with all the others."

He didn't say anything for a very long time. She understood how confusing it must be, knowing they had lived in a future he would never see, let alone understand. He didn't even know the meaning of the word engine, and yet he'd had a glimpse of what it could do.

"Are you all right?" she finally asked.

He pulled her into his arms. "Yes, because I have

learned something today that I did not know."

"You mean about the cars and airplanes?"

"Yes, I know that now, but I also know that my bones will be dust long before that happens, and that means it will be someone else's problem."

She laughed. "You are right. All we have to do is lay the first blocks to build it, and others will carry it on."

Before he could answer, Acat came running.

"Chak is with the new boys. I went in to bring them food and he was there. He is scaring them and I could not make him leave."

Cayetano didn't wait for Layla's reaction. He left the room in long angry strides. By the time Layla reached the hall, he was running. Their happy day had taken a dark turn she didn't like.

****

Evan was crying, and Adam was standing astraddle his brother's legs, refusing to obey the shaman's order to move.

They'd heard his thoughts the moment he'd walked into the room. Despite what he said to the contrary, they knew he was up to no good.

Chak stared at them without speaking. The twins knew he was trying to read their thoughts and promptly blocked him.

Yuma was clutching his awl like a knife, ready to defend his clan. Car building fun was over.

"Where do you come from?" Chak asked.

"We came with the others," Adam said.

"Then why are you here in the palace? Why are you not out there with your people?"

Yuma spoke up. "They are like me. They have no

family. Cayetano and Layla are our family now."

"Layla. Who is this Layla?"

"You call her Singing Bird. Where we lived, we called her Layla Birdsong."

Chak frowned. "Then she is not Singing Bird. She is an imposter and you just proved it! This is why bad things will happen here. The real Singing Bird is gone, and an imposter has come to take her place. Cayetano has been bewitched and will lead us all astray."

"Stop talking like that!" Yuma shouted. "You are wrong. Go away!"

Chak was in shock. This was worse than he'd expected. He took the bottle of poison out of his pocket and began moving toward the jug of water by the window as if he was going to pour himself a drink. He reached for the jug, poured a small amount of water in the cup and quickly drank it, then paused, waiting for the moment when he could slip in the poison.

"You strangers bring bad ways to Naaki Chava. Soon our children will see your behavior and begin arguing with their elders. You should go!"

Chak heard footsteps behind him and turned just as Cayetano hit him. The vial flew out of his hand and through the window.

Cayetano was furious. "You have come into these rooms uninvited, shouting at these children as if you have the right. You are a shaman, not their caretaker, and a shaman who gives me great anger."

At that moment, Layla burst into the room. Chak pointed at her, screaming every word that came out of his mouth.

"It is her fault this bad blood is happening. Even this boy knows the truth. She is not Singing Bird. She has another name. You are being tricked and we are overrun with strangers. We did not ask for them to come. Is she the chief now? Has Cayetano turned into a woman, and this false Singing Bird into our chief?"

"You are wrong. She had the same name, but it was only spoken in a different way. Bird song and Singing Bird mean the same thing and you know it. If you were not so old, I would strike you down where you stand!" Cayetano said. "Get your belongings and leave Naaki Chava now. You have no place here."

Chak was speechless. The Shamans often had differing opinions from their chiefs, and it was understood because they could 'see' things that mere humans could not.

When Cayetano shouted for the guards and ordered them to escort him out of the palace and out of Naaki Chava, he thought about begging. Then he saw the look in Singing Bird's eyes and knew if he didn't obey, Cayetano might kill him, and if he didn't, she would.

"You will be sorry," Chak muttered, as he pushed past Cayetano, only to find Singing Bird standing in his path.

"You have threatened my family. If I ever see your face again, my face will be the last one you see."

Chak's belly rolled as the guards moved in beside and behind him and escorted him out.

Cayetano walked out with the guards as Layla went to the boys and gathered them in her arms.

"I am so sorry that happened, but you were all very brave. Did he hurt you? Did he touch you... any of you?"

"No, but he was trying to sneak something into our water. I think it was poison. I could hear his thoughts, wishing he would be around to watch us die," Evan said.

Yuma pointed out the window. "Something flew

out of his hand when Cayetano hit him."

She went to the window to look out and saw the shattered vial lying on the ground, and the contents spilled and soaking into the earth. Birds were dropping down from the trees to peck about and then flying back up to the branches. As she watched, she saw a bird begin to falter, as if losing balance. As she watched, it fell forward through the branches onto the ground and never moved. Then to her horror, another fell, and another until the ground was covered in dead birds. She turned away.

Cayetano walked in and saw her expression.

"What is it?"

She pointed out the window. "Yuma said that fell out of Chak's hand when you hit him."

When Cayetano saw the broken vial and dead birds, his fingers curled into fists; his voice was shaking with rage.

"I should have killed him."

Adam slipped into the space between them. "I know something," he whispered.

"I do too," Evan hissed.

"Speak it," Cayetano said.

"We knew he meant harm. He hates Singing Bird, but he hates you more, Cayetano."

"Why?" Layla asked.

"His father knew Cayetano's father," Adam said.

Cayetano nodded. "Yes. They grew up together."

"His father believed he should have been chief instead of Cayetano's father. The hate started there," Evan added.

"But why me?" Layla asked. "Why does he wish me such harm?"

Cayetano sighed. "Even I know this. The easiest way to hurt me is to hurt you. Without you I die here."

He put a hand on his chest.

Layla felt his pain as surely as if it was her own.

"Then we have to make sure no one hurts you this way, because when you hurt, so do I."

Yuma had been silent, but no longer. He swung the awl up over his head.

"You saved me. You saved Adam and Evan. Now we will protect you. We have decided."

Now her tears fell freely.

"I don't want any of you feeling responsibility here. You are the children. We are the adults."

Yuma shook his head. "I may not be tall, but my childhood is gone. It died with my father. I am a man, and I will grow bigger, but my heart will stay the same."

Evan whispered. "We also know about your baby but we aren't telling anyone. She will change the world."

Layla glanced at Cayetano. He looked as stunned as she felt.

Yuma leaned against her hip and slipped his hand into hers.

"The baby will be named Tyhen, but people will call her The Dove and she will be mine. I will protect her with my life and she will love me."

In that moment, she remembered Windwalker's words.

Leave no one behind.

Now she understood. The future would never happen as it should, without the little boy she had saved.

Layla told Cayetano what they said, but he was in shock. Not only did these three children know the baby would be a girl, but they were giving her a name?

"What does this name Tyhen mean?" he asked.

Layla's voice was trembling. "It's the language of Layla Birdsong's people, the Muscogee. It means whirlwind."

She felt Cayetano flinch, but he didn't falter. It was another reminder that the child belonged to the Windwalker and not to him.

"That is a good name," Cayetano said. "A strong wind cleans. She will have a lot of cleaning to do to make so many tribes stop fighting with each other."

"But she won't be alone," Adam said. "She will have us."

Chapter Nineteen

Chak was preparing himself to die. He knew he wouldn't last long in the jungle, and was cursing Cayetano's life with every step. When he heard rustling in the trees behind him, he spun, expecting the next moments to be his last.

Instead, two men walked into view, as surprised to see him as he was them. They were each carrying a spear in one hand and a large bag in the other. When they recognized the shaman, they were afraid they would be cursed for interrupting some ritual.

Instead, Chak hailed them. "Where are you going?"

"To the City of the Sun. We have yams to trade at their marketplace."

The City of the Sun. Chak had heard it was led by a chief named Bazat, and that he was crazy. Still, crazy would be preferable to dead if he could find a way to turn this to his benefit.

"I would walk with you."

They both nodded in agreement and he fell in behind him, thanking the Gods for their arrival. He listened absently to their chatter as they walked, but when he realized they were talking about the death of a shaman in the City of the Sun, he interrupted.

"How did this shaman come to die?"

"They say he was cursed by the Little War-Gods," one man said.

Chak frowned. "There were War-Gods in the City of the Sun?"

"Yes, the twin sons of Sun and Mother Earth who are called the Little War-Gods. They fell out of the sky into the marketplace and Bazat took them into the palace. But then they disappeared."

Chak stumbled. The twins who appeared so suddenly in Cayetano's palace could also be the same twins! And if they were really the Little War-Gods, then that would explain what was happening.

First Singing Bird returned with all the New Ones, and then the twins appearing so unexpectedly could be the reason Cayetano was behaving strangely. He must be under a spell.

Chak began fantasizing about ridding Naaki Chava of Singing Bird, sending the strangers into the jungle to find their own place to live, and returning to the city a hero for recognizing what had taken place. Cayetano would be grief-stricken at the loss of his woman, shamed for falling prey to their wiles, and fall out of favor. It was the perfect revenge.

What puzzled him most was why he hadn't seen that in his dreams? His only explanation was the Little War-Gods had powers greater than his, and blocked his dreams to keep him from their truth. He began to question the traders more.

"So how did Bazat behave when the twins were gone? Did he want them back?"

"My brother's woman is from the City of the Sun. He said Bazat was angry and searched the jungle, but couldn't find them. He sacrificed two citizens of the city to appease the twins' anger, one citizen for each twin, and now his anger is done."

Now it was clear! Chak saw his path. He had been driven from Naaki Chava so that Bazat could learn the truth. And the shaman had died in the City of the Sun to make room for him.

His step was no longer dragging and he was no longer waiting to die. He had a place to be and a purpose to fulfill. He would pay Cayetano back. Singing Bird would die.

****

As the day moved on and Chak's threat was no longer an issue, Cayetano kept thinking about Yuma's toy, he was curious to see how the New Ones fared, and if they had any creations of their own.

Language was still an issue between the New Ones and the people of Naaki Chava, but he'd been told they were learning quickly and coping as to be expected. It was nearing the harvest celebration in Naaki Chava. Crops were being put in storage much faster than before because the New Ones were working side by side in the fields with the People, and that made everyone happy.

But he wanted to see for himself and went to find Singing Bird. If he had questions, she had their language, too.

****

Layla had finally found a place to be alone. She was struggling with more morning sickness and she wanted to think. She couldn't get past how close the boys had come to being murdered. It reminded her of how fragile their toehold was in this new place.

As she sat, she picked at some fruit, testing to see if it would stay on her stomach. So far, this morning sickness was the only physical connection she had with the baby she carried. It was too soon for her belly to grow, and far too soon to feel the child begin to move. In a way, the morning sickness was turning into a good reminder, because there were times when the pregnancy didn't seem real.

She chewed and swallowed the fruit, then waited to see if nausea hit. When it did not, she tried another small piece and then tore off some of the bread and popped it into her mouth, too.

Birds were squawking overhead as they flew past. Beautiful peacocks strutted through the courtyard, spreading the magnificence of their tail-feathers and then shrieking, as if to say, 'look at me! Look at me'.

Layla smiled and tossed a piece of fruit toward one of them but a monkey dropped down from a tree, grabbed the fruit and scampered off. She laughed.

"Sorry Mr. Peacock, but you were bragging too loudly and moving too slow."

I am here.

Layla turned around, expecting to see one of the servants, but she was alone. She shrugged off the moment and took another bite of the bread, chewing slowly and again, letting it settle in her belly before chancing another bite.

You cannot feel my heart, but I can feel yours.

Layla stood up. "Who's there? Who's hiding? Come out and show yourself."

I am not hiding, I am growing. I will see you when I am done.

Layla's heart skipped a beat as she put a hand on her belly.

"Is this you I hear?"

Yes, my mother, you can hear my voice, and soon you will feel me, as well.

Layla sat down to keep from falling. She thought

she heard a giggle, but was still in shock. It could have been a bird.

No. It was me.

Layla didn't know whether to laugh or cry.

Don't cry. Be happy. I am happy I will be your child.

"I am happy, too."

Tell Cayetano that it is not the seed that makes a father. It is the love that guides a heart.

Now Layla was weeping when Cayetano found her, sitting beneath a mango tree with tears running down her face.

"Singing Bird! Are you ill? Who has made your heart hurt?"

"These aren't sad tears, they are happy tears," she said, and threw her arms around his neck.

"What has made you happy?"

"I have a message for you from this baby," she said, and put his hand on the flat of her belly.

He frowned. "How can this be?"

"I don't know how it's happening, but I can hear her voice and she gave me a message especially for you."

The shock on his face was evident. "If she is this connected to the spirits, then she knows I am not her father."

"And that is exactly what the message is about. She said,

'Tell Cayetano that it is not the seed that makes a father. It is the love that guides a heart'."

Cayetano was too shocked to speak.

"So she already loves you, not the seed."

The scar at the corner of his mouth twitched. It did so when he was clenching his jaw, and she knew that was happening because he was trying not to cry.

"This is a good thing," she said. "Be happy. I am. But enough about me, I could tell by the way you were walking that you had something important to tell me. Am I right?"

"I will protect her with my life," he whispered.

"She knows that. I know that. Now why did you come looking for me?"

"I want to go into the city where the New Ones are living. If Yuma is making a toy I cannot understand, I am curious as to what the adults are doing, but I cannot understand them."

"Ah... you need a translator."

He frowned. "I do not know that word, but I do need you."

She smiled. "And I need you. So, I am ready to go if you are."

"Yes. The guards wait. Where are the boys?"

"With Acat and two others. They are not alone."

He nodded. "They must never be alone again while they are young."

"Yes, I agree."

"Then we go."

She walked with a lighter heart - partly because she walked with the man who filled her soul - because her food was staying down, and because for the first time, her baby felt real.

****

Nantay was working on what he hoped would turn into a ceiling fan that would be powered by a water wheel connected to the canal behind their house. It would take a little rigging but he knew he could do it. He was still fastening a fan blade to the frame when he saw a crowd coming down the street.

He stopped to watch and soon realized it was the chief and Layla Birdsong. It had taken all of them a while to understand she had once lived in this time as a woman named Singing Bird, and that after she brought them back in time, she would not have been able to live as the same spirit in two different bodies. Since it was a miracle they were still alive, it was easy to accept the miracle of Layla's transformation, as well. He knew that she had recognized him, but would she feel the same toward the Navajo here, as she had before?

****

Cayetano was observing great signs of change. Some of the New Ones were building their own lodges, or adding to the ones they'd been given so that they had more than one room in which to live.

And the children who'd come with the New Ones were playing games that the other children didn't know. Games that Singing Bird told him were called baseball, and hide and seek.

As they turned a corner, they saw two children sitting on either end of a fallen tree limb that they had balanced over the stump of a larger one. One child went up as the other went down, and they would reverse. Up down, up down. It was so intriguing that he laughed out loud. He was pleased by the long line of children, both from the People and from the New Ones, waiting to take a turn.

"Look at this!" he said, pointing and laughing. "What is this called?"

Layla was smiling. "It's called a teeter-totter."

"You did this as a child?"

She nodded. No need even trying to explain a

Ferris wheel or a merry-go-round, let alone a roller-coaster. This teeter-totter was enough of a revelation. She had been wondering how long it would take for the first bit of modern technology to be adapted into this life, and now she knew. Children were always the most adaptable to change. They would be the ones who embraced the new bits of technology far quicker than others.

As they walked a little farther, she caught a glimpse of a familiar face and took Cayetano's hand.

"Come see this man. Back in my other life, he was a policeman where we lived, like the guards who are around us now. When I was attacked, he came with my grandfather and stood guard outside my room as I healed."

Cayetano was anxious to meet such a man. He had a moment of jealousy as he watched Singing Bird embrace the man, then realized it must be the way friends greeted in those times, because she then embraced others standing beside him.

"Nantay! Leland Benally! It is so good to see you! Are you well?"

Both men were smiling widely, then Nantay asked the question they were both thinking.

"We are alive, which is a miracle we will never forget. We heard you were seriously hurt when you came through the portal. You seem well. Is this so?"

"It's true. My burns were bad. I could not see a thing for several days. It was a scary time, but as you can tell, I am well now. I want you to meet Cayetano. He is my husband here."

They both eyed the chief curiously, but with respect.

"It is an honor to meet you," Benally said. "There are so many of us, we are very grateful that you have welcomed us into your city."

Layla quickly translated and Cayetano was pleased.

"You are most welcome," he said. "Our shamans told us you were coming. We knew there would be many. If you have other needs, you must let us know."

Layla translated again then asked Nantay a question of her own.

"Have the New Ones had trouble assimilating into this culture?"

"It's been a learning experience for sure," Nantay said.

"When I saw you coming, I wasn't sure you would know me," he said.

"Oh, because I look different? You should have seen the fit I had when I saw my face," Layla said.

Nantay and Benally both laughed.

"I'm serious," Layla said. "I didn't know what would happen to us when we made the Last Walk. I just knew it was the path I was supposed to take to keep you safe. I didn't know we were coming back in time. I honestly thought we would be going into the Anasazi's future. This has all been strange for me, too. I still feel the same inside. I still feel like Layla, but now I remember Singing Bird, too."

Benally grinned. "Double whammy, but it looks like you hit the jackpot. Cool dude," he said, referring to Cayetano who was looking at the ceiling fan Nantay was building with great interest.

She laughed. "Yes, the chief *is* a cool dude. So how are the others treating you?" she asked. "You know they refer to all of you as the New Ones. It's kind of funny because, in truth, you are the old ones."

Nantay shrugged. "It is all good. Not easy, but anything new is not easy. There are things to be learned. My wife is struggling to accept no running water or indoor toilets, although her grandmother still lived in a Hogan down in the canyons."

"Where is Shirley?" Layla asked.

He pointed to the door of their dwelling. "Inside. She broke her leg on the Last Walk. It is healing, but she still can't put weight on it."

"Oh no! Could I talk to her?"

"Sure. Come inside," he said, and walked back into the house.

Layla took Cayetano's hand again. "His woman broke her leg on the Last Walk. She is a friend. I want to talk to her."

He followed her inside.

Layla was taken aback but the interior. It was very crude compared to the palace. And there was no comparison to the home they'd had back on the reservation other than four walls and a roof. Here, they had one small window, an open door, sleeping mats, a pot to cook in, and a jug of water nearby. She could only imagine how Shirley Nantay was faring.

"Shirley, it's me, Layla. I didn't know that you'd been hurt."

Shirley was a small woman with bright eyes and a ready smile – at least she had been. The woman lying on the mat was in need of a more comfortable place and her ready smile was gone. When she saw Layla, she stifled a gasp as she tried to sit up.

"Montford said that you had changed. I couldn't imagine how. Now I see."

Layla knelt at her side. "Only on the outside, Shirley. I am so sorry you were hurt. It makes all of this change even worse."

The sympathy was Shirley's undoing. She covered her face and began to cry.

Nantay was immediately upset and at the same time, embarrassed.

"She's in pain," Layla said, explain what was happening to Cayetano. "But most of all, I think she's overwhelmed by the change."

"Tell her that I will send Little Mouse. She will help."

"You are truly a good chief," Layla said softly, then patted Shirley's arm. "Cayetano is sorry for your pain, Shirley. He wants me to tell you that he is sending a healer to you. Her name is Little Mouse. You will love her as I do, but now we'll leave so you can rest."

They walked out, with Nantay behind them.

"Thank you! Thank you so much," he said. "Without any way of knowing what plants in this place are good for healing or dangerous to touch, I couldn't even make Indian medicine for her, myself."

Layla's eyes widened. She'd been so busy thinking of how the New Ones would change the way of life here, that she'd forgotten they would also need to be taught about the land into which they'd come.

"I will see to it that Little Mouse, and others like her, will teach all of you what you need to know. There are some good hunters in our people. They need to learn how to hunt here, as they did before."

"Yes, people have been talking about that. I will tell them it will happen. We want to make our living conditions better, but didn't have any idea of how to begin. We need more building materials and many other things that have to be foraged, and we don't know where to start."

"Did we get here with any tools? We had to leave so much behind when we started to run."

"Yes, we did. When we began lightening our loads on the Last Walk, I told the men who had tools and knives to keep them if they could. We have more than a thousand or so men who came here with different kinds of tools. We could build better, if we had the goods to do it."

She quickly translated to Cayetano, and just like that, he knew who to talk to get that started.

"What else?" she asked.

"Their weapons are crude. They have metals, but they are mostly ornamental. It would be helpful to them if they had metal tips on their arrows and metal heads on their axes instead of bone or rock," Nantay said.

"Even if you had the proper raw ore, you would have no way to-"

He smiled. "There are many men here who had held many different jobs. If we knew where to look, we could do much."

Layla turned again to Cayetano, her eyes alight with excitement.

"Are there people from Naaki Chava willing to teach the New Ones where to find supplies they need?"

"I will think about the right people and tell them," he said, then looked up at the sky. "It will rain soon. We go."

"I'll come back," Layla said. "Spread the word. We'll make things better. I promise."

And he'd been right. They had barely reached the palace before the sky unloaded the near-daily downpour. They never lasted long, but were part of why the tropical aspect of this place existed.

****

It was about a week after their arrival before Evan was allowed to move around. He had to be careful, but was happy to be upright and breathing without being in pain.

Layla's morning sickness was with her daily, but she endured it without fuss, and simply waited for it to pass before she put food in her mouth. She had not had another conversation with her daughter, and accepted that it would happen on the baby's time and not hers.

She began to spend a lot of time teaching the boys the language of Naaki Chava and they were learning quickly. But the day she caught the twins speaking in their own private language, she was intrigued.

When Adam realized she had walked into the room, he blushed then stammered.

"I didn't know you were there."

Layla was intrigued. "What language is that? I don't think I've ever heard it before."

"It's our language," Evan said. "We only speak it among ourselves."

"And Yuma. We're teaching it to Yuma," Adam added. "I might be useful one day if we could talk to each other without people knowing what we say."

Layla sat down on a stool as the boys gathered around her.

"Do you mean that you two made up an entire language that only you know?"

The twins nodded.

"Twin-speak," she said. "I've read about it when I was in college, but I've never met anyone who had done it."

Evan shrugged. "We had to. We knew how we came to be born and were afraid of what Mr. Prince would make us do, so we made up our own language. If he couldn't understand us, then he couldn't control us."

At that point, Yuma came into the room with Acat and slipped into Layla's lap. Despite his assurance that he was a man, there were times when he still wanted to be little, and this was one of them.

"I go to the marketplace," Acat said, explaining why she was leaving Yuma in her care.

"She's bringing back some sugar cane for all three of us," Yuma said. "I asked. Is that okay?"

Layla grinned. "Of course it's okay. Bring one for me, too," she added.

Acat giggled and scurried off.

"So, back to our conversation," Layla said. "What did you mean when you said, 'how we came to be born?"

Evan looked at Adam. "You tell," he said softly.

Adam nodded and began the tale. "Our mother was a gypsy who read fortunes. She could see the future and into people's hearts. Mr. Prince found out about her skills. He also knew a man who could feel no pain. People could cut him or burn him, and he never cried out. Mr. Prince paid my mother and this man to make a baby. He wanted to know how a child would be from two people like that. Our mother agreed, not knowing that he meant to keep us. After we were born, he wanted her to go away but she wouldn't. So he had her killed."

Layla was shocked by his lack of emotion.

"What about the man who was your father?"

"We don't know, but he didn't matter to us because we didn't matter to him."

"What did Prince think you two were going to do for him?"

Adam shrugged. "It was always about gaining power."

Layla frowned. "This is bad, but you are here now.

One day you will grow up and have a family of your own."

Adam frowned and Evan shook his head.

"No, we won't marry. We are able to feel a connection to people, and be bound by honor, like we are to you. But we can't feel love as you are intending. We love each other and that is all, but only because we are one and the same."

Layla frowned.

"You can't know this yet. You haven't matured enough to-"

Adam shook his head. "But we do know this. Our mother was psychic, and so are we. Our father could not feel pain. We feel pain, but we cannot feel love. This is how we were born."

"I am so sorry," she said. "But I'm glad the man who owned you died. Murdering your mother was a terrible crime, but what he did to the both of you was a crime against nature."

The boys shrugged. "He was a collector and we were part of his collection. He had all kinds of things that were supposed to be good luck and maps to hidden treasures. It was his portal key that got us here."

"Do you still have it?" Layla asked.

They nodded. "We stole it back from Bazat when we ran away."

"It needs to be hidden away," Layla muttered.

"It needs to be thrown away," Evan said.

"It needs to be destroyed," Adam said.

"We'll talk to Cayetano about this tonight. For now, just leave it wherever you've hidden it. The fewer people who know about it, the better off you are."

The twins looked at each other and smiled. She had not asked where it was hidden, or asked to see it.

Even more proof that she was not only a good woman, but one who could be trusted.

****

That night, she told Cayetano what they'd said.

"Do you mean they will never feel for a woman what I feel for you?" he asked.

Layla nodded. "That is what they said."

Cayetano shook his head in disbelief. "My heart hurts for them. The greatest thing about being a man is being with the woman he loves." He pulled her close, running his fingers through her hair. "You are *my* heart, Singing Bird. Without you, the best part of me would die."

Layla's hands trembled as she cupped his face. "One of the first things the Windwalker told me, was the same thing Niyol told me, and the same thing you told me."

The surprise on his face was visible.

"This is true?"

"Yes. Do you know what it was?"

"No."

"You all said... 'You belong to me, and you will love me'."

His nostrils flared. "And is this not so?"

"It is true. I do love you, with all my heart."

He smirked. "Then it seems we were very wise to have predicted such a thing."

As she laughed she remembered what she'd promised the boys.

"There is another thing. The boys have the portal key that brought them here. They want to hide it so no one can ever find it again. Can you help them?"

His eyes narrowed thoughtfully. "Yes. I will talk to

them myself."

"Thank you. Now my job for this day is done."

He growled, as he swung her up into his arms. "You have yet to make love to me this day."

A shiver of what was to come shot through her.

"Today, I would ask that you make love to me," she whispered.

He laid her down on the sleeping mat.

"It will be done," he said softly, and slid between her legs.

Chapter Twenty

The City of the Sun belied its name. The moment Chak and the traders entered, he felt darkness. He thanked them for their company and parted ways, anxious to explore. Yet even as he was walking through the marketplace, he sensed an underlying fear that was reflected in the people's faces. Their voices were subdued, raised only in arguments, and there was little laughter. It was nothing like Naaki Chava.

But, his belly was empty and he had nothing to trade but information. He didn't even know how to get an audience with Bazat without getting himself into trouble. The traders said this chief used beheading as a means of solving his problems, so he had to be careful.

The temple was easy to see, rising above the houses in the middle of the city. He moved toward it instinctively, hoping he would find more of his kind. They would know him as a true shaman and hopefully get him an audience with the chief. But upon arrival, his hopes were dashed.

The temple was abandoned. Only vultures roosted on the uppermost corners, which told Chak it was a place to which they were accustomed to finding food. When a large rat slipped out from a lower doorway and scampered along the base of the temple before disappearing into the jungle behind it, he shuddered.

This city was smaller than Naaki Chava. The

palace, just visible on the rise behind the temple appeared more ornate, while the dwellings of the residents were as unkempt as the people who lived in them.

He had a moment of hesitation, wondering if he wanted to insinuate himself here. If it had not been for Singing Bird, he would not be in this position. Hate grew as he saw the road leading up to the palace. If he took it, there was no going back.

As he stood, debating with himself about the wisdom of his intent, there was a rush of wind in his face, as if a spirit had passed by. He looked up and then gasped.

The sun! It was being eaten by the moon!

He threw up his hands and raced toward the palace to warn the chief, his heart pounding with every step.

****

Bazat was on his back, while the woman astraddle his body was methodically pumping herself upon his erection. A large blue bird swung on a nearby perch in perfect rhythm. She had been at it for a while and he was nearing release when he became aware of commotion outside his window, and then the sound of running feet inside the palace. He tried to push her off but she was so high on the dry mushroom she had smoked, she was oblivious.

“Get off!” he shouted, but she kept on humping and suddenly it was too late to stop.

Evan as he was shoving her off his legs, light was bursting behind his eyes; his seed spewing from his body.

“Bazat! Bazat! Come quick!” a servant said, as he

ran into the room.

He took one look at the moaning woman and the condition the chief was in and started to retreat when they began hearing screams down in the city.

At that point, Bazat was already on his feet.

"What is happening?" he shouted, and ran to the window.

"There is a shaman who asks to speak with you. He says to tell you that the moon is eating the sun," the servant cried.

A knot of fear tightened Bazat's bowels. "That is not possible!"

"It is so! Look up into the sky. The shaman was right! It is beginning!"

Bazat looked. The knot of fear grew tighter. "Send him to the great room."

The servant dashed away as Bazat put on his breechclout, stepped into his sandals, jammed his feathered headdress onto his head and began fastening the feathered cape around his neck as he strode to the throne room.

He wasn't accustomed to doing these tasks for himself, but there was no time for ritual. And after losing the twins, he did not want to anger another spirit by appearing before a shaman as anything other than the great chief Bazat.

He entered the throne room to find all the servants face down on the floor, praying to the Gods to spare them. This was the City of the Sun and the Sun was disappearing before their eyes. Would they be next?

"Go away!" he yelled.

They scrambled to their feet and ran; terrified they would become a sacrifice to the dying Sun.

A lone man in dusty clothing was standing in the

middle of the room with his hands clasped in front of him and his head down, showing his respect.

Bazat climbed up the steps to the throne and then sat. Because he was a small man, he chose to address those beneath him from a higher level.

"Look at me!" Bazat yelled, and the man looked up.

Chak was taken aback. The stocky little man with a beak of a nose and bowed legs was nothing like Cayetano in looks or demeanor.

Bazat pointed his finger. "You have brought danger to my city. Tell the moon to give back the sun or I will spill your blood to appease their anger."

Chak stifled a moan. "I did not bring this danger. I came to warn you of it," he said quickly.

"Then you came too late because it is already here," Bazat said.

"Yes, but I know why it happened," Chak said.

Bazat's frown deepened. "Tell me now."

"Did the twins of Sun and Mother Earth not flee from your city? Did a shaman not die here on the steps of the temple the same day?"

Bazat stared, his face expressionless. "I sacrificed to the twins. It is over."

"No. They are hiding in Naaki Chava in the palace of Cayetano. They laugh that they have deceived you. Cayetano's woman, Singing Bird is plotting to take away your reign in this city so that the New Ones she brought into Naaki Chava will have even more places to live."

Bazat leaped to his feet. "How do you know this?"

"I was a shaman in Naaki Chava. Cayetano banned me from the city because I saw into his heart. I saw his desire to take everything around him as his own, including the City of the Sun."

"This is so?"

Chak happily lied, thinking of the doom it would create.

"This is so."

Bazat stormed down from the throne, waving his arms and spitting his words in short, venomous bursts.

"I will kill them. I will kill them all."

Chak pointed to the window. "It is getting darker. But I believe it will get light again soon. I believe that this was only a warning to you. You must rid this jungle of the evil in Naaki Chava, or next time the moon will swallow the sun and take it to the far side of the earth, never to return."

Bazat began to pace. "What should I do?"

"Go out to the people! Tell them you will protect them, and that it will get light again. Don't let them know about the twins. That must be done in secrecy. You should not go to war with Naaki Chava, for there are three times more people there than you have here. You would be defeated."

Bazat stormed out of the room. Chak followed along behind, hoping this was enough to insinuate himself into the crazy chief's life.

****

Adam was sitting outside with Evan, entertaining his brother by throwing fruit to the birds and watching them fight for the treats, while Yuma stood watch.

He was the youngest, but he knew they would never be fighters, and so he'd taken it upon himself to be the soldier of the three.

"Come sit," Adam said. "I'll teach you some more new words."

"I am on duty," Yuma said.

Adam and Evan laughed. "The only duty here is bird duty."

Yuma frowned, but he didn't answer. He was seeing something they did not. The birds were starting to take to the trees as they did at night when they went to roost. Even more puzzling, the monkeys were suddenly silent.

"Something is wrong. Look what is happening," Yuma said, pointing to the birds that were already roosting.

Adam looked up, then past Yuma's shoulder to the sky. He stood up.

"Look. It's an eclipse!" he cried.

Yuma saw it and realized the birds and animals had known it first.

"Help me up!" Evan said. "We have to tell Cayetano!"

"Why?" Yuma asked. "It's just an eclipse."

"Because these people are primitive in understanding the universe. They will think it's a bad sign. You have to hurry," he said.

"I'll go," Yuma said, and rushed into the palace, leaving them to follow at a slower pace.

He was running down the hall when he saw one of the servants.

"Cayetano! Cayetano! Where is he?" Yuma cried.

The man pointed to the hallway leading to where the chief held court.

Yuma headed down the hall. Even as he was running, it sounded like the city was in riot. He ran into the throne room, shouting as he went.

"Cayetano! Cayetano! Come quick!"

****

Cayetano was with his second chiefs, discussing the upcoming harvest celebration. While there would be feasting and drumming, it was also a time for extra safeguards for the city. When everyone was in the streets celebrating the good year, their enemies would see them at their weakest.

He was, as yet, unaware that Naaki Chava was already in an uproar. The eclipse was now visible and the people down in the city were in a panic. They were prostrate on the ground, praying for mercy, certain that they would die, when Yuma burst into the meeting room, shouting.

Cayetano jumped up. "Has something happened to Singing Bird?"

"No, no. Come see the sky. Your people will be afraid. You have to tell them it is okay."

"What is it?" he asked, as Yuma led him to the window.

The second chiefs followed. Already, a shadow was moving over the face of the sun.

"Aiyee!" they cried. "A bad omen! What does it mean? We must call the Shamans!"

Cayetano was shocked and also afraid, but he couldn't let it show.

"Where is Singing Bird?" he asked.

One of the servants stepped forward. "Great Chief, Singing Bird went into the city."

Fear for her safety overshadowed the omen in the sky, but he made himself focus on the boy who kept tugging at his hand.

"It's not bad," Yuma said. "It has happened many times since, and doesn't mean anything to us."

Cayetano picked him up so that they were eye to eye.

"This is true? You would not lie to me?"

"No, I do not lie, Cayetano. It is the truth and all the New Ones will know it, too. If Layla is in the city, she will help calm them, because she has seen this before, and knows it means nothing to us."

"You find the twins and stay here in the palace with Acat," Cayetano said, and then gave the little boy a quick hug before sending him on his way.

The second chiefs were huddled together, waiting. When Cayetano turned around, he was smiling.

"It means nothing," he said. "It is something the New Ones have seen many times before. It means nothing to us, but we still go into the city to make sure calm is restored."

****

Layla had gone to the Nantay home with two of her servants, bringing dishes in which to put their food, stools to sit on, and pillows and thicker sleeping mats for Shirley's comfort.

Shirley was happy to see her, and in a much better frame of mind than before. Little Mouse had come with medicine for pain, and promised to teach them where to find different healing plants on their own. They had been talking for only a short while when she began to hear unusual noises.

"Something is going on outside. It's never that noisy here," Shirley said.

The servants who'd come with Layla were outside waiting, when they suddenly burst into the room.

"Singing Bird! Come quick! Something is eating the sun!"

"Oh wow, an eclipse," Shirley said.

Layla ran to the door. "Oh no, it is!"

Shirley frowned. "So what's the big deal?"

"If I remember my history, things like this were considered bad omens. It's probably time for some damage control." She glanced out the window and added. "And here comes your husband, so you won't be alone."

"Thank goodness," Shirley said. "Take care."

"Yes, I'll see you again soon," Layla said, waving at Nantay as she hurried off.

They headed for the temple, knowing that was where the people would gather. But she became trapped within the crowd and separated from her servants.

At first no one noticed her, but after they did, began shouting her name and pulling at her, begging for her to save them. No matter how loud she shouted, they couldn't hear, and the day grew darker as the sun continued to disappear.

She didn't dare stop, or try to slow down because the people were manic. Someone's fingers became entangled in her hair as they ran past; another pushed her aside in an effort to get ahead. Twice she stumbled and almost fell. It was the first time since her arrival that she felt physical fear. The ground trembled beneath the thunder of so many feet, and she knew if she went down, she would be trampled.

Suddenly, the forward motion ceased. The crowd had reached impasse; forced to stop where they were, pinning Layla against the side of a wall.

Be calm. Father comes.

Relief came swiftly. The baby had felt her panic and responded. She began to look for Cayetano, knowing he would stand a head above most.

****

Cayetano was anxious and uncertain as to what he would say to stop the fear. Everyone was going crazy. There was no way his voice would be heard. And while Singing Bird was nowhere in sight, he had a gut feeling she was in danger.

As his warriors ran with him, their war cries' grew louder, startling the crowd enough to part and let them through. He scanned the faces as they ran, looking, always looking for her. They were almost at the temple when he heard a voice telling him to stop and look, so he did. Moments later, he saw Singing Bird, her fist in the air, pinned against a wall without a way out.

His shout was nothing short of a roar. It shocked those closest into sudden silence.

"Singing Bird is there! Let her pass!"

Then he pushed his way through.

****

When Layla saw Cayetano and his warriors coming through the crowd, she screamed his name so loud it hurt her own ears, and still he kept moving.

I will tell him.

When Cayetano suddenly stopped and began to scan the crowd, she realized the baby had done just that. She thrust her arm in the air, her hand curled into a fist, and that was when he saw her. She knew he was shouting, but she didn't hear anything but the thunder of her own heartbeat and her baby's laughter.

And then she was in his arms.

Cayetano's heart was hammering against his ribcage as he pulled her from the crowd, carried her back to the warriors, then all the way to the steps of the temple.

"Are you hurt?" he asked quickly.

"No. I just got trapped. I am good. Help me up the steps. I can calm them."

He swung her up and then followed her.

As soon as Layla reached the top, she thrust her arms in the air.

"Hear me," she shouted.

The throng stilled.

She pointed to the sky. "This is not a warning. It is not a bad omen. It means nothing to us. It is something that happens only in the sky. The sun and moon are playing. One is passing the other just as I would pass you on the street. When the moon has finished saying hello to the sun, the light will return and nothing will change. You will see. I promise."

The crowd hushed. All eyes were on the sky, watching. More than half the sun was gone and the light was fading around them. They watched the birds fly to roost. Even the monkeys who scampered across rooftops were absent, their chatter as silent as the gathered crowd who kept looking to the sky, afraid they would be struck down.

Then one by one, the New Ones began to push their way through to the front. Their numbers were so great that, as they moved forward, they slowly pushed the residents of Naaki Chava to the back of the crowd. It wasn't until movement ceased that it became obvious that they and they alone, had the temple completely surrounded.

Layla's heart swelled with gratitude. The New Ones had seen the danger and come to her rescue, just as she'd come to theirs in a land that was dying.

"What is happening?" Cayetano asked. "Why have they done this?"

Layla whispered. “I think they feared the crowd might riot. They are protecting me. They are protecting you.”

Cayetano was stunned. He had not thought of the New Ones as anything but an added burden and a means to an end. It was the first time he thought of them as people willing to die for the woman at his side.

He stayed close to her as he scanned the crowd, searching for the absent Shamans. When he finally saw them struggling to push through the crowd, he shouted down. “Let them pass.”

The crowd parted, and the old men came up the steps one by one. By the time they reached the top, they were hesitant to look into Singing Bird’s face for fear she would have them banished as she had Chak.

Cayetano knew what they were thinking and gave them a warning look.

Ah Kin dipped his head and whispered softly. “My Chief, do you want us to pray?”

He tightened his grip on his woman. “There is no need,” he said. “Singing Bird says it means nothing.”

“But Cayetano, if we anger the Gods, they may not give back the light.”

His frown darkened. “I said, there is no need. You heard my woman’s words. The sun and moon are merely passing each other and the light will return.”

Layla knew what courage that took to deny everything he knew about Gods and omens, and take her at her word. She stood beside him, her head up, her gaze fixed on their faces. They looked away, and so the watch continued.

When the sun was completely gone, a gasp rose from the crowd. Layla felt their fear, but the New Ones held their ground, and she knew that they were safe.

When the first sliver of sun began to appear on

the other side of the darkness, there was another sigh, but this time, it was one of relief.

Cayetano's whole body relaxed and she felt it.

"See, my heart, my words were true," she whispered.

"I knew that," he said.

She stepped away and shouted out as she pointed to the sky.

"See, the moon is telling the sun goodbye and is going away. It will be light again soon, and the birds will fly and all will be as it was."

As they waited, the sky went from dark to dim, then from dim to dusk, and then finally the bright light of day had returned. The sun was whole. The moon was no more, and as Singing Bird promised, the sky was filled with birds, and the jungle woke as if it was a new day.

The crowd that had been in such a panic moved away, going back to their daily tasks with nervous laughter. Layla took off down the steps to the New Ones who had turned to face her. They were waving and shouting her name.

Layla was in tears as she stopped at the first tier of the temple. She began walking around it, calling out her thanks and waving, laughing as she recognized faces in the crowd. It was a homecoming long overdue.

She walked until she had circled the temple to find Cayetano waiting. She ran the last few steps, laughing.

He caught her as she ran, sweeping her off her feet and into his arms, unashamed of feelings for the woman who held his heart.

Late that night, long after the boys had gone to bed and the palace was finally quiet, Layla lay in Cayetano's arms, but she couldn't sleep.

The night was dark. The moon was gone from the sky. It was a dark so profound that she would have been afraid were it not for his presence. The air was cool, but his body heat kept her warm. She snuggled backward a little closer, taking comfort in the way his arms instinctively tightened, as if, even in sleep, he would not let her go. Finally, she laid one hand on his arm, the other on her belly, and closed her eyes. Her family was complete.

Chapter Twenty-One

The day of harvest celebration dawned with the sounds of jubilation. Many tapirs had been killed for the feast. The night before, the carcasses were wrapped in banana leaves and placed in fire pits, then piled high with fiery coals so they could cook all night. Squash and beans were in pots over cooking fires, while yams baked in hot coals. Women were pounding grain to make flat cakes they baked on hot stones and the scents of roasting pig and baking bread filled the air.

Layla had been sick again all morning and stayed in the room, but as the sun moved across the sky, her energy returned. The servants knew the Chief's wife was with child, which meant even more good fortune for Naaki Chava.

Cayetano sat with her, watching the rise and fall of her breasts as she combed the tangles from her just-washed hair, and seeing the laughter in her eyes as the boys sat around her feet. They were like little parrots from the jungle, always moving, always squawking; entertaining her with their chatter. She was a natural mother, and yet she would give birth to only one. It hurt his heart to know this was so, but reminded himself the journey they were on was no longer about them. They had both come back in time to right a wrong.

Layla caught him watching and flashed back to

the day she'd first seen his face. Time had taken care of her confusion between loving Niyol and remembering Cayetano. The man before her was beautiful in her eyes. He was flesh and blood real, not a spirit, and she was a woman with a baby in her belly. It was enough.

Suddenly, she wanted him, and knew the lust was on her face as she watched his eyes narrow and his nostrils flare.

She stood. "Boys. Go play for a while. Feed the birds. Find something to play outside. The day is too beautiful to be indoors and I want some quiet."

The boys left willingly, but the moment they were outside in the hall they began to giggle between themselves.

"They will make love," Yuma said, rolling his eyes.

The twins nodded.

"It's better than making war," Evan said.

Adam punched his arm and then all three of them went running down the hall.

Cayetano closed the door and dropped his breechclout; his erection growing even as he walked toward her.

Layla came out of her clothing to stand naked before him, wearing nothing but the necklace with the silver bird. When he took her hand, she pulled him down onto the sleeping mat.

He slid an arm beneath her neck as she turned to face him. Her breasts were heavy against his hand. The long fall of her hair was cool and damp on the back of his arm. He could hardly breathe for the want.

"I ache to feel you inside me," she whispered, and rolled over onto her back, making room for him to come in, and so he did.

She was wet and ready when Cayetano slid

between her legs, then into her depths. There was no waiting, no foreplay, no need. Her arms were around his neck, and when he took her, a sigh of satisfaction slid up her throat and against his ear. He closed his eyes and began to move.

Layla wrapped her legs around his waist as he took her right where she wanted to go. The lust between them was as hot as the love was deep. And so it went, body to body, heart to heart; giving into a primal urge as old as time.

She was on top, rocking against him when the climax began to roll through her in a white-hot burst of heat, shattering thought, and what was left of her control.

Cayetano felt her inner muscles suddenly clench. She was at her peak. With what was left of his control, he tightened his grip, pulled her down hard, and let go of his seed.

She collapsed on top of him, spent and trembling in every muscle – a feeling of completion like no other.

"You are my heart. You are my love," she whispered.

His eyes were closed so she could not see his tears.

"I said that you would love me," he whispered, and held her even closer.

He felt her laughter, and although she made no sound, it filled his soul.

****

Bazat waited for Naaki Chava's harvest celebration to seek his revenge. When morning dawned, he left the City of the Sun with six men and the shaman who had come with the eclipse. No one cared that they were gone, and a good many hoped they did not return. They would rather be a city without a leader, than to endure another day of tyranny under the little man with the dark heart.

For Bazat, the trek to Naaki Chava was oddly without incident, which left him with the belief that the Gods were watching over him, keeping the wild animals and big snakes from their path. They moved at a steady lope without talking, resting only when the shaman could not keep up.

Chak had seen into the wily chief's heart and it had put a knot in his belly that wouldn't go away. Bazat was using him as a means to an end. Once this day was over, Chak had no idea how his own fate would play out. Even though the death of Cayetano was something he'd wanted all his life, he had a bad feeling. But, he was on this path, and there was no stepping aside. So he trailed behind the warriors, at times struggling to keep up, knowing the only reason they hadn't run off and left him was because he knew a back way into the palace without being seen.

It was late afternoon by the time they reached the outskirts of the city. Chak led them into a secure hiding place behind the palace and pointed toward the back entrance.

"They will be in their quarters now, preparing for the evening feast. We wait until after dark and then we go in. They will be full of food and drink. It will be the perfect time to strike."

Bazat heard and settled the men into place, waiting for the sun to go down and the moon to come up; the only witness to their treachery.

****

The ceremony had come and gone without incident. The Shamans blessed the harvest, the offerings had been left on the temple steps, and the city was finally at rest.

Layla put the boys to sleep herself, and once she was satisfied all was well, went back to their private quarters.

Cayetano waited for her, hungry for a repeat of their earlier lovemaking. By the time they collapsed in a tangle of arms and legs, they were exhausted. He pulled a blanket up to their waists and moved her close against him before falling asleep.

Aware that on this day several thousand years ago, she had been murdered, Layla had a difficult time sleeping. She kept hearing noises and whispers, but they were only in her head. She couldn't tell if it was remnants of an ancient memory, or simply a bad dream.

The rooms were dark and she could hear screams coming from every direction. Someone was chasing her, but no matter how fast she ran, she couldn't escape.

Her baby was crying, run, Mother, run.

And then a voice from the past!

You will fight but you must not die.

Windwalker? Is that you?

She rolled out of Cayetano's arms, waking him instantly, and in the moonlight, he saw tears on her face. He shook her awake.

"Singing Bird! Open your eyes."

Layla gasped and sat up before she was fully awake.

"What's wrong?"

He touched her face. "You cry."

She swiped the tears from her cheeks. “It was a dream.”

“A sad dream?”

She frowned, remembering all too vividly the voice that she’d heard.

“I don’t know.”

He, too, was all too aware of the significance of this day. His gut knotted.

“Do you sense trouble?”

“Maybe. I’m not sure. Would you go check on the boys?”

He brushed a single tear from the side of her eye and pulled up her cover against the night chill.

“Yes, anything to make these go away,” he said softly, then got up and donned his breechclout, palmed his knife, and walked out of their room.

****

Bazat and his men were armed and already inside the palace, following Chak through shadowy corridors, moving soundlessly on bare feet past the servants rooms, past the kitchen where the scents of the food prepared earlier still lingered. Once they stopped abruptly, waiting in a back hallway for a pair of guards to pass by.

It was all Chak could do to keep Bazat from attacking right then. The little man was crazed with bloodlust and ready to kill, no matter who crossed his path. As soon as the hall was empty, Chak motioned for them to follow.

****

Even though Cayetano had gone to check on the

boys, Layla's uneasiness persisted. She got up, put on a robe that she often wore to the bath and went to the window overlooking the city. It was not for the first time since their arrival that she'd remembered other cities and the lights that burned in streets, and the businesses that stayed open all night. Remembering the way the shops would be decorated for different holidays, and how the seasons came and went, marking off their lives and the years. She remembered her grandfather's face, and how his eyes would crinkle up so tightly when he laughed that they nearly went shut. Remembering the sounds of that life and the civilization that came with it and knowing it was forever gone was like a fist in her gut.

When the air shifted behind her, she looked over her shoulder and suddenly shivered. The door was shut, but even though the sound was faint, she heard footsteps. She turned abruptly, facing the door. There were too many footsteps for it to be Cayetano. That was when the message hit her.

You will fight, but you must not die.

She grabbed her knife and slipped into the darkest shadows of the room, her heart pounding; her eyes wide and fixed upon the door.

****

Cayetano moved with a long confident stride as he walked to the boys' room. This was their stronghold – it was the safe place. Yet he wouldn't discount Singing Bird's dream. She was a woman of many faces, and had powers now she'd never had before.

He reached their door and then slipped in. His plan was just to check on them without waking them, but the moment he crossed the threshold, Yuma sat up, clutching a knife.

Cayetano knelt. “It’s me. I came to see if you were well.”

Yuma’s gaze was blank. He was still asleep.

Cayetano started to wake him when Yuma jumped to his feet and pointed at the twins.

“Bazat is in the palace!”

The twins had heard Cayetano’s voice, and were waking up even as Yuma stood. The moment he did, their intuitions kicked in and they screamed in unison.

“Bazat and his warriors are at Layla’s door!”

A wave of horror went through Cayetano as he pointed at the twins. “Hide yourselves.”

When he turned to run, Yuma was nowhere in sight. He bolted out of the room, screaming for the guards as he ran.

****

Chak heard the shouts.

“They know we’re here!” he hissed.

Bazat pointed to his warriors. “We do not wait to fight. Attack those who follow!”

His men ran toward the shouts as Chak bolted in the opposite direction. His intent was to get to the temple. The other Shamans here would hide him, and when Cayetano and his woman were dead, they would be in charge.

Bazat burst into the room, expecting to see the chief and his woman in a state of sleep. Instead, the sleeping mats were empty. It was instinct that made him turn as she came at him from out of the dark. But Bazat was well-versed in the art of war. He feinted to the right and ducked under the blade just before she would have separated his head from his neck.

Layla didn't know who the little man was, but she felt the evil emanating. He was laughing, even as he came at her in a crouching leap.

She spun away, but he caught her by the arm and slashed downward with the knife. Instead of hitting flesh, the blade caught on the chain of her necklace. The bird went flying, but her father's necklace had saved her life.

And that was when Layla's fury kicked in.

Bazat was enjoying the fight when she suddenly screamed, but it wasn't in fear. It was nothing but pure rage, and it sent a chill up his spine. He'd never had a woman fight him like a warrior. It was time to finish this.

He darted sideways, and when she moved to follow the motion, he took a quicker step back in the other direction and just like that, the tide had turned. Layla's knife went flying, and she was on her back and fighting for her life.

Fury lived in every facet of her being. She wouldn't give – she wouldn't roll over and die – not again. Not like this. She gripped his wrist with both hands, kicking her legs, bucking her body beneath him in an effort to throw him off as she struggled to keep the knife from her chest.

Her fight was eerily silent now. Nothing but the fierce grunts and short gasps for breath, as his greater weight and physical strength began to take its toll. Unless a miracle occurred, this was a battle she would lose.

He was laughing as he finally broke her grip on the knife. He pinned her wrists over her head with one hand, and held the knife above her head with his other.

"Scream now, Singing Bird! It is your night to die!"

Layla caught a flash of movement over Bazat's shoulders a split second before she heard the solid thud of what sounded like a fist to flesh. Then it seemed as time stood still.

As she watched, he let out a tiny whine - like letting the air out of a balloon - then fell forward in a convulsive shudder, pinning her to the floor with his lifeless body.

She was pushing and screaming, "get him off, get him off," when Cayetano burst into the room, followed by guards carrying torches.

The moment there was light in the room, she saw Yuma in a half-crouch beside her. His eyes were wild, his face splattered in blood, and she could tell from the angle of his body that he'd tried to throw himself between her and Bazat. Then she saw a knife, stuck to the hilt in the middle of Bazat's back and shuddered.

It was Yuma who had saved her life!

Leave no one behind.

Even as Cayetano was shouting her name and pulling the dead body away, she was reaching for Yuma's hand. The moment that she was free, she sat up and pulled him into her lap.

He was trembling, but his voice was as steady as her heartbeat.

"He is dead, right?"

"Yes, my little warrior, he is dead," she whispered. "You saved my life."

He nodded. "And Tyhen. I protect her with my life. She belongs to me."

Layla looked up.

Cayetano was stunned. This child had not only saved her, he'd also broken the curse. The man who had killed Singing Bird was dead, but not by his hand.

The twins came running into the room, their eyes wide with shock.

"I told you to hide," Cayetano said.

"We couldn't" they cried - not when they had information the chief needed to know. "Chak led them here. He is running to the temple to hide."

"Go," Layla said. "He was the one who betrayed you before. He is not part of the curse. He is unfinished business."

Cayetano issued quick orders, leaving part of the guards at their door, and left the palace on the run with the others behind him.

Layla sent servants to clean the blood from the floor while others carried away the body. As she was issuing orders, the twins got a wet cloth and began wiping the blood from Yuma's face. He sat without moving as they cleaned away the spatter.

They didn't speak because they knew he would not be able to answer. A few seconds later, Layla took the cloth from their hands and finished the job.

"Is he going to be okay?" Evan whispered.

"He's in shock," Adam offered.

Layla nodded. "Yes, he's in shock." Then she pulled him up to her lap. "Yuma, look at me."

His gaze shifted as he focused on her face, and as he did, reality sank in.

"You did a very brave thing," Layla said.

Tears began rolling down his cheeks. "Before our world died, my Daddy told me that it was hard to be a man, but that I would know when it was my time to grow up. I told you I was a man. When I get taller, you will see."

Layla's voice was shaking as she hugged him close. "I don't know how you could be any bigger of a man than you already are."

****

Chak was running in an all-out sprint into the city. His heart was pounding to the rhythm of foot to ground, his gaze taking in the familiar sites. He'd been born in this place, and tonight he would die here. Bazat had failed. He'd known it before he'd cleared the palace, which meant his last chance of escape had also failed. All he wanted to do now was just get to the temple. It was where he'd been happiest. It was where he belonged.

A baby cried somewhere in the distance, but there would be no tears shed for him this night. He was about to die in shame.

The sounds of shouts and running feet were a good distance behind him, but they were warriors and he was not. They would catch him, and so he ran because it was all he had left to do.

The temple loomed in moonlight with a beauty almost as great as when bathed by the sun. It wasn't too much further. He could do it. Just keep putting one foot in front of the other, although the men were closer now; their steps almost in unison.

He didn't need to turn around to know Cayetano was leading them. He didn't need to see his face to feel the rage. His legs were giving out; the muscles burning all the way to the bone, while blood shot through his body at an erratic pace.

When he finally ran into the playa surrounding the temple, he almost stumbled. He'd made it! The wild animals that had been eating from the harvest offerings quickly scampered away.

Only a few more yards and then it would be over. His ears were roaring from the blood-rush, his legs no longer moving as they should.

He heard a shout! Someone called his name.

No, he screamed, only to realize too late that he never voiced it.

Something hit him in the middle of the back with such impact that the breath left his body. He looked down in shock at the spear protruding from his chest as pain began to radiate into every limb. His knees buckled as his heart gave out. The silence that swept over him was as welcome as the peace that moved through him.

It was done.

****

Cayetano's chest was heaving, but it was nothing to the rage in his heart as he stood over Chak's dead body.

A second chief eyed the near-perfect throw of Cayetano's spear that had pierced the chest from back to front. "What do we do with him? Should we put him with the offerings?"

Cayetano's eyes narrowed angrily.

"We do not curse our own offerings with the body of a traitor. Get the Shamans. I would speak with them."

Two of the guards ran into the temple, as the others waited there with their chief.

The air was still. The stars seemed close enough to touch, which lent calm to the night. They waited silently until the Shamans came running.

Ah Kin was the first to arrive, and the first to recognize Chak's body.

"Aiyee! What is this?"

Cayetano pointed. "That is the man who led a

killer into the palace. The killer is dead and now so is the traitor. Do with him as you will and know this. If your heart is as angry as Chak's was, then you have no place here."

By now the others had arrived to receive the full measure of their chief's threat. They were vocally upset on the behalf of Naaki Chava and of their chief, and Ah Kin had the good sense to agree.

"We will bury Chak in the proper way, and let the Old Ones deal with his spirit," Ah Kin said.

"Get him out of my sight," Cayetano said, and watched until the Shamans were gone before heading back to the palace.

But it was a good trip. They walked when before they'd been running. Justice had been done.

Cayetano knew there would be little sleep tonight, but he needed to see Singing Bird's face now, just to be sure that the curse had been broken.

He was tired, but oddly satisfied as he strode down the halls toward their quarters. As he entered, the last of his anxiety disappeared. Singing Bird was there, sound asleep on her mat, with the boys snuggled close around her.

His heart was full as he dropped his weapons and his clothes, dragged up another mat and stretched out. He pulled a cover up to his waist, and then pushed up on one elbow long enough to make sure he wasn't dreaming.

Singing Bird opened her eyes.

"Is it over?" she whispered.

"It is over," he said softly.

"Then it was all worth it," she said, and went back to sleep.

Epilogue

Eight months later:

A cry broke the silence of the night, piercing in its clarity. It was a cry of dismay for having left the warmth and safety of a mother's womb that was soon silenced with an offer of the mother's breast.

Layla was exhausted from the labor of birth, and relieved to have her body back to herself. It would take time to recover, but she had that luxury. She was Cayetano's woman and he was her heart.

She looked down at the baby cradled against her breast and sighed as the little mouth finally found her nipple to nurse. She would soon forget the pain of childbirth, but never would she forget this night. She had felt the earth shift the same moment the baby took her first breath. Change was in the wind.

She knew she had not imagined it when Cayetano, who had never left her side throughout the nine hours of labor, suddenly jumped as if in fright.

They looked at each other, and then down at the baby.

"It is beginning," Cayetano whispered.

She nodded.

A short time later, Acat appeared at the doorway.

"The boys want to see her."

"Let them come in," Cayetano said.

The twins entered first.

In the past eight months they'd grown in height and in stature. Here, they were not only accepted, but loved and valued for more than their abilities. They knew what this baby meant to the future, and were prepared to devote the rest of their lives to making sure nothing went wrong.

They entered with smiles on their faces, each carrying a gift they had made.

Adam laid a small doll at Layla's knee and then stroked the thatch of black hair on the tiny baby's head.

"She's so small," he said, and then laughed when she tugged even harder at Layla's breast.

Evan laid another doll beside the first.

"There are two of us. She should have twins as well."

Cayetano grinned.

"Thank you," Layla said. "When she is a little bigger, she will love them."

And then she saw Yuma. He was still standing in the doorway and with a look of awe upon his face. Something dangling from his hand as he came forward and she recognized the necklace Bazat had cut from her neck. She thought it was gone and had grieved for the loss. She was glad to see it again.

But it was Yuma, above all, who had changed the most in the past eight months. Not only had he grown in height and breadth, but his hair was longer, his features less like the child he'd been – more like the man he would be. He moved with the assurance of knowing his worth and place in the world, and knelt at Layla's feet.

"When she is old enough," he said, and laid the necklace he had found and repaired near her knee.

Layla nodded. "I will save it for the time when she

will wear it, rather than eat it."

Again, everyone laughed.

"She is so beautiful," Yuma said softly, and like Adam, laid a hand on the top of her hair.

At his touch, the baby stopped nursing. Her eyes opened, and it appeared to Layla as if she was trying to focus.

"Yuma, come stand behind me," Layla said. "I think she wants to see you."

Yuma knelt then peered over Layla's shoulder, straight into the baby's face.

"I am here," Yuma said.

Layla watched the baby trying to follow the sound of his voice, and when her eyes suddenly opened wide, Layla smiled. "She sees you."

"I see *you*, Tyhen. You will call me Yuma. I will protect you with my life, and you will love me."

The End

THE DOVE

BOOK 2

THE PROPHECY SERIES

The prophecy continues to unfold as the Windwalker's daughter becomes a woman, fulfilling the destiny for which she was born, and bringing truth to a young boy's vow.

Coming in 2013

CPSIA information can be obtained at www.ICGtesting.com
Printed in the USA
BVOW011848220413

318819BV00010B/168/P